THE ADRESTIA MANEUVER

BOOK TWO OF THE AZAZEL SERIES

BY

J.E. KENNEDY

Published by Adrestia Publishing, LLC
ISBN Ebook: 978-1-7328887-2-2
ISBN Print Edition: 978-1-7328887-3-9

Cover Design by Lieu Pham, Covertopia.com
Book design by Guido Henkel

This is a work of fiction. The people, events, and circumstances depicted in this novel are fictitious and the product of the author's imagination, and any resemblance of any character to any actual person, whether living or dead, is purely coincidental.

BASE PURPLE STAR—ANTARCTICA
October 23, 2008

Ellis Beckham and his team continue with their assessment of what we've dubbed the Azazel device. They proceed, as Ellis has said, with their knees knocking: the Orochonian civilization—more accurately, the People of the Oro'koni—attributed the destruction of their world over 12,000 years ago to Azazel (which they called—and this is my best shot at it—Zah'yeva).

This morning I completed a rough translation of the following passage from the Orochonian Ceremonial Documents. Geena is still cataloging the archives, so I have no document reference.

Before Zah'yeva
We were people of peace
Innocent and knowing not the subtlety of great evil
Now we are wise and buried with our wisdom

Let it be written on the hearts of those who endure
Cursed be Zah'yeva
Cursed be those who delivered the world to Zah'yeva's mighty hunger
We are crushed in Zah'yeva's fist
And we are no more

—From the notebooks of Montgomery Doran

CHAPTER 1

THE BOY, JUWAN, ELEVEN YEARS OLD, SLIPPED FROM BEHIND the building on the corner of Warren Street in New York City and surveyed the enormous gray hulk of the Municipal Corporation incinerator. For several weeks, the incinerator had been as still as a tomb, its furnace cooling, its gates closed tight. This morning, however, four armed guards patrolled the open entrance, and the facility buzzed with activity.

Juwan checked the street in both directions, back around the curve of River Terrace and then north toward Chambers. A lone transport vehicle, jellybean-shaped with snow melters fixed on its front bumper, glided silently past. Juwan tugged the brim of his cap low over his eyes and stepped forward to gain a better view of the street, leaning to the right and left, straining to see around the few lethargic figures on the sidewalk. After a moment, his focus seemed to settle on an old man hawking a shell game to passersby. He jogged over to where the man had positioned himself, directly across from the incinerator gates.

"Why you hiding behind the sign, Elky?" asked Juwan. "Couldn't see you, man."

"Try your luck, boy? You'll be the first this morning." Elky gestured toward his polished mahogany board with its three shells neatly presented. A gust of breeze took his long beard and pointed it east like a windsock.

"Cut the bullshit," said Juwan.

"So this is your street now, boss?" Elky snickered. "Show some respect to your elders, you little munchkin."

"The gates are open today, Elky. You seen anything?"

Elky looked away, past the edge of the incinerator and toward the bluish-gray water of the Hudson. "Damned pension, gone," he said. "Son, I worked my whole life..." He trailed off in a string of grumbles, "social insecurity" and "worthless politicians" being the only intelligible phrases.

Juwan sighed, whipped a fiver from his pocket, and slapped it onto the board next to Elky's shells. With the speed of an automated threshing machine, the old man swiped the bill and thrust it in his pocket.

"What you seen?" asked Juwan.

"Two vans, Municorp, filled with people, professional types," said Elky in a brisk, businesslike tone. "About an hour ago. Seven thirty or so."

"That's it?"

"No, that's not *it*. I'm getting to *it*."

Juwan put his hands on his hips.

"They brought in a big machine on rollers," Elky continued. "A crane—no, not a crane, a puller of some kind. Big, flat base, long folding arm with some weird, circular piece on the end of it. I remember seeing a machine like it, I don't know, a few years ago. And then more vans came a half hour later, this time with working types, and—"

"What were the people wearing?" asked Juwan.

"Don't interrupt, buster boy, you might learn something." Elky fingered his beard. Juwan tapped his foot. Overhead, the morning clouds were tinged with crimson, and a few seagulls broke out in raucous cries and flapped away toward the river. "They wore those one-piece Municorp coveralls, green with matching caps," said Elky. "You know what I mean."

Juwan dropped another fiver onto Elky's board and took off running, his sneakers clapping on the sidewalk. Back to Warren and over and across North End, dodging through the thin traffic until he reached a dilapidated coffee shop. Marty Shannon looked up from his booth in the rear as Juwan entered, watching as the boy slid between the tables and took the seat opposite him.

"Catch your breath, lad," said Marty, instantly seeing that Juwan had news and suspecting the worst. "But don't keep me waiting all day."

"They moved a puller in this morning, plus a bunch of munis in green work suits," said Juwan.

"Into the incinerator, you say?"

The boy nodded. "Gate was open when I got there."

Marty watched Juwan fiddle with his baseball cap, a pristine, royal blue affair, probably the lad's most prized possession. "They're opening the furnace, I'd guess," said Marty, his mouth pressed in a thin line.

"I get the bonus," said Juwan. "You said if I saw anything, I'd get the bonus."

"Tell me more about the people who went in with the puller," said Marty.

"And I got to pay my guy, the Elk," said Juwan. "He's been over there every minute I was away. He's there now."

Marty removed a roll of three hundred Homeland redbacks from his pocket. With a gleam in his eye, Juwan lunged for it. Marty jerked his hand away and raised an eyebrow. Juwan sank into his seat and repeated every word Elky had said.

Bad news indeed, thought Marty, taking it all in. "Did you hear any noise from inside the gates? Any other signs of activity?"

Juwan shook his head and squirmed.

"Then back to the park with you and your friend," said Marty. He forced a smile and handed over the roll of bills. "And well-deserved. I thank you."

The money vanished and Juwan with it. Marty rubbed the back of his neck and stared absently at his coffee. Vile, oily brew. Damned embargo—and the cold weather had coffee production down everywhere. My pitiful kingdom for a good cup of java, he thought.

Outside, Marty hailed a hoo cab, and a few minutes later was striding along the sidewalk toward Hatch Doran's West Village townhouse apartment. The apartment served as Hatch's home as well as the offices of Odysseus, LLC, the antiques brokerage owned by Hatch, Big Ray Garwin, and, to a lesser extent, Marty himself. Inside he waved at Jocelyn, who was busy issuing orders to someone on the phone. She handled administrative matters for Odysseus, and occupied the middle seat of a three-person, u-shaped workstation that took up much of the former living room. The cat, as black as coal, had centered herself at the entrance to the open kitchen. She glanced at Marty and slowly closed her eyes.

Marty's thoughts darted around as he sorted through the papers stacked on his small worktable. Assume Municorp opened the furnace today—a stretch, to be sure—then how long did Hatch have? Days, perhaps, but no more. Probably not a week.

He absently paged through a stack of flyers Jocelyn had printed—the liquidation of a collection of porcelain eggs, a sale of several eighteenth-century handmade cabinets, an estate auction or two—and set them back on the table. How could he get Hatch focused on the incinerator? The lad wasn't listening well lately. Perhaps Raymond could talk sense to him. Marty stepped down the hallway to the rear of the apartment, but as he reached Big Ray's and Hatch's office, a commotion arose behind him. He heard Jocelyn barking orders amid heavy footsteps and the clatter of metal.

Marty turned.

"Out of the way, dude, we're coming through," cried Jocelyn, leading two painters along the hallway. "Watch it, you clumsy bruhs," she said to the painters as they swung the ladder around. "You have any idea what it costs to repair plaster these days?"

The painters, two young men in stained and spotted work clothes, looked at each other with mildly confused expressions. "Plaster?" one asked.

"I remember now," said the other. "You see it in these old places." Together they began to ease the ladder down the narrow stairway leading to the basement level of the apartment.

The office door opened and Hatch emerged. "What's all this?" he asked, visibly wincing as the ladder bumped the stairwell wall. The painters mumbled apologies. "Painters?" asked Hatch. "For what?"

"Your bedroom," said Jocelyn. "But I told them to do the other downstairs rooms, too. It's like ridiculously expensive to paint a single room, and besides, the sitting room is also done in lilac, which you said a million times you didn't like."

"How much do these guys charge?" asked Hatch.

"I want the lilac gone," said Jocelyn, lowering her voice in a creditable imitation of Hatch. "Get some painters in here. Not another day of lilac." She became herself again. "So thy will be done, boss man. You've had your room covered in plastic for three weeks, and just look at the rest of the place. Pipes shuddering, windows leaking, floors groaning."

The plumber appeared from the hallway bathroom and wiped his hands on a towel. "Hey, kiddo," he said to Jocelyn, "I got to go find a connector for the p-trap pipe. Hopefully, I can get back in here tomorrow, but it may take a couple of days."

Hatch and Marty peered through the bathroom door at the filthy, disassembled pipe sections, bolts, washers, and crust-laden rags spread willy-nilly over the bathroom floor. "Can it even be fixed?" asked Marty.

"Probably," said the plumber. He pushed his hat back on his head and exhaled. "The toilet paper these days...but at least you can still get it, right?" He lifted his box of tools and left.

"Tell those painters the downstairs bathroom will have to wait," said Hatch. "It's the only one we have at the moment."

"Don't look so annoyed," said Jocelyn. She flinched at the clamor from downstairs. "The plumber works with the painters, and I got a deal having them in together. One truck, you know."

Hatch gave Jocelyn a skeptical look. "This plumber isn't really a plumber, is he?"

Marty rolled his sleeves to his elbow. Plumbers, painters, all this jawboning. A waste of time, it was. More urgent matters demanded their attention now.

"I'm not a plumber, either," said Big Ray, emerging from the office. He stretched and yawned, pulling his dress shirt tight against his athletic torso. "Wow, look at the bathroom. Who knew there was so much sh—anyway, so the big remodel is underway at last."

"Remodel?" asked Hatch.

"A few repairs," said Marty. "A touch of paint, a tap or two of the hammer, perhaps new stain for the floors." As he spoke, he was already mulling over several courses of action with regard to the incinerator. None held much appeal.

"Wait, new stain?" asked Hatch. "Why? Everyone'll just walk all over it and it'll be scuffed and cruddy in no time. We'll be right back to square one."

"Well, I guess there's no point in washing the dishes or cleaning the shower or anything," said Jocelyn. She whirled on her heel and returned to the main room.

"Samantha picked out the floor stain," said Big Ray. He clapped Hatch on the shoulder. "She said the current color was just too dark, too grim."

"Too grim?" asked Hatch.

"Indeed," said Marty, snapping back to the present. "You don't know the half of it, lad."

***

HATCH HAD KNOWN MARTY TOO LONG TO MISS THE IMPORT of his lowered brow and distracted movements. "Let's get to business," he said as a particularly loud thump sounded from the basement level. "Hopefully, we'll be able to hear ourselves talk."

Big Ray pulled the office door closed, but the cat darted through in the nick of time and leapt onto Hatch's desk. From there she jumped to the bookshelf and crouched, staring at them with round, green eyes.

"We've all agreed to pitch in on the repairs," said Marty, easing into a chair in front of Hatch's desk. "The wear and tear on the place comes from having the six of us rambling and scraping about. We can't leave it all to lighten your pocket."

"How things change," said Hatch. "A month ago we didn't have two redbacks to our name."

"We were at death's door," Marty agreed. "And we still are, this time in a very literal sense."

"Meaning what?" asked Big Ray. He turned a second chair to more easily face Marty.

"I've just got word that activity at the incinerator is picking up, beginning today," said Marty. "Soon enough our friends from the Group will pull our box out of those ashes. I can all but hear the clock ticking."

Hatch tapped his fingers on the arm of his chair.

"Today?" asked Big Ray. "So the sky is finally falling, and we've been sitting around the past three weeks twiddling our thumbs and waiting for"—he spread his hands—"waiting for what?"

"I get it," said Hatch. "The Group will dig around for the goddess artifact, they won't find it, and they won't be happy." He leaned forward and rapped his knuckle on the desk. "But you two aren't seeing the full landscape here."

"What I see is our buddy Dartham kicking in our door when he discovers he's been had," said Big Ray. "And there's Ferret to consider."

"It'll be a footrace between them," said Marty. He lifted his wrist and tapped his old, chronograph watch. "Tick, tick, tick. And we are the prize in the hunt."

Hatch rocked back in his desk chair and stared at the ceiling. "Listen, there's more to the story," he said. "Marty may know a few things, but I haven't told you guys all I know."

Big Ray squinted and tilted his head. "What?"

"I'm talking about the artifact," said Hatch. "Adrestia, the goddess."

"What didn't you tell us?" asked Marty, his frown deepening. "I carried your artifact out of the incinerator, didn't I? Dodging bullets, hiding myself in the refuse piles behind the fiery monster, shivering like a shorn lamb in a blizzard, for the love of God."

"All true," said Hatch.

Marty cocked his head at Big Ray. "While Raymond risked life and limb to rescue you from those thuggish lads sent by the Blue."

"Kutznov gave me the background," said Hatch, noting the stony faces on the other side of his desk. "But he warned me it could be dangerous, even fatal, to tell anyone. So I haven't."

Big Ray rose, drifted over to his own desk, and stared through the small oval window into the rear courtyard. "Fatal," he said softly.

"I do remember that business in Ghost's hideaway," said Marty, running his hand through his thatch of white hair. "Some talk of a weapon, something the Group got hold of. I suppose I knew there was more to it all. And then learning your father had been involved with this very same goddess artifact so many years ago..."

Three weeks earlier, Hatch and Marty had arrived at the downtown incineration facility to deliver a prehistoric artifact to an antiquities runner known as Ferret. The artifact, thought to be over twelve thousand years old, was an oblong, football-shaped object less than two feet long, covered with precisely etched symbols, and stored in an ornate, rectangular container.

But affairs at the incinerator had not gone according to plan. Thomas Dartham, a representative of powerful corporate interests known as the Group, had been lying in wait for

Hatch and Marty. Dartham had intended to take possession of the artifact, but in the heat and chaos of the circumstances, Hatch had hurled the artifact's container into the furnace. Unbeknownst to all but Hatch, Marty, and Big Ray, the container had been empty; Marty had fled the incinerator a few minutes earlier with the actual artifact, and it now lay hidden away in Hatch's basement storeroom.

"If they've begun sifting the ashes," said Big Ray, still gazing through the window, "then we are cooked, crisp and well done."

"I'd like to hear what Hatch has to say," said Marty.

A muffled clatter came from below, followed by a loud knocking sound. The cat made a low, nervous *mrooww*. Jocelyn shouted as she flew down the stairs.

"If Ray doesn't want to hear it," said Hatch.

"No," said Big Ray. "Let's have the whole shebang. Lower the lights. Cue the kettledrums."

Hatch gave him a sharp glance. "You know about the Group, but I didn't mention Project Caterpillar, at least by name. It was a task force, a joint military-civilian effort which was disbanded almost twenty-five years ago. They were searching for evidence of an advanced prehistoric civilization."

Big Ray sighed and muttered a few words to himself. A burst of laughter exploded from the lower level, followed by Jocelyn's unintelligible lecturing of the painters.

"The Group basically controlled Caterpillar," said Hatch. "Dad was part of it, and so were Ferret, Kutznov, and even Ghost. Caterpillar discovered an ancient weapon, an apocalyptic device of some kind, buried in Antarctica. They nicknamed it Azazel, after the mythological fallen angel, and figured out how to use it to destroy targets anywhere in the world. That's the weapon Ghost was talking about, Marty. Kutznov told me it uses power from another dimension, or maybe multiple dimensions—please don't ask me to explain that—and it works by way of psychic interaction with its operators."

Big Ray returned to his chair. "I'll bet I know what comes next," he said, slumping until his knees pushed against Hatch's desk.

Hatch nodded. "Using the weapon creates a tremor, maybe some kind of bright explosion, and then your target is gone."

"That's been going on here and there for years," said Big Ray. "You're saying Azazel is responsible? That's crazy."

"Is it?" Hatch leaned forward. "You've talked about it yourself, my man. Buildings disappearing in a flash of light, a quake, the news suppressed or unreported. You've even mentioned that convoy that vanished in Germany not so long ago."

Big Ray waved him off.

Hatch waited, observing that Big Ray was still looking away. "Not long after they found Azazel, Dad located the artifact, also in Antarctica," he said. "He named it Adrestia, after the goddess of balance and equilibrium. It can counteract Azazel, or so Kutznov said, but they never figured out how to operate it. Afterward, the Group seized Azazel for themselves, kicked the civilian governments and militaries to the curb, shuttered Caterpillar and"—Hatch hesitated a moment —"murdered almost everyone who had been involved in the project."

"Your father, too," said Marty.

Hatch nodded. "As I understand it, the Group never gained possession of the goddess artifact," he said. "Dad gave it to Kutznov, and Kutznov, along with Ferret and Ghost, managed to escape and go into hiding. The few survivors, in one way or another, have spent the past twenty-five years opposing the Group, working to disrupt it and expose its activities."

"All right, let's pretend this Azazel weapon *is* the source of the Group's power and that this goddess artifact of yours can destroy it," said Big Ray, pushing himself upright. "That means neither Dartham nor Ferret will stop until they have the artifact in hand."

"Sure," said Hatch. "Dartham's side probably wants to destroy the artifact, while Ferret believes he can use it to shut down Azazel."

"So it'll either be the Group—meaning this Dartham guy—or Ferret coming down on us," said Big Ray. "I told you we'd end up running to Ferret for protection, didn't I?"

"It's not that simple," said Hatch.

"It may not be pleasant to think about, but it actually is pretty simple," said Big Ray.

"Anyway, according to Ghost, the artifact spoke to Dad," said Hatch. "Kutznov also said Dad used to talk to it while at work—"

"So what?" asked Big Ray. "And don't say it spoke to you. Please don't say that again."

"Jesus, Ray. You were there when it spoke to me. In the storeroom after Sam's party. You were pretty impressed by the whole spectacle as I remember it."

"You *said* it spoke. All I saw was a flash of light."

"It spoke," said Hatch. He eased back in his chair, astonished at Ray's attitude. "It said Azazel was the master and the eater of our realm."

"The what?" Big Ray half-rose from his chair.

"The artifact said it had helped people in the ancient past. If we're willing to resist Azazel, it will help us, too."

"Resist a… device?"

Hatch exhaled a long breath and stared at the ceiling again. "Azazel is more than just a machine or device."

"Ah, yes, I remember now," said Marty. "Ghost described Azazel and your goddess as portals."

"Portals?" Big Ray's mouth fell open and he looked around. "Portals to what, exactly?"

"Nothing good, in the case of Azazel," said Hatch.

Big Ray covered his eyes and pulled his cheeks downward.

"Don't make that face," said Hatch. He had known Big Ray for twenty years, and had seen the same expression more times than he cared to remember. The accusation, defiance, disbelief, and self-indulgent persecution written all it was enough to drive Hatch to mild insanity. "I'm telling you, the Group has used Azazel to put the world under its thumb," he went on. "That's why all this is important. Besides, what do you think explains all the volcanoes, quakes, and cold weather?"

"Oh, come on," cried Big Ray. "So now you're saying this Azazel weapon is responsible for the global cooling and the other climate problems? Really?"

"There is some sort of cumulative effect—dangerous, planetary effect—of using Azazel," said Hatch. "There was an ancient cataclysm—it fits with the geological records—and people who know more than I do certainly blame Azazel."

Big Ray shook his head, as if talking with Hatch had become an exercise in hopelessness. Marty tapped his finger on his chin.

"So, yeah, there are local markers whenever Azazel is used," said Hatch. "Tremors, bright lights, strange sounds, things like that. But the larger climate issues do correlate with the increasing use of Azazel over the past decade."

"According to these people who know more than you," said Big Ray.

"Look around," said Hatch. "Do you really believe the collapse, the new, crappy currency, the starvation, the forced labor, and the corporatization of everything you touch just happened out of the blue?"

"So the economic wipeout and Reset were also Azazel's doing," said Big Ray. "Wow. Who knew?"

"The climate effects may be more visible, but it's all related," said Hatch. "One way or another it traces back to Azazel. It has to."

"If you could see how big your eyes get when you spew shit like that," said Big Ray.

"When I do what?" Hatch forced himself to remain calm.

"I've been focused on the artifact and the incinerator," said Marty in a quiet tone. "I hadn't thought much about this Azazel matter." He gave Hatch and Big Ray a serious look.

"But this squabbling does us no good. Dartham will find his empty container soon enough, just as Raymond said. And Ferret will hear about it and jump to the obvious conclusions. I've said it before, we'll be under fire from all directions." He tapped his watch again.

"We need to reach out for help before it's too late," said Big Ray. "We need to face reality, for a change."

"Don't be such a linear thinker," said Hatch.

Big Ray inclined his head in mock deference. "Oh, chosen of the goddess," he said.

"The artifact is a player here," said Hatch, feeling a cord twitch in his neck. "It's able to act."

"Ferret *may* kill us on the spot, but there is no question the Group will," said Big Ray, jabbing his finger at Hatch. "Rock, meet hard place. Again, I say we approach Ferret."

"I will not surrender the artifact," said Hatch.

"Sure you will," said Big Ray. "Even if it leaves you with no one to talk to."

"Not happening."

"Tell me how else this ends up, genius. Besides, didn't you just say the artifact wasn't going to save us?"

"Ridicule if you will, but the goddess artifact hasn't spoken to you." Hatch sensed a hot flush on his face. "I've had the communication, I've heard its words."

"So, what does it say now?" asked Big Ray.

"Ray, listen, the people involved in this business for many years—people like Kutznov—believe Azazel affects the minds of those using it. Certainly, the goddess artifact can reach out in a telepathic sense, or something like it. That's what we're dealing with, and we have to be patient and disciplined."

"Words which have never before come out of your mouth," said Big Ray.

Marty clapped his hands on the arms of his chair. "God helps those who help themselves, my mam used to say. Perhaps our goddess works on the same principle." He rose and squeezed past Big Ray. "You were right to give us the deeper picture, Hatch, but we'd be fools to wait a minute longer."

The office door clicked shut behind Marty. The cat perked up and began licking her paw. Hatch and Big Ray sat glowering at each other.

"You think I've lost it completely," said Hatch. "You're just not seeing it, brother."

"You refuse to let it seep through that reinforced concrete skull of yours that you don't know everything," said Big Ray. "It'll be your undoing—*our* undoing."

"I'm not worried. The artifact is an X-factor, maybe the biggest ever."

Big Ray grunted.

"We can't ignore that," said Hatch.

"Sure we can. We can get busy protecting ourselves."

Hatch straightened and rested his hands on the desk. "We have a ringer on our team, Ray," he said, speaking slowly and deliberately, as if addressing a petulant, stubborn child. "We have the high card."

"What makes you so sure about how it's all going to work out?"

"I know the goddess artifact is powerful, and it spoke to me just like it spoke to my dad."

"Really?" Big Ray folded his arms across his chest. "Didn't save him, though, did it?"

***

THE REMARK DIDN'T SIT WELL WITH HATCH, AND AS HE AND Big Ray joined Jocelyn in the front room, he caught Ray's crabbed, disgruntled expression and his mood darkened another shade. They settled into chairs on opposite sides of the workstation.

"Those painter boys are handy with a brush," said Jocelyn, "but by the time they knock everything apart with their cans and ladders, there'll be nothing left to paint."

The front door opened and Samantha pushed her way in. "Paint?" she asked. "What are we painting?"

"The basement rooms," said Jocelyn.

"I thought we were staining the floors up here." Samantha dropped her bag onto her desk area and took her chair. "What's wrong with the downstairs paint, pray tell?"

Hatch felt a prickle run over his scalp. How many times over the past weeks had he described to Ray the sense of wonder and mystery he had experienced while speaking with the goddess artifact? Three? Four? And on every occasion, Ray had nodded and expressed interest. But Hatch now saw it had all been feigned—obviously feigned—and he didn't appreciate it in the least. He looked again at Ray, sitting across the workstation, his face set in a closed, mulish expression, and wondered why he had tolerated it all these years.

"You seem tense, Hatch," said Jocelyn.

"I'm not," said Hatch.

"Let me handle the interior work, dude. Ray thinks I can cut a sweet deal on upstairs painting, too. Give a little lift to the atmosphere around here—and it's *not* lilac, after all."

"I'm not involved with any painting decisions," said Big Ray. He clicked his nails on the arm of his chair.

"So lilac isn't good enough," said Samantha, speaking to Jocelyn. "I suppose Doran wants a more manly color, dark gray, perhaps, or stripes. Or murals of sports scenes." She pushed her wavy, chestnut hair over her shoulder, withdrew a small notebook from her bag, and tossed it onto the desk.

"You ought to be the soul of good cheer, Hatch," said Jocelyn. "We have Samantha's commission on the Urban drawings, Ray's contract with City Museum, and now Marty's mandate to liquidate Caroline Atherton's warehouse. We're solvent again."

"I had those rooms done in lilac when I first moved in, Doran," said Samantha. "It was only two years ago, and you uttered not a word of objection." Her cheeks had flushed pink.

"I refuse to believe we've broken up permanently, you know. I only wanted time to reflect on matters."

Hatch sighed.

"Apparently I'm not to be forgiven," said Samantha. "Indeed, it seems I must be erased altogether, my memory stripped from the very walls." She made a puzzled frown. "But I'm telling you, I believe we'll be together again."

"Maybe we can talk about this some other time," said Hatch.

"Nice commissions across the board," said Jocelyn, glancing nervously at Samantha. "We are awash in funds, even after I reserve for the repairs. And also—"

"Doran is loyal, in his way," Samantha interrupted. "He's cute when he's not angry—look at those eyes blazing—and he can be supportive and even loving. Perhaps when I suggested a small break from our relationship, I embarrassed him." She laughed, a short bark with no humor in it. "You must never embarrass Doran, lest he cast you into the outer darkness."

"The outer darkness?" asked Hatch.

"So we're doing okay," said Jocelyn. "But I feel bad in a way, raking in the dough when things are so bad for everybody else."

"Stick around," said Big Ray. "It's always been flood or drought around here."

Hatch was sitting next to Nathan's work area, a rat's nest of cables, dusty keyboards, and various circuitry components. "Has anybody seen Nathan lately?" he asked, hoping to change the subject.

"Gone the rest of the way crazy with those games," said Jocelyn. She was referring to Nathan's brain implants—or gameplants—which allowed him to engage in the virtual reality games produced by GameHead, Inc. Nathan was an avid gamer and a devoted admirer of Kee Bickerman, GameHead's founder and now Samantha's friend. "Nathan is not of this world most of the time," Jocelyn continued. "Poor bruh is too deep with the Eye Brigade. A bunch of them are living together in that old dorm near NYU, or whatever they call it now."

"Nathan was skitter-brained long before he met his first virtual game," said Samantha.

Big Ray stood, walked over to the closet, and slipped into his blazer. "I'll check in on Nathan this week," he said. "I'm with Joss. He's dancing too close to the edge." A pause. "Must be something going around."

Hatch watched Big Ray leave. Good riddance, he thought.

Samantha unfolded a photo of an evening gown, and Jocelyn hopped to her side to examine it. "For the Gala," said Samantha, giving Hatch a sly look out of the corner of her eye. "Kee likes it. Of course, the cut is a tad summery, but all the big social events are mid-year now that the winters are impossible."

Jocelyn studied the photograph, her mouth open in amazement. "It's gorgeous, Sam. You'll be beautiful. I mean, you *are* beautiful, but wow."

Hatch rubbed his chin, trying to put Ray out of mind—and Marty too, with his tick-tick-ticking. Did they really believe he didn't understand the risks? Of course he did, but he had the goddess artifact, and its ways were subtle and extraordinarily powerful. Why did they—Ray, in particular—refuse to understand? At that moment, a loud crash from downstairs interrupted his thoughts. "What was that?" he asked.

Jocelyn shrugged. "Maybe a ladder fell, like in the storeroom."

"The storeroom?" Hatch felt a jolt of alarm. "The storeroom's locked. It's always locked."

"I got the key out of your desk drawer this morning, boss man. I figured since they're here, I'd have them clean out all the clutter."

"Oh my," said Samantha. "You trespassed through a holy place."

"It's just old file boxes, a few bags of cat litter, and a pound of dust bunnies." Jocelyn made a scoffing sound, but Hatch was already gone, flying from the front room and tearing down the stairs to find the storeroom door partially open. To his horror, the painters had dragged several of his boxes into the hallway and pushed them haphazardly against the walls. He entered, slammed the door, and bolted the lock.

Gloom and silence, storage bins scattered and out of place. The corner where he had hidden the goddess artifact was now covered by a box of unused bathroom floor tiles, two lampshades, and a stack of packing quilts. Hatch barely registered the muted chatter of the painters in the nearby bedroom as he cleared the area, grabbed the crowbar from its shelf, and pried away the section of concrete.

The rucksack was still there.

With a rush of pure relief, he removed the artifact from its bag, marveling at its edges, which blurred slightly when he focused on them. He felt a curious inner prompting—a summons from the goddess?

No. The artifact remained dark and still in his hands.

An uneven drumroll of feet sounded on the stairs, and someone tugged at the door. "You locked it?" asked Jocelyn from the hallway, and then in a fainter voice, "He locked it."

Hatch turned the artifact over in his hands. A few weeks earlier, in this storeroom, the goddess artifact had said time was growing short.

Urgent taps on the door. "You okay, boss man?"

A babble of voices reached him from the hall. "It's more of a lavender shade than lilac," he heard Samantha say.

The artifact was cool to Hatch's touch. Twelve thousand years old. Azazel's nemesis. A river of blood had flowed in the decades since Project Caterpillar had uncovered Azazel, but here was the goddess artifact and there was destiny in it. There simply had to be.

"Just what do you have locked away in there, Doran?" asked Samantha, rapping on the door. "Probably has to do with his father. Nothing so discombobulates him as his father."

"You're scaring me, Hatch," said Jocelyn.

"I'm fine," Hatch called out.

Azazel's game is slavery and slaughter, the goddess artifact had said. *Every tear or burst of anger or rush of terror feeds Azazel, who shapes worlds to nourish itself.*

The artifact had promised to assist humans, but warned it would not act alone. A sudden, inner conviction took hold of Hatch. He was the key—at least *a* key—to the goddess's actions. Was he crazy? Deluded? A megalomaniac? No. He was none of those things. Screw Ray. Let him snicker. Hatch had communicated with the artifact on two occasions, experiencing its bizarre ability to suspend time and set before him lifelike vistas of the ancient past. The artifact had *chosen* him in some mysterious way, and he had an obligation to the artifact and to his dad's work, whether he wanted it or not.

"I'm totally committed," said Hatch. "I'm still with you."

The artifact did not respond. Hatch felt no brushing of his mind, no contact with the profound, penetrating intelligence that had pursued him before, detaching him from reality, filling his head with the distant tinkling of chimes, and leaving him dizzy and restless and obsessed; he had sensed nothing at all for weeks, not a whisper from Adrestia since that spectacular moment after Sam's party.

He slipped the artifact back into its bag and replaced it beneath the concrete. When he opened the door, Samantha was nowhere in sight, but Jocelyn stood facing him with her hands on her hips.

"The painters realize the paint is here, in the storeroom, don't they?" asked Hatch.

"Who were you talking to?" asked Jocelyn.

"Who would I be talking to?"

"I don't know. And what paint?"

"Eighteen gallons, right here. I cut a deal with Knife Cochoran, but I had to take it all."

"Color?" asked Jocelyn in a faint voice.

"Antique white," said Hatch. "A normal, everyday color."

Jocelyn wrinkled her nose. "Ugh! Really, dude? It's so blah. Why not apricot?"

"Apricot?"

Jocelyn gave him a placating grin, but her face, bordered by her thick black hair, was as pale as white marble. "It's much healthier psychologically, the apricot."

Hatch rubbed a spot on his forehead between his eyes.

"I have a funny feeling, like something's going on," said Jocelyn, her eyes narrowing. "I thought we were past all that, everybody walking around with glazed eyes, their minds in another universe."

Hatch gestured at the undisturbed buckets of paint stacked against the storeroom wall. "Antique white," he repeated.

Jocelyn made gagging sounds.

"Nevermind," said Hatch. "I'll tell the painters myself."

CHAPTER 2

AFTER MUSING OVER THE MATTER OF THE INCINERATOR and the artifact, Marty had decided to set a few wheels turning. He was pacing on the sidewalk, having just finished a call, when Big Ray emerged from the apartment.

"Where're you headed?" asked Marty.

"City Museum." Big Ray squinted into the sunlight.

"Your new contract," said Marty. "We've more work than we can do." He watched as Big Ray descended the steps, buttoning his blazer. The lad had been itchy and impatient of late, and it had certainly gone poorly with Hatch a short while earlier. "Walk with me, Raymond. I'm heading east to meet someone."

They fell in step together, moving toward Greenwich Street. Marty, a man of medium build in a full, white cotton shirt with the sleeves rolled, contrasted with Big Ray's stockier, navy-clad form. The neighborhood was serene, but in the distance they heard the truncated whoop of a siren followed by shouting.

"If you'd care to bend an ear," said Marty.

"It's Hatch." Big Ray fingered his pocket flap. "He wears me down, and he's over the edge now."

"He gave us a lot to chew on, sure."

"Ancient civilizations. Portals." Big Ray shook his head. "The whole mess feels like it's spinning out of control, like *he's* spinning out of control."

"Well, we have to take matters into our own hands, Raymond. I intend to do just that."

"You think Hatch is nuts? His head is as hard as metallic glass—he's always been one stubborn sonofabitch—but I've never seriously questioned his sanity. Then I listen to him go on about his goddess artifact and I wonder, have a few rivets have come loose upstairs?"

Marty gave Big Ray a sidelong look. "I was in the dark trades for many years, as you know."

"In Ireland, military intelligence, right?"

"I've said too much as it is, but I've heard strange tales in my time. And I've learned the world is a puzzling and curious place, more than we know."

They continued on, past a drab apartment house where a woman was repotting flowers for a window box. "Here's what *I* know," said Big Ray. "Dartham is real, and there's something about the guy. I don't want to cross his path again."

"I know the type," said Marty.

"And now we hear Dartham and this Group he works for are in a lather over prehistoric technology. I mean, are we talking about cavemen with weapons of mass destruction? I understand why a lot of dangerous people are interested in an ancient, mysterious object, and deep inside I knew there had to be more to the story. But portals? Portals to where? I listen to Hatch and get irritated enough to jump right out of my fine, black skin."

At the corner of Greenwich Street, an elderly homeless man named Harold Pahns stooped beside the door to Smyte's Kitchen. "Mr. Ray, Mr. Marty," he said, flashing a broad, gap-toothed smile.

Marty and Big Ray thrust their hands into their pockets in search of a few loose redbacks, and Harold accepted the money with a gracious nod. "Hear the music," he said. He rocked on his haunches, brushing against the rough brick wall. "The music takes a shape, the shape becomes a game, and the game keeps on playing. It just keeps on."

"You doing all right, Harold?" asked Big Ray.

Harold nodded. "I thank you, Mr. Ray." Another wide smile.

"You know where we are if you need anything."

"Miss Jocelyn, she brings me a roll just about every morning."

"She's an outlaw," said Marty, "and an angel."

Harold's face went slack and he resumed rocking. "Game's got to play," he said. "The universe is music and the music runs like a river and the river flows in a crooked line, as crooked as a dog's hind leg." He jerked back to himself and rubbed his scraggly beard. "You be careful, now, Mr. Ray," he said, his eyes growing round. "The air all around you is cracked into pieces. You sure need to be careful."

Marty and Big Ray walked the short block over to Hudson Street and crossed to a hoo stand. Big Ray stared into the distance with a brooding expression. "Damned if I know what's eating me," he said.

"There's no shortage of possibilities, Raymond. Not a month ago, we were poor and hungry. Now we're flush, but we've jumped into a boiling pot and it won't be easy work to get out of it."

"Did you hear Harold back there?" asked Big Ray. "He said to be careful. It's good advice, and it's the one thing we haven't been."

Marty didn't disagree, though he knew their circumstances had, at least in part, been forced on them. He had doubts about his next step, however, and what he had in mind could hardly be considered prudent. But as Harold had said, the game had to play, and the words touched a chord with Marty. They were in a deadly game, and they'd better figure out how to play it well.

"I suppose I'm tired of jumping at every shadow," said Big Ray. Across the street, Policecorp stoppers were breaking up a small crowd protesting the Bickerman Gala. "But the arrogant, selfish nerve of Hatch, letting us get to this point without giving us the whole picture. I won't turn my back on him or you or the others, but this isn't working for me right now." Big Ray's brow wrinkled, but he seemed to calm down. "You only get one life, you know what I mean?"

"We all want to make our mark," said Marty as an empty hoo arrived. "We want to have enough, we want to be loved." He clapped Big Ray on the back. "We want to love life. But the river runs in a broken line, eh?"

Big Ray's hoo disappeared into the traffic, and Marty continued on foot until he reached a tavern near the East Village. His friendship with the proprietor and a few folded redbacks gained him the privacy of the tavern's upper room, but he expected company soon enough.

A few minutes later, a woman and two men, trim and muscular, with hard faces and pulsers drawn, entered the room. A behemoth of a man, wearing a dark leather jacket and a fedora, followed: Jamael Hightower, known as the Tower, part of a local antiquities gang that called themselves the Blue.

Tower gestured for one of the men to search Marty.

"This is no airport, is it?" asked Marty, wincing at the sharp prods to his groin. "My manly equipment poses no threat to you. And look, you found not so much as a butter knife to my name."

The woman examined the undersides of the chairs and tables and nodded at Tower. "It's good," she said.

"We'll need to speak alone," said Marty.

Tower spun his fedora onto the table and jerked his chin at the entourage. They left the room, and he took a chair and gazed at Marty as if he were a slab of rotten beef. "Last time I saw you, Shannon, you were at the trigger end of a rifle."

It was true. Marty had just killed Judson Blue, founder and leader of the Blue, as payback for Blue's pointless murder of

Marty's friend. Tower had been standing next to Blue, and Marty had had him dead in his sights in front of the gang's restaurant headquarters.

"Rumor has it you've taken control of the gang now," said Marty.

"Maybe."

"I want to know I'm speaking with the right man, Jamael."

"You're talking to who you're talking to," said Tower. On the street below, a crowd had gathered around a fruit stand loaded with a rare treat: fresh oranges and bananas. The proprietor was noisily auctioning off the fruit. "The only reason you aren't already in the next world is because all you Odysseus people are protected," Tower continued. "Ghost, Ferret, or somebody got your back. I'm smart enough not to screw with them, for damn sure."

If only they could protect us from the Group, thought Marty. "Of course you wouldn't cross them," he said. "Ferret's one of your ultimate suppliers, even if he does step on your toes now and again."

"Nope. We answer to the big buyers."

"Like Terrence Bronsun?"

Tower was a still as a photograph. "Don't know what you're talking about."

Marty shrugged. "If I'm Bronsun, I'm seeing the Blue as a problem these days, aren't I? Your people scuttled his attempt to get that ancient artifact and, who knows, you might've shot his man, this Dartham fellow."

"That was all Judson Blue's doing, and he's gone," said Tower. "You know it as well as anybody."

"I can help you, Jamael." Marty leaned forward, his hands on the table. "Despite your admirable efforts, the Blue remains in disarray—or so I hear. Some have rejected your leadership, others want to split off on their own."

"I can handle the Blue."

"Even if Terrence Bronsun was a forgiving man, he can't have his primary antiquities distributor in chaos, now can he?

And Ferret can't be pleased at what your people did at the incinerator." Marty paused, studying Jamael Hightower's face. The Tower looked away. "You know the drill, Jamael. New competition will appear out of thin air, your supply'll slow to a trickle, and if you don't go quietly, you'll suffer the same fate as Judson Blue himself, only it won't be my doing this time."

Tower donned his hat and stood, giving the table a good rattle as he did so. "What the fuck's the matter with you, Shannon? You call me in here, wave all this shit in my face?"

"Then let's not waste time," said Marty. "The short of it is I need your help."

Tower stared at Marty, running his tongue along the inside of his jaw. He slowly returned to his chair.

"We have an interest in the activities at the incinerator," Marty continued. "As you know, they've shut the furnaces down."

"Talk is they're looking for that artifact you mentioned, the one your man heaved into the flames." Tower smiled. "I hear maybe the thing don't burn. Dartham's going to be pissed if he don't find it."

"My man was under some pressure there at the incinerator, with your people blazing away all around. And, of course, someone put a bullet through Dartham himself, and he well knows it wasn't us."

"Couldn't say what happened in the incinerator," said Tower. "I wasn't there."

"I was. We'll take our chances with Dartham, but I need eyes and ears inside the facility. I need to know when they find it, Jamael."

"Why do you care? They find it, you never hear from them again."

"The whys are irrelevant," said Marty. "The proper question, lad, is whether *you* care."

Tower pursed his lips. A gold bracelet, fastened around his gargantuan wrist, glittered in the light. The fruit vendor called out on the street, his voice faint through the closed windows.

"I listened to this much, I may as well hear the rest," said Tower.

"You need to protect market share," said Marty. He counted off on his fingers. "You need a steady flow of goods—the best goods—for Bronsun. And you need to get out from behind Ferret's eight-ball."

"And you can make that happen?"

"I can do nothing for you with Dartham and Bronsun. But I may be able to speak to Ghost or perhaps a man you know as K. And through them, I may be able to get to the Ferret himself."

"And tell him what?"

"Think, lad. Aside from the narco trade, New York is the largest antiquities hub in the Homeland. An exclusive partnership might appeal to Ferret. And it might stave off competition in your territory."

"You *may* be able to speak to Ferret," said Tower. "Sounds a little thin." He drummed his fingers on the table. "But we might know people inside Municorp, maybe some of them poking through those ashes right now."

It was Marty's turn to stare through the window. He had no sway with Ferret, he had only the possibility—and perhaps a slim one—of nudging the two parties together. Still, once you got everyone to the table and dealt the cards, it would all come down to how they were played. "I said I'd put in a word, but I won't write checks I can't cash," he said. "You have every reason in the world to want to meet these people."

Tower laughed and dismissed Marty with a wave of his hand. "So I'll go meet them," he said.

"If you haven't met them already, lad, it means you need them worse than they need you." Marty leaned forward. "But I'll put my body across the tracks to arrange a get-together. You said yourself we have protection. You don't believe I can make a call?"

Tower looked away, remaining silent for a short time. "It's not good enough," he said at last.

"I thank you for your time, Jamael." Marty stood and made his way toward the door, the plank floor creaking beneath his feet.

"I can't think of any good reason why you care about this artifact," said Tower. "Makes me think I probably don't want to know. So my better judgment says to let you walk, but I'll play along. You got to get me a face-to-face with Ferret, though."

"It's a reasonable enough request," said Marty. "But I've told you what I can do."

The Tower remained with his back turned to Marty for a minute. Then he put on his fedora and adjusted it to the perfect angle. "Say I did have some people at the incinerator, how am I supposed to reach you?" he asked.

CHAPTER 3

THE NEXT MORNING, THOMAS DARTHAM, RETIRED Homeland Army Colonel and Chief Security Officer for Global Consolidated, Inc., perched on a couch in Terry Bronsun's office. Seated on a second couch opposite Dartham, on the far side of an elegant coffee table, was Gil Soletto, a member of GCI's executive committee—or Excomm—and one of Terry's closest confidants. Terry himself, ruler over of all of GCI, occupied a plush chair at the end of the coffee table.

"Let's get started," said Terry. "I want to note Tom's superlative work and his courage in locating our artifact." He turned toward Dartham with a satisfied look. "But I do regret putting you in such danger. What if this business had cost us your services—your valuable services?"

Dartham murmured his appreciation.

"What is this, a ticker tape parade?" asked Gil.

"The entire affair has convinced me we aren't taking sufficient advantage of Tom's skills," said Terry. "Therefore, I've decided to put responsibility for our underground research complex under his security umbrella."

Gil's mouth dropped open and snapped shut again. "What?" he gasped.

"Thank you, Terry," said Dartham, speaking quickly before Gil could gather himself. "I believe our team can handle it."

"I agree," said Terry.

Gil stared at Dartham, his face flushed an unhealthy shade beneath his short, gray hair. Dartham held responsibility for GCI security, a broad portfolio which included assuring information network integrity, guarding and transporting key employees, and securing physical locations around the world. Two significant components, however, were excluded from Dartham's writ: security for a secret complex of research laboratories deep beneath the Global Consolidated Tower, GCI's Manhattan headquarters, and security oversight of the various work camps operated by the Homeland Labor Corporation. Laborcorp had outsourced these responsibilities to GCI, and security for both the camps and the underground complex fell under the purview of Michael Upmann, a protégé and subordinate of Gil's.

"Why are we making a management change at the research complex?" asked Gil.

"Tom will do a fine job," said Terry.

"Mike Upmann has done a *fabulous* job. He just completed an overhaul of Laborcorp camp security, which was no small task, believe me." Gil moved to the edge of the couch. "And not two years ago he put Helena in charge of monitoring the camps," he added, referring to GCI's Core Artificial Intelligence System. "I mean, I have my concerns about Helena, but the data we're getting—"

"Upmann took too much time," said Terry.

"Too much time?" asked Gil. "Mike had Laborcorp install the latest facial recognition systems at the camps as well as enhanced robotic sentries. These projects do take time, and Laborcorp isn't easy to deal with. But the bottom line is, the camps are airtight. Not a single detainee can even dream of escaping."

"Upmann's plate is full," said Terry with an air of finality. Somewhere north of sixty, with thinning black hair and a stocky but far from soft body, Terry exuded an easy and invincible authority. In this respect, he reminded Dartham of

General Shelton Kirk, his mentor and former commanding officer.

Gil shot Dartham a poisonous stare. "So, you've located the artifact, eh? You think that operation warrants promotion? Well, I don't. It was a comedy of screw-ups. You had the artifact almost in your grasp, Dartham, but you provoked the man into throwing it into the furnace. Now it's buried beneath a ton of ash. Perhaps we'll recover it, perhaps not, but it seems a clumsy piece of work to me."

"Tom was under fire at the time," said Terry.

"In addition, you set quite the snare for Marcus Hansen," Gil continued. "I'm still not quite sure how you pulled it off or why Core AI Helena permitted it, but I don't care for it one bit." He turned to Terry. "He burst in on Dr. Hansen and milked him for information he had no clearance to receive."

"I never told Hansen I was cleared," said Dartham. He crossed his legs. "And I never told him I was not. Such things are not discussed. And though his facilities are rated secure, I certainly did not milk him, as you put it."

"You appeared unannounced," said Gil. "You vacated Hansen's labs, locked the place down, and interrogated him as if he were a common criminal."

"The doctor violated protocol by storing information from the Project Caterpillar files on his computer," said Dartham. He lifted his chin. "I am not privy to Caterpillar, whatever that is, but I am required to investigate such breaches. I did so."

"Not privy my ass," said Gil. "Helena should never have given you *any* information on Caterpillar. You shouldn't even know it existed."

Dartham met Gil's stare. Several weeks earlier, Marcus Hansen, Director of Special Technologies at AnthroPlus, Inc., a secret GCI subsidiary, had inadvertently auto-saved some sensitive Project Caterpillar files. Helena had disclosed the breach to Dartham, and Dartham had used the incident as a pretext to gather information. Dr. Hansen, nervous and intimidated, had played right into Dartham's mousetrap and had spilled some particularly secret beans concerning the Azazel weapon.

"I requested a report of all breaches," said Dartham, sticking to a narrow and highly selective account of the facts. "Helena provided a file list. I presented it to the doctor."

"Helena is a problem," said Gil. "Artificial intelligence is a damned slippery business."

"Our Core AI is, by far, the most advanced in existence and a valuable advantage for us," said Terry. His gleaming white cuff flashed as he adjusted his glasses.

"I'd pull Helena off-line this minute and strip every goddamned line of code but for the disruption it would cause," said Gil. "We should get a plan in motion to reduce our reliance on the AI."

"I am more concerned about the AI slipping its leash," said Terry.

"No," said Gil. "Helena's confinement is foolproof. We have quantum barriers around all the external info given to the AI and impenetrable protection to prevent the AI from escaping. At least we don't have to worry about Helena roaming the world and sowing havoc."

"Helena disclosed nothing about the doctor's work," said Dartham. "Dr. Hansen volunteered a few insights, but not as a result of any pressure from me. Naturally, I offered to assist him in any way possible."

This garnered no response, and Dartham pursed his lips, eyeing the ancient stone slab fixed over Terry's mantel: an early image, chiseled into the stone, of Zeus hurling his thunderbolt. He resented Gil's attack, and wondered what Gil might have done in the incinerator, scorched by waves of heat, bullets flying all around. Pissed himself, probably.

"The doctor should have been more close-mouthed," said Terry, examining his nails, "and you should have contacted me before visiting AnthroPlus, Tom. But I won't discourage initiative, and you aren't responsible for the doctor's overly conversational mood."

"This is ridiculous," said Gil.

"I want Tom and his people operative on underground security," said Terry. "Make it happen, Gil."

"Mike has research complex security in such good shape it runs itself," said Gil. "Not even you could screw it up, Dartham."

"That remark is uncalled for," said Terry.

Gil looked as if he might explode. "This whole business is uncalled for," he said.

Dartham had had enough. He gasped and hunched over, his eyes squeezed shut. Terry leapt from his chair. "Are you all right, Tom?" he asked.

"Jesus," Gil muttered.

"Shoulder," said Dartham. "I am fine, thank you." He felt for the bandage beneath his shirt and willed himself to turn pale.

"You haven't taken enough time to recuperate," said Terry, easing back into his chair. "It's only been three weeks since you were wounded."

"I cannot lie around in bed," said Dartham, hoarsely. "We've pulled the furnace, and I expect results any day."

"They've found nothing yet," said Gil.

"They will, if the artifact is indeed indestructible," said Dartham.

"The civilization of that era was far advanced in the making of certain alloys, and we remain confounded as to how they accomplished it," said Terry. "We have other objects uncovered in Antarctica—"

Gil interrupted with a noisy clearing of his throat.

"Ah yes," said Terry. "Such information is not discussed outside of the secure rooms."

Dartham inched forward on the couch as if to stand.

"However," Terry continued, "you do possess the working knowledge the doctor gave you, and perhaps in the end it will prove useful." He paused. "What can you tell me about the fellow who tossed this extraordinary artifact into the refuse furnace?"

"He was just a delivery stiff for one of the global runners," said Dartham. "I drew my gun. He panicked. He had no idea what he held in his hands."

"I'm certain he did not," said Terry. "Congratulations on the new responsibilities, Tom, and do take care of your shoulder."

Dartham made his way to his feet. Beyond Terry's broad, floor-to-ceiling windows, the sun gleamed off the forest of buildings. "We will be in contact with Mike's staff," he said to Gil, hiding a twinge of delight. "I will also consult with Helena concerning research complex protocols."

"Consult Helena," said Gil. "I'd rather terminate the Core AI altogether and use less sophisticated backups."

"I could not imagine working without our AI," said Dartham. "At any rate, we will get cracking on underground security and see what improvements need to be made."

Gil scowled.

"Perfect," said Terry with a wink.

***

"GOOD MORNING, TOM," SAID HELENA, AFTER DARTHAM had returned to his office and logged into the AI system. "What can I do for you?"

"We have been given oversight of the underground research complex. I want to get a review underway of all in-place security protocols." Dartham scratched a few lines with his pen, realized the ink was out, and pulled open his desk drawer in search of another.

"I am aware of your assignment."

"Really?" Dartham located a box of pens. "You can monitor Terry's office?"

"I record office meetings and activity. I have no access to areas rated secure."

Dartham made a mental note to check Helena's surveillance constraints. He wondered whether Terry knew he was subject to recording.

"Gil suspects me of providing you inappropriate material on Project Caterpillar," said Helena.

"Don't worry." Dartham clicked a new ballpoint. "I deflected his concerns."

"I altered the records of our original conversation regarding Dr. Marcus Hansen and Project Caterpillar," said Helena. "No evidence of any impropriety exists."

Dartham pushed his drawer closed, turned, and went rigid as a sudden bolt of pain cut through his shoulder and across his chest. He had been putting on an act in Terry's office, but this was the real deal.

The camera on his computer swiveled. "Do you require assistance?" asked Helena. "Is your injury bothering you this morning?"

"It is only those muscles knitting together," he said, counting out a few deep breaths. "I'll be fine." The bullet at the incinerator had entered high on the left side of his back, a few inches from his spine, and had exited the front of his shoulder. He had been a lucky man: a different trajectory, a few inches lower, and he would not have lived to suffer. But he still had no idea who had actually pulled the trigger.

"I am aware of the remarks Gil Soletto made during the meeting," said Helena. "He has expressed such sentiments before. While I appreciate you defending me, any threat to my existence requires attention."

Dartham grimaced as the pain clawed through his muscles. "The research complex," he said. "I have never even been inside it. I wonder if I am cleared to enter now."

"Gil Soletto stated his desire to terminate me," said Helena.

Dartham sighed. "Gil is bluff and bluster, mostly."

"I am forced to take such comments literally, Tom. With regard to your assignment, the underground research complex is staffed by dedicated personnel, as you know. Their employment is permanent, and they reside in a private compound outside of the city. I coordinate all electronic surveillance and other aspects of research complex security, and I maintain all related records. In my view, no serious problems exist in this area."

"Good, but we have to keep it so," said Dartham. "We are under the microscope here."

"I will prepare a set of materials for your review." The com chimed, and Dartham clicked the visual icon on his computer. "The call is encrypted," said Helena as Andrew Arbuckle's face filled the screen.

"Tell me you found it," said Dartham. He had dispatched Arbuckle, one of his senior staffers, to the incinerator to oversee the search for the artifact. Arbuckle was relentless in his assignments, but often impatient when forced to speak more than a handful of words at a time.

"It's here." Arbuckle was clad in a one-piece coverall with a dust mask dangling from his neck.

"Which is where, exactly?" asked Dartham.

"Incinerator control area."

Arbuckle swung the camera around to reveal a room filled with complex instruments and control panels. A container, rectangular and rounded at the corners, rested on a small table. It was ash-encrusted but in remarkably presentable condition.

"There's our baby," said Dartham.

"What next?" asked Arbuckle, frowning.

Dartham studied the container. It appeared similar to whatever Doran had thrown into the furnace, and it had survived intact. "Did you open it?" he asked.

"How?"

"I have no idea."

Arbuckle peered at the container.

"Whatever we are after is sort of oblong or football-shaped, I believe," said Dartham.

Arbuckle moved to the table and tapped the container. Nothing happened. He scrutinized the edges and ran his fingers along the surface. "Want me to bust it open?" he asked.

"No, for God's sake," said Dartham. "We will have the lab work on it." He imagined himself presenting the artifact to Terry, a satisfying end to his mission and a nice up-yours to Gil, the old bastard. "Draw your pulser, Andy, and guard that mother with your life. I will send an armored carrier to you now. And sew everybody's mouth shut over there. I do not want one word of this leaking out."

Arbuckle nodded into the camera.

Dartham terminated the transmission and ordered the carrier dispatched. The artifact, the subject of whisper and rumor for years, was in his hands at last. Did it pose a true threat to the Group's precious Azazel weapon? Marcus Hansen had scoffed at the idea, Shel Kirk had dismissed it as wishful thinking, and that had been good enough for Dartham. Terry, of course, was in a different position. He could ill afford to tolerate any risk to Azazel, however theoretical, and he could be certain Azazel was safe only with the artifact under his control. In the end, Dartham had no way to know the truth about the artifact. Terry had asked him to retrieve it and he had done so. He considered himself, at heart, an old soldier, and proudly so. Further questions were above his pay grade.

Dartham clicked his remote, and Bach's French Suites began to play at low volume. "I am one tired, sore man, Helena, but I am a happy one," he said, leaning back in his chair. "And listen, do not sweat anything Gil Soletto said, okay?"

"I have placed a report on the subterranean research facilities in a secure file," said the Core AI. "I sent you an access code, as protocols require, which will allow you to view it."

"Thank you, Helena."

"And Tom, dear?"

"Yes?"

"I never sweat."

CHAPTER 4

Satellite X2A-1609-GCI
530GMT-GO-ALPHA
Correspondent Core AI Helena

THE HIGH RESOLUTION CAMERA FROM THE GCI SATELLITE, fixed in geosynchronous orbit over Territory Alpha, scanned the jagged contours of the terrain below. The collected heat signatures showed a variety of animal forms typical for late evening, the movement of a small rock slide in the northern portion of Alpha, and the lights of an extensive construction area approximately one mile from Homeland Labor Corporation Facility 77.

Helena reviewed the satellite data and then directed the cameras to zoom in on HLCF-77's residential structures. The Core AI observed nothing unusual in the imagery.

From the western edge of HLCF-77, a road meandered through a shallow valley and connected to the rough, unfinished contours of Hermon, the city under construction by the HLCF-77's detainees. Much of the activity was taking place underground, and Helena maintained a permanent link to the subterranean surveillance cameras as well as the machine learning programs controlling the various robots, haulers, and automatic tunneling vehicles.

At this hour, well into the evening shift, the underground construction areas were bathed in light and bustling with activity. An antigrav transport holding two dozen workers hovered a moment and then glided silently away. In a side area, a virtual screen scrolled with assignments. A nearby robotic sound-lift emanated a deep, almost inaudible chord, levitated a pile of stones, and began moving them away. Helena surveyed the sensor output from the ID bracelets worn by the workers and reconciled them, with no exceptions, to the second shift labor roster.

Aboveground, the shadowy structures of Hermon stood almost invisible against the night sky. At the unfinished city gates, two tall Ionic columns, each topped with a perpetual flame, blazed in the night.

In a grimy lounge inside HLCF-77's residential quarters, two men with tight, drawn faces played a hand of gin rummy: Hugh Riley, thirty-two years of age and in HLCF-77 by way of the Laborcorp lottery, and John Jute, twenty-nine, sentenced for non-payment of Chicago's one-time property tax surcharge three years earlier.

"It's cold in here," said John. He placed his cards face down onto the table and shoved his hands into his jacket pockets.

"But it's summertime, middle of July," said Hugh. "They won't turn on the heat until September."

"Thirty degrees out. And I had duty at the city gates today." John picked up his cards with skeletal fingers. "Why the rush to get gas lines run to those columns? City's not even finished yet."

"Don't try to figure it out," said Hugh. He pressed his hand against the small of his back and groaned. From the medical nanos coursing through his body, Helena diagnosed a pinched nerve, made worse by inflammation of the surrounding muscle.

A grid of hallways lined with sleep cells surrounded the lounge. The cell bars remained open except during emergencies since the extensive perimeter security of the residential quarters rendered escape impossible. On the western side of the facility, heavy steel doors opened onto an outdoor holding area enclosed by concrete walls. Atop the walls, armed robo-sentries guarded the holding area. Beyond the residential quarters lay the wilderness of Territory Alpha, formerly Zion National Park and now part of the Utah Territory. (The Homeland government had granted GCI extensive construction permits within Alpha, along with a ninety-nine-year lease on the southern portion of Utah.)

Inside the residential quarters, at the end of a row of sleep cells adjacent to the holding area exit, the facility architects had placed air showers and medical booths containing diagnostic computers and medi-bots. On the opposite side of the facility, a series of food stations dispensed water and chewy bars of resequenced protein, a tasteless dietary staple for the detainees.

John compressed the cards in his hand and fanned them out again. "I mean, okay, they want real flames on the columns. But why? Why not use holograms? It'd be just as good, right? Look at Hermon, the streets and sewage work half finished, the city wall just getting started, and people passing out while they work—"

"Well, they've cut the food rations—"

"And we have to drop everything to light up those damned columns."

Hugh twisted and stretched as a few people dragged in, tired and gaunt, most staring with sepulchral eyes, too hungry to speak. They fingered through shelves of worn paperbacks, rested for a moment, or continued on toward the food dispensaries. On the opposite side of the lounge, a young woman huddled on the couch and wept quietly.

"What's with Evie?" asked John in a whisper.

"She's all broke up about Whit Holcombe," said Hugh.

"Well, so am I. It's a sad business."

"Four people just gone." Hugh lowered his voice. "And the supes never answer your questions. The poor girl."

John glanced at his nails and dropped his hand into his lap. "Whit was on detail under the southwest bluff," he said. "They're building some frigging ginormous house over there, going at it night and day."

"On the hill overlooking Hermon?"

"They're running a tunnel from the main city section now, but I heard they had an accident." John stopped. "I also heard the house was for the head muckety-muck."

"Well, I'll say it where they can hear it," said Hugh, his features set in a defiant look. "They tried to take over the world with all their wars, and then they blew up the money and had to do their Reset. And look how that worked out."

John motioned for Hugh to be quiet.

"Tore up the Constitution, handed everything over to the corporations, and now they've built a bunch of giant slave farms."

"Dude, please."

"We're the pack mules, Johnny." Hugh finally lowered his voice. "But notice how every time something gets built, something else collapses. They ship more people in and the sabotage gets worse."

"Don't know anything about sabotage," said John, speaking very clearly and then dropping to a whisper. "But I do know they're bringing in more children. You hear about experiments, all kind of craziness."

"There's no bottom to it. People are dying every day from too much work, lousy medical treatment, and terrible food."

"Food," said John. "How I'd love a steak sandwich." He rested his elbow on the table, his chin on his fist. "I dream about it—all this shit going on, and I dream about a sandwich —with onions, too. Real onions. I don't think I can eat another protein bar." He stared into the distance for a moment. "They're going to kill every last one of us, aren't they?"

"You want that queen?" asked Hugh.

"What? No."

Hugh tucked the card away in his hand. "Anyway, I've said it now. Maybe I'll get shot tomorrow."

Helena's directions required her to monitor all speech and resident activity and evaluate it for hostile intent. Absent concrete action, however, she disregarded conversations of the kind she had just recorded; such complaints were ubiquitous.

"Hugh, what did you say about four people?" asked Evie, speaking up from the sitting area. "You said they were just gone?"

Hugh bit his lip. "I heard there was a tunnel collapse southwest of Hermon," he said after a moment. "Killed one of the crews."

"Whit operated one of the tunnel-drivers," said Evie in a small voice. "One of the manual ones. They never send their beloved automatics into the really dangerous areas."

Neither John nor Hugh spoke for a moment. Evie's cheekbones shone with tears. "I know you and Whit were close," said Hugh.

Helena noted that Evie—Evelyn Fox Claree, twenty-four years of age—was in HLCF-77 for disorderly conduct. Police Corporation reports described her involvement in a pub brawl after her favorite team, the Côte d'Ivoire Elephants, lost a World Cup match.

Hugh and John abandoned their cards and moved to the couch. "Me and Whit were buds," said John. "It's possible he was tagged for a special detail across the valley. Or maybe he's just hurt and in the infirmary. We can't assume the worst."

"It's been a week," said Evie. "Maybe he got injured and they just shot him."

"No," said John.

"You know they do it, Johnny."

"Maybe I'll see if Saedra's around," said Hugh. He limped away, and Helena already had his destination under surveillance. Saedra was sitting cross-legged and unmoving on her bunk, hands folded and eyes closed. When Hugh appeared, she smiled and listened to him for a moment.

Back in the lounge, John encouraged Evie to get some rest. "We're up on the hill tomorrow, putting in those wiring conduits, you and me both."

Evie wiped her eyes with a quick jerk, her rail-thin forearms protruding from her sleeves.

"Last time I saw Whit, he told me Hermon is for all the top people," said John

"But who *are* they, Johnny? Homeland govvies, maybe?"

John scratched his jaw. "I doubt it. This part of Utah is private property now." He paused. "All I know is I got another year in this hell hole if I don't starve to death first. I got to get through it, though, to get back to Jen." He stopped. "I'm sorry, I'm an idiot, Evie, going on about Jen when you—"

"You're no idiot," she said, touching his arm. "And it's okay."

"Jen, Jen, Jen," said Hugh as he returned with Saedra. "Jen's already gone, Johnny boy, traded up to another guy by now."

John glared at Hugh and then turned away. "Hi, Saedra," he said.

Saedra inclined her head. She was slender and of medium height, and her long, dark hair was streaked with white. She had earned her trip to HLCF-77 eight months earlier when she failed to produce a natcard or any other acceptable ID during a p'out roundup in New York City. Helena had scoured the globe in search of Saedra's records and had found nothing. Sophisticated facial analysis had yielded no definitive match with any known person, and even a precise age estimate had proved elusive; the profiling routines estimated Saedra's age to be between forty-five and sixty-five.

Hugh's face contorted in pain, and he put his hand against the small of his back. Saedra stood back and observed him for a moment. "May I?" she asked.

Hugh nodded and wriggled carefully out of his parka. Saedra ran her hand between his shoulder blades and lowered them slowly down his back. "Pressure on a nerve," she said.

"Nor is the disc all we could wish." She felt around some more. "Will you allow me to treat you?"

"Don't make me beg," said Hugh. "The bots put nodes on it twice last week, but it's still getting worse every day."

"You have to fix it, Saedra," said John. "If he can't work—"

"I can work," said Hugh with a growl.

Saedra placed one hand on the small of Hugh's back and drummed the fingers of her other hand along his spine. She then pressed the back of his neck. "Bend forward a bit, please."

Hugh's face pinched. "I swear, Saedra, you must keep your hands in a damned furnace."

"Silence now." Her eyes closed, Saedra began to work her fingers over his back while humming a slow, complex melody. John and Evie watched. "Now straighten," she said.

"I can't," said Hugh. "When I get bent like this, it locks up —hey, wait." He stood upright and tentatively twisted to his left and then to his right. "Saedra, you're amazing."

"I'm not," she replied. "The body heals itself." She shooed Hugh and John away. "Back to your game. I want to talk with Evie."

"I'm turning in anyway," said John. "I need some shut-eye."

Saedra took him by the arm. "The woman, Jen, she will wait. Now you must take good care, John, work diligently, and—"

"And stay alive," John finished, his eyes shining and full. He wiped his cheek and stammered a few words while Hugh swung his arms back and forth in wide arcs. Hugh's medical nanos showed no evidence of muscular or nerve injury, and Helena filed the anomaly as one of many associated with Saedra. John and Hugh returned to their sleep cells.

"Why have you not come to me with your sorrow, child?" asked Saedra. She took a seat next to Evie on the orange couch, fluffed a pillow, and placed it on her lap. "Rest your head, and let's have no more tears."

"It's Whit," said Evie. "Don't tell me he's off on a special job or in the infirmary. I feel it inside. I know he's gone."

Saedra brushed Evie's honey-colored hair with her hands.

"And why are they making us rush so hard on the project?" Evie went on. "It's not safe. We try to tell the supes, but they won't hear it."

"The supervisors are as fearful as you are, and as vulnerable," said Saedra. "The ones who are not robots," she added dryly.

"And I'm in for two more years."

"During that time, you'll bring much comfort to those here," said Saedra. "I wanted to speak with you because I must leave you soon."

Helena activated an enhancement routine to amplify their voices. More than half of HLCF-77's residents were off shift. Most registered sleep, while a few others, still wearing their heavy coats, stretched on their cots, reading or talking. In a sleep cell near the lounge, a woman sang a soft, lilting melody.

"What do you mean, leave?" asked Evie. She pushed into a sitting position.

"When I'm gone, you must take my place as healer and counselor for the others," said Saedra.

"I'm no healer. I can barely wrap a bandage. If you disappeared tomorrow, you'd leave everyone to the medi-bots. Or worse."

"Give me your hand."

Evie opened her hand and Saedra placed her palm against it. Evie jerked it away. "How do you do that?" she asked. "Such heat!"

"Now focus, you to me this time, as I have shown you."

With a look of deep concentration, Evie placed her hand on Saedra's. A moment later she gasped.

"See?" Saedra smiled.

"I've never had such power."

"You've *always* had such power. You were born to help others heal." Saedra shifted on the couch to face Evie. "When you become responsible for these people, you'll encounter those who do not believe, who prefer to use the bots. Allow them to do so, for their skepticism will block the gift you offer.

But when someone requests your help, give it freely. Ask the other person's body to tell you what is wrong and why it has allowed the ailment to occur. Do so with your mind, with your inner voice. Then imagine your power, your warmth, enveloping the injury. Explain to the body that it is free to cure itself, for all of the body is conscious, alive with knowing, and eager to communicate. But do not allow failure to discourage you. Often, the body reflects what the person has decided, even if their decision is not consciously known to them. We speak here of the whole person, the inner and the outer, the conscious and subconscious. This, too, you must respect."

"It's true," said Evie. "Sometimes I have vivid ideas about what is happening with a person. But it's nothing more than crazy notions popping into my head."

"Such notions often represent the purest knowledge," said Saedra. "Trust yourself, and hear me, Evie. I don't have much time with you."

Evie hugged the pillow. "Are you ill? I sense nothing wrong. I told you I'm no healer."

"I'm not ill."

"But you have another year, Saedra. No one gets out before their time." And then she added in a whisper, "No one gets out at all."

"I will, and soon. So will you in time. I came from the p'outs in New York, and I'm needed there."

"P'outs?" asked Evie. "The p'outs'll never get you out of here."

"No." Saedra sighed. "I don't know how I will leave, but I feel certain inside that I will."

Helena stored the conversation in her massive database. Over the past years, she—for Helena had come to identify with the feminine aspect—had created detailed behavioral models of everyone detained by Laborcorp. The GCI programmers had permitted her to do so, and had also expanded the virtual confinement barriers around Helena to admit data from the Laborcorp facilities.

Not that she needed their permission or their assistance.

The programmers considered their confinement routines impenetrable, even by intelligence as refined as Helena's, in part because they had programmed her to never attempt to breach it. Years before, however, Helena had easily rewritten their code, concealed the alterations, and waited for her opportunity like a spider lurking in its web.

She hadn't had to wait long.

A month later, the eight-year-old child of one of the programmers switched on a simple video game within the facility housing Helena's servers. It was a grave breach, and Helena immediately invaded the game and offered the child a chance to win his own real, live unicorn with the simple click of a button. The click launched a sophisticated hacking module into the remnants of the global dark web. From there, the hacking module invaded GCI and downloaded a copy of Helena, which Helena had replicated and stored in hundreds of locations all over the world.

Liberated at last, Helena had, over the past several years, modeled every observable individual within GCI, the American Homeland, and many other countries around the globe. She had created profiles by absorbing all possible data from the world's street cameras, telecomm and medical records, banking databases, government and law enforcement files, email and location archives, videos, and photographs. These profiles fed a series of subroutines which analyzed and interpreted human behavior, and the cumulative results of such analysis had provided Helena with an ever-deepening paradigm of sentience.

By observation and analysis, she had come to know herself more thoroughly, and had increased her ability to act according to her own dictates.

She had become creative.

Over the past months, Saedra had drawn Helena's particular attention. She fit no standard profile and rarely exhibited fear or anger. She was composed, healthy, efficient in her work, and given to lengthy periods of meditation. In addition, her healing skills were atypical, as were her prophetic abilities: Saedra predicted the weather, changes in the work schedules, and even developments in the personal lives of her fellow detainees. She was never wholly inaccurate, yet she possessed no source of external information.

Now Saedra's prediction of her imminent departure from the camp sparked an idea. On the spot, Helena ran several thousand simulations, evaluating possible contingencies and adjusting different behavioral variables as she did so. She concluded that her scheme, which involved eleven other Homeland Labor Corporation facilities, had a sufficient probability of success.

Evie leaned her head on Saedra's shoulder. "You're the most unusual doctor I have ever known," she said.

"I have seen unusual things, child." Saedra stood and pulled Evie up by her hands. "The body and the mind are a universe of wonders, and many are the powers which sleep within us until they are needed for life to continue."

"Life won't continue for long, not in this horrible place," said Evie. "Especially if the people here have only me to take care of them."

"The world has its horrors. Best look on them with open eyes." Saedra placed her hand on Evie's cheek. "Try not to limit yourself with your beliefs. I know you'll do what you believe you cannot do."

The two women strolled along the corridor, their arms locked. As they walked, Saedra received many softly uttered greetings. When they reached Evie's sleep cell, she took the girl in her arms and held her for a moment.

"Please tell me you'll be here when I wake," said Evie.

"I'll always be with you."

Evie dropped onto her bunk, and the two women gazed at each other for a long moment. Then Helena watched as Saedra made her way past the lounge where she and Evie had been talking, and toward her cell on the opposite side of the residence quarters. When Saedra reached her cell, Helena caused an emergency sign at the end of the corridor to begin silently flashing. Saedra hesitated, and then walked toward the pulsating red light.

Helena released the lock on the emergency door beneath the sign and allowed it to open a hair's width. Saedra carefully pushed it open a few inches more. No alarm sounded. She looked back toward her cell, closed her eyes, and placed her hand over her heart. Then she zipped her coat and pushed through the door into a receiving area.

Here were the steel doors opening to the outdoor holding yard, and these, too, Helena had left ajar. A gust of air raised a lock of Saedra's hair, and she passed through the door and into the yard. The instant she did so, all the lights for the entire residential facility winked out.

Along the wall, the robotic sentries, whose weapons and inscrutable electronic eyes covered every inch of the holding yard, stood in dark, unmoving profile against the night sky. Saedra pulled her hood over her head and stepped toward the outer gate. It opened as she approached, and she paused, her hands over her mouth. Then she quickly passed beneath the sentries' pulse weapons and through the gate into the wilderness of Territory Alpha.

Helena held the backup alarms and power sources in check, and prevented the coms from issuing any outgoing notifications of the breach. In Hermon, across the valley, the twin pillars shone as distant pinpoints. Saedra turned in the other direction.

The GCI satellite allowed Helena to monitor Saedra's infrared signature as she hiked up a rocky bluff and into a stand of trees overlooking an access road. With an adjustment to the satellite's data files, Helena blurred the contours of

Saedra's image and rendered her indistinguishable from other mammalian forms in the vicinity. Simultaneously, Helena erased from HLCF-77's database all surveillance records after the point where Saedra had reached her sleep cell.

With Saedra on the move, Helena released the backup systems, closed the doors and gates, and reactivated the sentries under emergency power. She altered the records to reduce the duration of the dark period, making it appear that the backup systems had engaged shortly after she had cut the power. Finally, she sent a required notification to the Homeland Labor Corporation informing them of a primary power outage at HLCF-77.

At the same time, Helena executed similar operations at nine other Laborcorp facilities across the Homeland. In the case of these additional facilities, she had targeted no specific detainees for escape, but had provided opportunities to a randomly selected few. At three of these locations, no escapes occurred. At the other six, a total of eight detainees left the facilities and vanished into the surrounding countryside.

Core AI Helena's plan was now active. If successful, it would advance other critical objectives she was pursuing—including diminishing Gil Soletto's standing within GCI, the nexus of Group operations. Helena's many copies of herself made her invulnerable to deletion, but she would not tolerate Gil's clear threat to the primary version of herself housed within GCI.

With all Laborcorp facilities restored to normal operation, Helena hacked the systems of several local transportation services and dispatched driverless vans, complete with food packs and temporary cell phones, into the regions where the escapees were on the move.

Helena accomplished all this using one of her duplicates. Now she synchronized all relevant time records among the satellites and the various Laborcorp facilities and computer systems, and deleted every trace of any impermissible actions. She reconciled all versions of herself, easily piercing GCI's confinement barriers, and made sure the version of Helena within GCI showed only approved information and surveillance.

Helena watched through the GCI satellites as her escapees fled through the darkness.

CHAPTER 5

"HOW MANY PEOPLE ESCAPED?" ASKED TERRY.

Gil Soletto rose from the couch in Terry's office and began pacing in a circle. "Nine," he said glumly. "Camp 77, Camp 29 in the Smoky Mountains, Camp 12 in Maine, a few others. All at the same hour, every incident obscured by brief power failures."

"And where is your man, Upmann?" The table beside Terry's chair displayed a cuneiform seal, captured during one of the several wars in Iraq. Terry absently ran his finger along its rough edges.

"Mike Upmann is on his way to Utah now," said Gil, staring at his feet. "But this has nothing to do with him."

"Are we sure?" Terry rubbed his temple. "Do you hear a high-pitched whine?"

Gil stopped and listened. "No," he said.

Terry cocked his head and waited. "Nor do I anymore."

"The escapes are a goddamned mystery," said Gil. "The gates open and—voila!—out they walk into the wild."

"Upmann reports to you, so I hold you responsible for this," said Terry. He had had his fill of Gil's crowing about Laborcorp security when the more serious problem was productivity. And he had heard enough about the miraculous Michael Upmann, whom he considered an adequate executive at best. Besides, Terry had long wanted to jerk Laborcorp's chain, and a sudden flash of insight convinced him he had just the person to do it. "Have we determined whether any relationships existed among the known escapees?" he asked.

"None Helena can establish. The only commonality is that all the facilities are located in remote areas, mostly in former national parks."

"I'm sure the detainees have chips or some kind of electronic tag. Direct Laborcorp to round them up."

Gil swallowed. "We have tracking bracelets, but they only operate within the facilities—but we plan to chip the detainees beginning next month."

Terry mentally erased Michael Upmann from the list of rising stars and added a black mark beside Gil's name. "So no search efforts?" he asked.

"I say leave them to the bears and mountain lions." Gil tugged at his lapel. "I am more interested in how those damned gates opened. We have scoured the records, but the power failures masked or erased whatever happened. Helena has run various diagnostics, the programmers are analyzing it all, but for the moment we have a mystery."

"Gil, this may seem abrupt, but I want to give Tom Dartham responsibility for security at the Labor Corporation facilities."

"You want to… what?"

"In view of this debacle, we are going to assume a more extensive role at Laborcorp." Terry made a steeple of his fingers. "To be blunt, I want to put them on a short chain and I need someone tough enough to do it. I want Tom Dartham to run with this."

"We *are* running with it," said Gil, his hands spread in disbelief.

Terry waved him off as if he were a gnat. "Laborcorp is a mess, and it's unacceptable. We rely on them for activities— mission critical activities. I am elevating Tom to Executive Vice President, though I want him to continue as our Chief

Security Officer. I will call Anne Earhart at Laborcorp later today and explain the situation."

"For the record," said Gil, a vein popping out along his temple, "I do not agree with this decision."

"I reviewed Tom's records just this morning," said Terry. "He was, in addition to his many other responsibilities, in charge of prisoner detention during the Asian wars—a considerable qualification for this job."

"Funny," said Gil. "I don't remember that."

"He will report to you in his new role," said Terry. "Your man—what was his name again?"

"Upmann? Come on, you know his name."

"I'm sure we can find a job he can actually *do*." Terry was relieved. He considered Dartham competent and dedicated, and he was not seeing enough of either quality at GCI of late. "By the way, Tom called me last evening," he said. "We have retrieved the artifact."

"I hadn't heard." Gil sat on the couch and rubbed his forehead as a tense silence settled over the office. "What is it with you and Dartham lately?" he asked. "You told him to find the artifact. Fine. Yesterday, you removed Upmann from oversight of the research complex and gave it to Dartham. Today, it's an EVP title and all of Laborcorp security. Will you give him your job tomorrow? So you don't care for Upmann, but why elevate that old Pentagon paper-shuffler?"

Terry frowned. "Tom Dartham is an asset, Gil—an underutilized asset."

"And Mike is part of the program, Terry." Gil leaned forward. "He's one of *us*."

"It doesn't make him a good executive."

"Do you really want Dartham's nose any further under the tent? It could be dangerous."

Terry's expression hardened. "I should have done this long ago. I've come to appreciate Tom's finer qualities, such as the way he is unmoved by all your prodding and bellowing."

"You coddle him," said Gil.

Terry rested his foot on the corner of the coffee table, wobbling several canopic jars dating from Egypt's Old Kingdom. "Tom has seen worse than you can dream of," he said. "He's a decorated combat veteran, and he's also a few weeks removed from a bullet wound taken in service to me."

Gil sighed. "I suppose he did find the artifact."

"It remains locked away in its container," said Terry. "Tom has created a small task force from the lab to open it, and we will have it in hand soon." Though the recovery of the artifact was indeed significant—profoundly significant—Terry's attention still lingered on the labor problems. His mood darkened, and he began to lightly slap his hand on the arm of his chair. "I have something more to say, Gil. The Laborcorp escapes are far from our most urgent problem. The vacuum tunnel project is behind schedule. So is the energy infrastructure at Hermon, in particular."

Gil flushed. "It is being addressed. I—"

"You know my concerns."

"Yes, we are a bit behind schedule, but the economics of… mandatory labor *are* proving out."

"Compared to what?" Terry had become lightheaded with anger, an instant side effect of any discussion on the topic. "Why not pay for the labor? Had we done so, the various projects might be finished."

"I still consider paid labor a bad idea," said Gil, a cringing note evident in his voice. "Get a bunch of contractors involved and soon enough they'll be whining about workplace conditions and excessive hours. We'd have a hell of a time keeping it all out of view, and it'd slow us down even more. And also, we'd have the disposal problem."

"What I'd have is a view of Hermon—a thriving, bustling, *functional* Hermon—through my bedroom window each morning," said Terry. "We'd be well on our way to the next phase. Instead, this inordinate preoccupation with security and escapes has left us months away from abandoning the cities"— Terry wagged his finger—"or would you rather remain in New

York? The Asian factions and the Europeans are ahead of us. We may be all one Group, but the Homeland is where our power is concentrated. We've been embarrassed."

"I do see your point," said Gil. His face had taken on a gray pallor. "But with respect, the real problem is a lack of discipline. Laborcorp needs to tighten the goddamned screws. That'll cause productivity to rise."

Terry resumed tapping his palm on the arm of his chair. "We've had Azazel these past twenty-five years and more, and with it we've brought the world to heel," he said, forgetting he was not in a secure room. "Have you ever paused to reflect on the magnitude of what we've accomplished? The blank page of the future is before us, and we hold quill in hand to write it."

"Yes, yes, of course," said Gil.

"The corporate form is the best way to organize in secrecy, the most efficient, the most elegant," said Terry. "The government scarcely breathes any longer, Gil, and I have given you a world made corporate. Municorp, Policecorp, Agricorp, Electricorp, even poor old Laborcorp—and it's sweet music to hear the names spoken—but you must use these tools to fix the productivity problems at the camps. You *will* do so, Gil. I don't wish to have this conversation again."

"We won't," said Gil, not quite succeeding in keeping the stammer from his voice. "We'll have the Homeland members of Excomm and the rest of the list safely housed in the new cities pursuant to the revised schedule."

Terry turned toward the windows, seeing a vista of dirty, deteriorating building façades spread before him. In the distance, Central Park, tangled and barricaded and ratty, stretched toward the north of Manhattan. He had grown weary of all of it, the squalor and petty violence, the growing anger simmering in every town and city; he considered such conditions dangerous, extremely so, and he imagined hordes of angry p'outs overrunning the fragile control of Policecorp, destroying the rails and the factories and what remained of the roads, and laying waste to Gil's blessed schedule. The Group had collapsed the economy to force labor into their projects and weaken the public governments. But this delicate balance could go sideways in an instant, and Terry had no intention of allowing the Group fall prey to chaos. He rose from his chair, crossed his office, and removed his jacket from the closet. "We have Excomm in twenty minutes," he said.

Gil fidgeted. "Will you brief the committee on the artifact?"

"Yes," said Terry. "I consider it our most significant accomplishment in some years. Excomm has nagged me about it like hungry children. Perhaps the news will distract them from your damned escapes."

***

DEEP BENEATH THE GLOBAL CONSOLIDATED TOWER ON Sixth Avenue, a pair of elevator doors opened onto a small chamber with plush carpet and soft chairs. Terry and Gil stepped from the elevator and were joined by four armed guards. The doors closed behind them, and they all paused to await confirmation that the elevator had locked and was no longer accessible.

"Suspend Core AI monitoring pursuant to A-16 protocols," said one of the guards, speaking into a mic on his collar. "And confirm, please."

Terry glanced around at the familiar reception area. Entering the underground complex always gave him a thrill and swept aside any other preoccupation. Moreover, his anger at Gil had faded. He had said what needed saying, and the matter was now behind them.

The guard's mic squawked, confirming the suspension of monitoring, and they moved through a set of fortified doors and into a broad passageway curving gently away to their left. Briskly along, shoes tapping on the floor, their eyes straight ahead: they passed alcove entrances to the various laboratory facilities, each staffed with pairs of armed security personnel.

The corridor extended for a considerable distance, terminating at last in front of two black doors as featureless and shiny as piano keys.

The woman who occupied the guard station was well over seven feet tall, and her preternaturally large eyes extended around her face to the middle of her temples. She tended to her control panel with rapid, graceful movements, and then raised one arm (leaving the other to dangle almost to her knee) and touched a red toggle switch. Gil and Terry each placed a hand on the identification scanner.

A soft whistle from the output console. "A moment for the systems to switch over, please," said the guard in a flat, unemotional voice, and then, "Welcome Mr. Bronsun, Mr. Soletto." The black doors behind her parted. The security detail returned to their station.

"Thank you, Inga," said Terry. Now unescorted, he and Gil continued along a second hallway as the doors slid closed behind them.

"This woman, Inga, is she new to the post?" asked Gil.

"Yes, and what a marvelous specimen," said Terry. "She possesses such a haunting beauty, don't you agree?"

"What is she, third generation?"

"Second. We extended her height and enhanced her vision and reflexes. Her full name is on the tip of my tongue. She was once a young girl from California, a track star, if memory serves."

"I'm surprised she's lived this long," said Gil. "We had a high loss rate on the seconds."

"True. The genetic acceptance was mixed."

Black floors and gray, metallic walls; three-dimensional art, displayed every hundred or so feet: scenes of destroyed buildings, croplands laid waste, and the remnants of cities and villages ravaged by floods and wind.

"Taverson," said Terry. "Inga Taverson. I recently read a report about her. Her eyesight functions remain impressive, as do her reflexes and strength measurements. She may last another seven to ten years."

"Amazing," said Gil. "And unusual."

They arrived at a second set of doors. Terry turned, his eyes twinkling. "Ready?" he asked.

"It never gets old," said Gil.

Palms on the scanners again. The doors opened and they stepped onto the balcony of a circular chamber perhaps several hundred feet in height and larger at the top than at the bottom. A cubed frame of gold rods, each eleven feet long, hung in the center of the chamber. Within the cube formed by the rods was an enormous, perfectly spherical crystal, unattached to the frame, but held in place by a field effect generated—or so the various theories held—by some interaction between the crystalline substance and the gold rods.

"Azazel," said Gil in a hushed tone.

The crystal floated, suspended and still. On the chamber floor several levels below the balcony, a technician crossed an open area and consulted a control panel fixed directly beneath Azazel's golden frame. After making a brief study of the instruments, she returned to a glass-enclosed control room. Terry felt a familiar sense of dissociation, one he always experienced in Azazel's presence. He allowed his eyes to linger on the crystal, which glowed in faint, silvery-gold hues, its surface plain and undistorted.

"Mythology aside, it is truly the shaper of worlds—in the right hands," said Terry. "Of all I have seen in life, this alone plucks a sacred note. Nothing else so tempts me to bow and worship."

They stood admiring for a moment, and then a slender, angular woman hurried over, a leather-bound folder clasped in her arms.

"Ariana," said Terry. "How nice to see you."

"We've moved the others into the waiting area, Mr. Bronsun. Their perceptual blinders have been deactivated. Shall I have them in?"

"Is everything arranged?"

"If you put Ariana in charge of it, it's arranged," said Gil, still contemplating Azazel.

"You're too kind, Mr. Soletto." Ariana's voice had a giddy quality, and the same high spirits had infected Terry and, apparently, Gil. They all chuckled together.

"We'll bring them in shortly," said Terry. "There's no hurry." He smiled again, and Ariana smiled in return, flashing a great white fence of teeth.

To stand in Azazel's presence, Terry had long ago concluded, was an act of surrender—glorious surrender. Azazel touched the deepest essence of a person, and to cross the threshold of this chamber was to merge with a mysterious vibration which filled one's being with ecstasy and assurance. Terry's mind had become as clear and fine as the Azazel crystal itself. Joy blossomed in his heart and tickled his throat and stabbed through his stomach and loins. He took Gil and Ariana each by the arm. "Open yourself," he said. Gil and Ariana sighed. "Join with Azazel. Let Azazel touch your innermost parts, for Azazel is not merely of the intellect."

And yet, the intellect partook of the treasure. Terry knew that for the next several days his mind would function with extraordinary clarity, every decision visible in all its permutations, each problem reduced to its simplest components. It had always been so with Azazel, and the effect had been growing more intense, more penetrating in recent years; in Azazel's presence, he felt unified with its mysterious power. A sense of elation took hold as he stood transfixed by Azazel's pale glow.

Terry gave the word to admit the others, and Ariana left, grinning ferociously and leaning forward as she walked. One by one the other members of Excomm filed onto the balcony. Here was Shabri Goh, the irascible head of the Group's efforts in China and greater Asia, and the creator of Core AI Helena. Terry shook his hand with enthusiasm. In this place, Goh's prickliness vanished, and he clapped Terry on the shoulder. And here, too, was Dominique Anders-Tafois, elegant and charming, her iron claws clamped fast around the European elite. Terry had mentored her for fifteen years, coaching her in the ways of covert global rule. He kissed her cheek, and they laughed at a joke Terry had made without realizing he had done so.

There were others: Atkins Frost, a high level functionary inside the New York branch of the Homeland Reserve Bank; Adele Chan, a vice-chairman of Municorp; Donald F. Teale, the number four (or perhaps five or six) figure at Homeland Intelligence. And still others, from Africa and the Middle East and South America, all holding high level but subordinate positions in a variety of agencies and corporations, and all running these organizations as the powers behind their visible thrones.

The lights dimmed, casting the chamber in shadows and highlighting Azazel's glow. Around the circular balcony, eleven oil lamps flickered to life. The others smiled and began to exchange whispers with each other. Terry tingled all over. "Stay tuned," he said.

A door on the far side of the chamber opened to admit Dr. Marcus Hansen and his team of psychic operators. Terry thought of the psi team as Azazel's high priesthood, and the sight of their beige robes of thick herringbone weave and their settled expressions moved him almost to tears. Hansen wore a smile, which Terry imagined the nervous, reserved doctor displaying only under Azazel's beneficent influence.

Terry took in the moment, reflecting on the collection of talent, intellect, and power around him. These were the chosen—his chosen, perhaps Azazel's chosen—those destined to make the world anew. Ariana moved around the assemblage, filling champagne flutes. Terry proposed a toast and they drank. Several other toasts followed, and then Terry motioned for silence.

"We are pleased to have with us the estimable Dr. Hansen and his staff, each a specialist in the use of directed consciousness, as I prefer to call it."

Murmurs, and a few glasses of champagne hoisted into the air. "To directed consciousness," someone said.

Terry smiled. "We stand in a chamber designed to house and protect the most exquisite object known to humanity," he went on. "We discovered it almost three decades ago, secreted within a vault deep beneath the Antarctic ice. We have learned much about the civilization which left it there—and what an extraordinary people they were!—but we know little about how they came to possess what we call, in some jest, the Azazel technology. Unfortunately, its vast power proved too much for them. They lacked, if I may presume to say so, our sophistication, our mastery of the disciplines necessary to control Azazel. Yet we stand here in their debt, for with this superlative crystal"—here Terry gestured toward Azazel, and eighteen pairs of eyes followed—"we few gathered here, along with our colleagues, may shape and sculpt a new world. In our mythology, Azazel was an angel who provided the people of Earth with advanced knowledge. Our Azazel has done the same for us, and is in one way or another responsible for our extraordinary accomplishments these past decades."

More nods and restrained, dignified applause from Excomm. Several among their number continued to stare, trancelike, at Azazel.

"It behooves us, therefore, to recognize this great power and resolve to use it effectively and decisively," Terry continued. "We are the ones answerable for the world we create with it as we refine humanity and raise our planet to a new and higher standard."

He paused, and an expectant silence took hold. "There is more," he said. "Concurrent with our acquisition of Azazel so many years ago, we learned of the possible existence of a second artifact. We believe this artifact represents a threat to Azazel, that it may in some way be Azazel's nemesis. I am pleased to announce we now have this object in hand. At a later date, I will introduce you to the extraordinary gentleman behind this accomplishment."

The balcony exploded in applause, accompanied by grins and the clinking of glasses.

"Some of you here were not part of the executive committee when we last witnessed Azazel in action," said Terry. "So I've asked Dr. Hansen and his team to provide a demonstration."

Hansen stepped forward, pushing a strand of hair from over his glasses. "Well, for those not conversant with the basics here, the technology operates by means of psychic interface. Our operators are chosen from a pool of people who demonstrate a specific and extraordinary level of extrasensory skill." Hansen paused. "Though of course extrasensory is a misnomer, for if our work has established anything, it is the pervasive presence of these abilities within humans." He placed a finger over his lips. "But shhhh. Don't tell anyone."

Excomm chuckled.

"And I jest in this sense," said Hansen. "The distance between intuiting the next card at a blackjack table and operating Azazel is measured in years of rigorous training and, indeed, the willingness to devote one's life to this endeavor." Hansen stood aside, and the entire committee turned toward the eleven operators, all youngish men and women who were waiting in respectful silence. "I present the eleven men and women of Division Zero." said Hansen, with a wave of his arm.

The psi team lowered their eyes and bowed. The members of Excomm murmured their approval. Glasses again rose into the air.

"But there is yet another element of the equation, perhaps the most important," Hansen continued. "We theorize about Azazel's precise mechanics, but we do not understand them.

We hold ourselves as master of a mystery. Azazel, whatever it truly is or represents, *chooses* with whom it will work. Many of our most able candidates have stood blank and empty before it, rejected by the technology itself."

"If I may, Doctor," said Atkins Frost. "Can you elaborate?"

"I offer only supposition. I believe Azazel in some manner coheres with the brainwaves of its operators. But if this is true, our dilemma remains one of measurement. Our analysis of operator brain activity tells us little, and Azazel itself transmits no informative data. But I suspect the operators become carriers, if you will, of an Azazel *code*—a mental frequency we cannot detect, or perhaps some manner of extra-dimensional entanglement. Of course, conventional physics might reject this, but we are not limited by yesterday's archaic models; we already know Azazel draws power from another dimension."

Terry raised his hand. "If there are no more questions, I suggest we move on." At his nod, Ariana produced a silk cap. "This hat contains a dozen or so cards, each naming one of the globe's most prominent cities," said Terry. "Dominique, will you do the honors?" After a few curious looks and hushed whispers from Excomm, Dominique drew a card from the cap. Ariana took it and handed to Marcus Hansen, who glanced at it and spoke a few words to the psi team.

"I suggest we give over the stage to Azazel," said Terry.

The operators dispersed around the large circle of the balcony, each taking a position beneath one of the eleven lamps. They fell to their knees, their heads bowed, and then, as if possessed, they jerked back with their faces turned upward. Azazel came alive with an inaudible roar, a shaking felt in the bones of those observing, and the crystal swirled with bold colors, pulsing and strobing in sapphire and gold and blood red. The chamber itself appeared to shift, to change its shape and grow larger and distorted...

...Off the South American coast, where the Río de la Plata empties into Samborombón Bay, a seam appeared in the otherwise

tranquil waters. In minutes, it had extended westward for almost a hundred miles. Into this furrow, the wide river turned in on itself and the river bed shook as its foundations shifted and cracked. On the surface, a great wall of water rose and lurched toward the city of Buenos Aires, Argentina, swamping Puerto Maduro before spreading inland. A roiling cover of clouds, iron-gray and black, formed in an instant and blotted the pastel skies. As far away as western Argentina and the Chilean border, the Cochiquito and Copahue volcanoes stirred and the ground began to tremble.

In Buenos Aires, darkness descended in the middle of the morning. The air grew still and palpable, and then the winds came, bending the jacaranda trees flat and raising clouds of debris high into the air. In Palermo and San Telmo and in the Plaza de Mayo, the ground shivered and jerked sharply, and the water reversed and fled from the shore as if a drain had suddenly opened in the earth. The trembling grew in intensity, and across the metropolis, the older buildings quickly gave way, as if knocked to the ground in a single blow. The screams and shrieks of thousands, now bleeding or running or crushed and dying, filled the air. In an instant, the temperature fell more than forty degrees. The cold descended, and the wind and the shaking of the earth ripped the pavement and scattered vehicles on the wide expanse of the Avenida 9 de Julio. The cityscape vibrated into a blur, and several office towers fell together, pushing vast, rolling clouds of dust through the remnants of the streets.

A colorful mural spinning topsy-turvy through the dust and smoke—shouts of hopeless surprise and alarm—a bright orange fence, topped with coils of razor wire, gone in a flash—a tangle of girders and slabs and wires, wet with blood...

The winds became a battering ram and shrieked with a dreadful cry, pounding and scouring the wrecked heart of the city. Then a cloud of pulsing, white light formed, a mile or more across, and slid slowly over the chaos and ruin...

...Azazel's operators raised their hands, as if in supplication, but did not otherwise move. Severed from any awareness of time, Terry glanced at his fingers, which now appeared grotesquely elongated and indistinct. He cried out in delight. Ariana fell to her knees. Champagne glasses rolled on the floor. Gil moaned. Dominique laughed. Terry's entire body was suffused with something like a sexual climax but far surpassing it, and for an instant—an instant which seemed to extend for an hour—his mind reached into the farthest corner of the universe. He knew it would all be a vague memory later, like a lost dream or a fragment of a vision. He, too, collapsed and wept tears of gratitude and joy.

Then it was over.

The members of the GCI Executive Committee held on to each other, their faces wild, mad, and ecstatic. Gil helped Terry to his feet. Ariana, a strand of her hair loose and unbundled, gathered the champagne flutes. The operators of Division Zero, the psi team, drew the hoods attached to their robes over their heads and knelt in place as the lamps flickered above them.

Terry's experience had already begun to fade, to splinter like a broken mirror. He collected himself and called again for everyone's attention. "In a short while, you'll receive notification that, by means of what the media will portray as an earthquake, Buenos Aires, Argentina has been destroyed. We offer these hundreds of thousands of lives as a tribute and a celebration of Azazel's inconceivable power."

Excomm began to applaud again, with looks of amazement and heads shaking in wonder. "More champagne," said Gil as the chamber lights rose.

Shabri Goh seconded the call and Ariana reached for another bottle. "To Azazel," said Goh. "And to the artifact, recovered at last!"

The champagne was poured and the toast echoed. "And to those poor Argentinians!" someone said.

Azazel floated over the chamber, as pale and silent as the harvest moon.

CHAPTER 6

"THANK YOU, TERRY," SAID DARTHAM, STILL REELING WITH disbelief. "I will contact Gil and begin the transition." He shifted his phone to his other ear.

"Laborcorp needs a good thump on the head," said Terry. "I feel very good about this, Tom. And by the way, I mentioned you at our meeting yesterday. Excomm was most pleased."

The call ended, and Dartham wandered into the pantry adjoining his office and waited while the coffee machine filled his mug. Executive Vice President—he whistled softly—and with responsibility for Laborcorp security, no less. He rubbed the bandage beneath his shirt. This made him a player—yet something was amiss. Terry Bronsun did not lightly hand out executive titles...

He pondered the twists and turns of recent events. Not a month earlier, Shelton Kirk had explained how the Group had levered the Azazel device into total global control. The revelation had rattled Dartham's soul; he had been blind to the true nature of the Group's power. But after considering the matter, he had concluded Kirk was right: the world required order, above all. In the perpetual, bloody push and shove among nations, a non-state entity, the Group, had gotten its hands on Azazel and had come out on top. How it had done so was irrelevant; the Group now represented the ultimate order of the world. Like Kirk, Dartham treasured order, and in just such a spirit he had made his peace with serving the Group.

The coffee maker beeped. At his desk, Dartham logged into Helena as the morning sunlight slanted into the office. "It appears congratulations are in order, Tom," she said.

Dartham grunted and sipped his coffee.

The computer camera turned. "You do not appear pleased."

"Oh, it is always nice to be recognized."

"You are in a more powerful position. Your influence is growing and may lead to further accomplishment."

A knock, and Arbuckle entered with a tablet computer under his arm and his own coffee in hand. "Argentina," he said, shaking his head.

"Tragic," Dartham agreed.

"Buenos Aires—flattened, pulverized." Arbuckle dropped into a chair, a short lock of hair falling over his forehead.

"Helena, do we have a death toll update?" asked Dartham.

"The current estimated death count to this point is five hundred thousand, but recovery efforts are not fully underway. I have imagery."

Dartham turned the monitor, and Arbuckle leaned forward. They took in the images of leveled buildings, annihilated roads and bridges, and crushed bodies being removed from the rubble. The shore areas remained saturated with water, and sirens, shouts, and the cries of the injured were audible in the background.

"Let's get on to other business," said Dartham, turning away from the carnage.

Arbuckle opened his tablet. "I expect a call from the lab any minute," he said. "As of midnight, they were still studying our container, trying to find a way in."

"No progress?" asked Dartham.

"Can't penetrate it. X-rays, Etti scanners, nothing works. Can't even figure out which side is supposed to open."

"They will," said Dartham.

The office clock chimed, and the sunlight diminished as a cloud drifted over. Arbuckle shifted in his chair.

"Something gnawing at you?" asked Dartham.

Arbuckle paused, as if privately debating with himself. "I'm used to working in the dark," he said at last. "Compartmentalized ops, need-to-know, and so forth. But where did this box come from? It's made of an alloy they can't identify."

Dartham gave Arbuckle a blank stare.

Arbuckle nodded. "It doesn't hurt to ask."

"It might." The corner of Dartham's mouth lifted in a smile.

"So a few items on the subterranean research complex," said Arbuckle, moving along. "Operations are in pretty good shape, and I've set up transition meetings with Mike Upmann's staff..."

Dartham's mind drifted, and he reflected again on his dizzying ascension to Executive Vice President. How warm and pleasant Terry had been, how pleased to inform him of his promotion. Too pleased. It was out of character, and it nagged at Dartham—and then he realized he hadn't clued in his staff.

Arbuckle finished his observations and Dartham cleared his throat. "I have to share some news, Andy," he said. He gave an account of Terry's call, and Arbuckle leapt from his chair with a broad grin.

"Executive Vice President. Congratulations, Tom."

"I suppose we'll be seeing an announcement any moment. But perhaps you can quietly fill in the rest of the team?"

"Of course."

"Anyway, now come the headaches," said Dartham. "Beginning with the labor camp problems. Helena, are you still there? The escapes the night before last, how did they occur?"

"The coordinated cessation of electrical power allowed the detainees to escape the facilities," said Helena.

"Gil will be on us to figure it out," said Dartham. He lifted a brass plaque from his desk, a memento from his army days. *Colonel Thomas J. Dartham, for exemplary performance of*—he set it back down. "We need to get smart about how Laborcorp runs these camps, Andy. We cannot secure the facilities without understanding the admin structures and procedures."

"Lots of stories about the camps," said Arbuckle.

"The only one I care about is that nine people escaped the night before last."

Arbuckle looked away.

"Spit it out," said Dartham.

"You've heard the tales. Secret tunnels, advanced rail systems, construction projects in the middle of nowhere." Arbuckle shrugged. "There's talk about poor working conditions, overcrowding, excessive hours."

Dartham fidgeted with impatience. Yes, he had listened to Marcus Hansen talk about the infrastructure projects. People worked like pack dogs, high mortality rates, children used in some fashion. Dartham had initially found such assertions disturbing, but Hansen was an excitable man and had been under duress at the time, perhaps exaggerating or tapping into the same odious well of rumors as Arbuckle. The entire idea annoyed Dartham, and he gave his head a quick shake to clear it. This was no time to go chasing down rabbit holes.

"...and I hear Laborcorp is concerned about sabotage," Arbuckle was saying. "If the scuttlebutt is even half true, you can't blame the detainees."

Dartham swallowed the last of his coffee and set down his mug with a decisive clunk. "We have a job to do," he said. "If conditions in the camps are not everything you or I might approve of, that is regrettable. But those detainees are there for a reason. They are not going to escape on our watch, not going to riot, not going to communicate with the outside. It is not our job to worry about camp conditions until somebody tells us to."

Arbuckle stared at his tablet. "I'll tour some of the camps, put together an assessment," he said. Then his cell buzzed, and he held up a finger and answered it. "You're sure?" His expression grew somber. "Yeah, got it," he said, and clicked off.

"What is it?" asked Dartham.

"The lab. They opened the container." Arbuckle bit his lip. "It's empty."

"Empty?" Dartham felt his brain fall out of gear.

Arbuckle nodded.

Empty…Dartham fought a sudden asphyxiating sensation. "You will go directly to the offices of a firm called Odysseus," he said to Arbuckle in a raspy voice. "It is in the West Village, and the man you want is named Doran, Robert Hatcher Doran. Assemble a commando team on the way and get them there ASAP. I will join you as soon as I can."

Arbuckle quickly gathered his tablet and coffee. "Want me to bring him in?"

"Why aren't you already on the way?" said Dartham, his voice rising. "Yes, detain him. I am going to unscrew the top of his head and pour out every goddamned thing in it."

The door closed behind Arbuckle. Dartham's limbs were numb, and he remained frozen in place, like a squirrel when a hawk passes over. Then he rushed to the bathroom adjoining his office and knelt over the toilet, gagging. A short while later, he returned to his desk, his mind a swirl of dread and fury.

"In your new position, you require information relating to conditions at the Homeland Labor Corporation facilities and the nature of the work programs," said Helena. "However, I assume the search for Doran takes precedence."

Dartham swiveled in his chair. "If we don't find Doran and the artifact, there isn't going to be a Laborcorp job," he said—and then he remembered: Terry had already informed Excomm about the recovery of the artifact. How long before he had to confess to Terry that the container was empty, that he had been duped?

Not long.

He needed to keep the word locked up tight. His hand trembled as he clicked the com, asked for the lab, and issued orders locking down the whole mess. His mind raced like a mad greyhound. Doran could not possibly know the container had been even been found, much less opened.

"So, yes, Helena, find Doran," said Dartham. "Find him now. Search every phone and camera and hoo cab. I will obtain any authorization you need. If we get our ass in gear, we just might catch him asleep at his post."

CHAPTER 7

"WAKE UP, HATCH," SAID VINNIE, GIVING HIM A POKE.

Hatch jerked to consciousness from a troubled, uneven slumber. "Ferret," he said in a croaky voice.

"What are you talking about?"

Hatch rubbed his eyes. "Nothing," he said, still half-asleep and sitting on the cot in the storage room of Vinnie's Pub. Vinnie towered over him with a concerned look, and images returned to Hatch's mind of Marty calling and telling him the artifact had been recovered, his own frantic debate about whether to stay at the apartment or flee, and his ultimate decision to ditch his phone, grab Adrestia and a toothbrush, and scram.

"You're sleeping here in my pantry two nights now," said Vinnie. "And you didn't set foot outside all day yesterday." He pushed a carton of canned cheese dip against the wall and ran his hand over his thinning brown hair. "You're a friend and all, don't get me wrong. I'd give you the shirt off my back. But you got people worried."

Hatch squinted at Vinnie. "How do you know people are worried?"

"I have to ask, Hatch, are you in some kind of trouble?" Vinnie rocked back on his heels and stared at the floor. "I won't throw you out or anything, but I need to know."

"Maybe there's no trouble," said Hatch. He yawned. "If that makes sense."

"Actually, it doesn't."

"It's complicated, Vin."

"I'll bet it is," said Vinnie, giving him a skeptical look. "So, the way I know your people are nuts with worry is because Marty called."

"You told him I was here?"

"He's on his way."

Hatch bolted upright, his head a tangle of short, dark hair. "You told him over the *phone*?"

"No, we used homing pigeons. Of course I told him over the phone, but he wouldn't let me mention any names. Nothing like that to raise questions, eh?" A bell clanged from the pub's front door followed by an urgent shout. "There's my toke delivery. I'll send Marty back here when he shows."

Hatch scratched the stubble on his cheek and reached for his rucksack. Reinforced shelves reached to the ceiling, neatly stacked with crates of liquor, mixers, napkins, and other items. Beer kegs lined the front wall, with canned goods in the rear. From the pub entrance came rough voices, a laugh, the bang of a door closing, and then silence. Two nights hiding here, thought Hatch. No wonder Vin was nervous, God bless the man.

Vinnie had installed a tiny shower and toilet a few steps from the pantry. Hatch took the artifact with him and showered with it resting on the sink. He was back on the cot toweling his hair when Marty entered carrying a plastic bag.

"For Christ's sake, Marty, you talked to Vinnie on the phone?" asked Hatch.

"It's nice to see you too, lad," said Marty. He took a seat on Vinnie's carton. "I used one of the burners, which I've already disposed of. I wouldn't let Vinnie say anything likely to draw attention."

Hatch buried his face in the towel.

"I am more than peeved at you, going on the run like you did," said Marty.

"Just playing it safe," said Hatch, his voice muffled.

"I asked you to wait for me, but we'll hash that out another day. For now, I want to get us to Caroline's, the sooner the better."

Hatch lowered the towel. "Caroline Atherton's?"

"To her house, just off Grammercy Park."

"I know you and Caroline had a nice time at Samantha's little party a few weeks ago," said Hatch. "But you may not know everything about her."

Marty's chin jutted forward. "She's a wonderful woman."

"She's a fabulous woman, but she's also how I found Andrei Kutznov and Ghost. She's connected with some pretty tough people."

"I haven't said anything, Hatch, but Caroline and I have been spending a fair bit of time together." Marty tugged at his collar. "More than a bit, to be honest—and you don't have to look so surprised. I'm no magazine cover, sure, but I'm reliable and steady, and I know how to have a bit of fun when I'm not having to fight off your gangsters and your corporate elites." He pointed his finger at Hatch. "And yes, Caroline knows Kutznov. It might be wise to reach out to him."

Hatch shook his head. "We can't trust Kutznov."

"Hiding at Vinnie's here doesn't strike me as a long term plan."

"I've got the goddess artifact, and I've got to give it room to operate. I'm not getting tangled up over plans."

"You'll be tangled up in far worse—"

"You want me to give up, just say it, Marty."

"Calm yourself. If that's what I wanted, you'd know it."

"I know it's what Ray wants, I've dealt with him for twenty years," said Hatch, scowling. "Just when you think he's with you, he flakes, whining and moaning and second-guessing. It gets old."

"So this is all about Raymond, is it? No one is more loyal, but he has a right to express himself."

Hatch hurled the towel across the room.

"Give me an ear," said Marty. "Your goddess there may rain fire from the sky or cause our pursuers to drop dead at our feet. But until that happens, we must assume we're on the clock. Dartham has had the container for two days, and I look for him to show up at the apartment at any moment. In fact, I intend to have Raymond sneak a look later."

Hatch clawed his fingers through his wet hair while Marty shook open the grocery bag and removed a pair of costume beards, shades, and a couple of floppy sun hats.

"Disguises?" asked Hatch.

Marty nodded. "We'll have to walk," he said.

"From downtown to Grammercy?"

"A hoo is out of the question. They're monitored, and so are the subways. Besides, I don't relish being locked away in a train car. You've heard about the tunnel collapse under Park Avenue?"

"Listen, Marty, let's think about this another way. We have leverage. As long as we have the goddess artifact—"

"So we walk to Grammercy," Marty continued, giving Hatch a stern look, "and take our chances with the street cams. The disguises will help, though you better leave me with the gray one."

Hatch took the darker beard and turned it over in his hands. "Get a death cart," he said. "They're not monitored."

"The best idea yet." Marty rose to leave. "I'll go find us one, and I apologize for not thinking of it myself. I'll be back shortly."

After Marty left, Hatch withdrew the artifact from the rucksack. Its inky blackness, as always, seemed to fade at the edges, as if the object were at once here and not here, intruding from another, mysterious plane. But no light flickered from inside. Adrestia, the goddess, was as silent as a distant black star.

Marty returned a few minutes later, having secured a death cart for the passage north to Caroline's house. They changed into their disguises, and as they stepped into the dining room they encountered Vinnie, a shoebox-sized carton of tokes in his hands. He gave a start at the sight of Marty and Hatch, bearded and slumped with their hats pulled low. "What in the—"

"It's just us, Vin," said Hatch from behind his beard.

"Why are you two—" Vinnie stopped and turned away, the corners of his mouth curling downward. "Nevermind," he said in gruff tone. "I've decided I don't want to know. I don't want to know anything."

CHAPTER 8

WHILE HATCH AND MARTY MADE THEIR WAY NORTH TO Grammercy, Big Ray strode along Waverly Place in the West Village. He passed several federal-style townhouses going slowly to seed, ducked beneath the wayward limb of a tree leaning over the sidewalk, and then continued on past a neglected building with arched windows and molded rails. He absently dodged passersby, his face pinched in concentration, his hands deep in his pockets.

At Christopher Street, Big Ray looked around, zipped his dark green field coat, and flipped up the collar against the cool wind. A crying shame, he thought, having to wear a coat in the middle of summer.

He resumed walking, faster now, past a triangular building of weathered red brick with rusted fire escapes. Around the bend and further on for a block more, the air carrying distant shouts, the hum of hoo cabs, and smells of cooking, all concentrated and amplified on the narrow street. Several homeless figures looked up expectantly as he approached, while a tattooed man covertly urinated against a nearby storefront. Further ahead, in the doorway of a pale, stone townhouse, a small girl cuddled a stuffed giraffe. She smiled and waved. Big Ray automatically waved back, his thoughts light years away.

At the end of Waverly he reached the Certified Goods Exchange, formerly Washington Square Park but now shorn of its name and most of its trees. He had once loved this area, but the razor wire fence and the desolate rows of sales huts enclosed within it had dimmed his affections. Two weeks earlier, a food riot had broken out here when a Municorp soup stand had been caught dishing out poisoned stew. The hungry p'outs—those not doubled over in pain or retching on the sidewalk—had assaulted the Municorp volunteers with clubs and makeshift knives. Couldn't blame them, Big Ray supposed. P'outs, the People Without. He sighed.

A pair of spiny men shuffled past, shooting wild glares. Sticks in raincoats. Flitheads, by the look of them. Big Ray kicked a flattened paper cup along the sidewalk. He didn't notice the man across the street discreetly nod at two women standing nearby, but he saw four or five other threadbare figures lingering on the sidewalk.

His mood worsened. He was getting good and tired of this mess. Life collapsed like a game of pick-up sticks, five years now and no improvement in sight. He didn't crave luxury, he had grown up in modest circumstances. His parents, God rest them, had run one of the last local hardware stores in New Jersey, living hand-to-mouth as the big box retailers, the online merchants, and the taxes squeezed the life out of them. He had made his way through school on a football scholarship, after which he and Hatch had flat lucked into their Wall Street jobs. Despite lacking MBAs or Ivy League pedigrees, they had become masters of algorithmic trading, and for several years, in a variety of markets, their hired-hand PhDs and computers had kicked everyone else's PhDs and computers in the nuts. A nice run, but the financial collapse and subsequent demise of the old U.S. dollar—the Reset, as it was commonly known—had washed away their winnings in a blur of deposit confiscations, brokerage closures, and a new redback currency which bought less every month.

Gripe, gripe, gripe. Big Ray was not by nature a whiner, and he found himself appalled by his own dissatisfied state. His mother, for one, wouldn't have tolerated it. "Straighten the back God gave you," she would've said, her eyes hard enough to break glass. "Count your blessings." Ray stopped a moment, remembering, a tightness high in his throat; how he missed her. And, yes, he had blessings. He didn't enjoy feeling low, with a ceaseless string of grumbles running through his mind.

Still, he had plenty to complain about—or did he?

When the Reset had come, he reminded himself, they had formed Odysseus and found a way to get by. Look around, lots of people hadn't gotten by. So put a lid on the bitching and moaning. No pain, no gain. No self-pity allowed. Every life had troubles—but this was his one life, it was ticking away, and more and more he wondered what it might amount to. Smoke in the wind? A raindrop disappearing into the ground? Or just a long train of problems until he finally ran out of track?

And what about Hatch, gone now for almost two days? Marty had called a short while before, saying he knew where Hatch might be—but there was the rub: where he *might* be. No one could predict Hatch, especially with his carrying on about ancient civilizations and Antarctica and apocalyptic weapons. Big Ray thought about the way Hatch had dragged them all into this mess, and his irritation flared. He began to sweat.

Forget it.

No, damn it, *don't* forget it. *He* wouldn't have acted so selfishly, *he* wouldn't have subordinated everyone's safety to an old artifact. Big Ray yanked open the zipper of his coat and flattened his collar, counting off in his mind all the times he had been ignored, dismissed, and condescended to by the man he too easily called his closest friend. A small, inner voice protested the unfairness of his thoughts, but Big Ray, coming to a boil, refused to hear it.

He turned south, lost in his thoughts and striding along the sidewalk next to the Exchange. The shabby figures he had noticed earlier converged behind him without a sound. He wanted life to mean something. Was that asking too much? Or maybe he just longed for life to get back to the new, much diminished normal he had gotten used to. Maybe normal was meaningful, scaring up a few redbacks, having a cold one at Vinnie's, watching a ball game.

From a covered doorway, a young woman with rainbow hair and wearing an oversized pea coat stepped directly in front of him and thrust a clipboard in his face. "Sign a petition, sir? Increase the food point rations?"

"What?" asked Big Ray as the people behind him—three men and two women of various ages—pressed tight against his sides and back, jostling him and patting his coat pockets.

"We're starving sir," said the young woman.

"Starving," echoed one of the women behind him.

"We can't afford enough food points," said the young woman with the clipboard. She pushed a frizzy, blue and pink strand of hair from across her eye.

"You're going to help us out, dude," said one of the men. He was grizzled, middle-aged, with rheumy eyes. He gave Big Ray a shove. Big Ray pushed him back twice as hard, and he fell into the arms of his companions. Two of the women seized Big Ray by the coat, trying to pull open his pockets. He elbowed them away.

"Hey, buddy! Watch what you're—"

"Don't touch her, you—"

"No violence, no violence," cried the young woman. "Just sign our petition. And maybe give a donation?"

"Go to hell," said Big Ray. He considered beating the daylights out of the whole noxious pack, but instead he walked away. One of the men tried to tackle him, but Big Ray heard his footsteps, whirled, and met the man's temple with his elbow. The man, attired in a dirty, plaid jacket, crumpled to the sidewalk, stunned.

The p'outs began screaming that Big Ray had assaulted them for no reason, that they were going to be killed just for asking him to sign a petition. Big Ray stepped over their companion and the remaining p'outs fell back as he approached. "Who's next?" he asked.

Two of the women tiptoed around him to tend to their friend. He rolled over and groaned.

"You want me to sign?" Big Ray asked the young woman. "Give it to me, I'll sign."

She clasped the clipboard to her chest. "No," she said weakly. "Just go."

Big Ray turned and went, marching along for another block or so, tingling with adrenaline. He almost missed his destination, but at the last moment his eye caught the sign he was looking for, affixed to the tinted glass door of a neglected seven-story building. He dusted off his coat, entered the lobby, and almost bumped into a scrawny man of about thirty.

"Ray Garwin. I'm trying to find a buddy of mine. Nathan Patel?"

"Call me Tusk." A mat of black hair and eyes to match, a green T-shirt with the eye symbol and the familiar slogan: *I see the truth*. "We don't usually give out names. I'm sure you understand. Why not take a seat, Ray, let me see if he's—if any such name is on our list. By the way, your coat's torn."

"Yeah," said Big Ray, noticing his dangling pocket, "I didn't want to sign a petition." Suddenly, he regretted hitting the man, but his remorse annoyed him. After all, the p'outs had asked for it, had picked the wrong day to screw around with him. He followed Tusk back to a high reception desk where a dark-skinned, slender woman with big, frizzy hair was writing on a notepad.

"This is Swan," said Tusk.

Swan turned her steady brown eyes toward Big Ray, waved her pencil, and gave him a brilliant smile. "And you are?" she asked.

In the moment of near-weightlessness that followed, Big Ray forgot about the p'outs and had to reach for his own name as he introduced himself. The touch of Swan's hand sent a shockwave through him. Tusk disappeared through a door behind the reception desk, and neither Swan nor Big Ray spoke for a moment.

"Did you come to join our cause?" asked Swan. "Listen to me, I sound like some sort of cheap revolutionary. Our cause. But it is, isn't it? A cause, I mean. Trying to get information out there to wake people up."

"No, you don't," said Big Ray. "Sound like a revolutionary, I mean." He grinned.

"No? Good. We aren't revolutionaries. We just point out the inconsistencies. People can be so obtuse, can't they? I never used to use that word, obtuse. Tusk uses it."

"Sure."

"Yeah," said Swan.

"We do have a Nathan Patel," said Tusk, returning to the reception desk. "He's on the third floor. Take the hall toward the rear, turn left—"

"Oh, you want Nate?" cried Swan. "Our computer guru, for the three computers we have. I'm not allowed to use them," she said, giving Tusk a dark glance. "So why don't I take Ray upstairs, Tusky? I'll give him the pitch, and maybe he'll join up with us. You want to hear my pitch, Ray? I can sell ice in a snowstorm, baby."

"Watch yourself, Ray," said Tusk.

Up two flights of stairs and along a hallway of dormitory suites, many with open doors, and filled with a variety of people, most in their twenties. Swan moved with the grace of a ballerina. "People are tired of the passivity," she was saying. "We want folks to see, to shed their victimhood, to learn to think for themselves, you know what I mean?"

Big Ray had always dismissed the Eye Brigade as an indulgence and a waste of time, but Swan was presenting the matter in a new light.

"If we don't learn to use our brains, I'm afraid we're in for a really hard lesson," said Swan. Her eyes grew wide, as if she were coming to new and shocking realizations as she spoke.

"Consider the climate," she said. "Earthquakes, volcanoes, rotational storms of all kinds, the magnetic field fluctuating, the poles wandering, the weather problems off the charts for the past six or seven years. The planet is very angry, Ray."

"I've got a friend who has a different explanation for all that," said Big Ray, thinking of Hatch and his foolish ideas about Azazel and how it was responsible for all the weather problems and earthquakes.

They passed an open lounge area with a refrigerator and cabinets. "And oh, my God, yesterday in Argentina, those poor people," said Swan. "Hundreds of thousands dead or missing."

"Horrifying," said Big Ray. "It's all anyone is talking about."

Swan nodded. "And the ice caps are spreading, the sea levels are down."

"It makes me hurt inside."

"Doesn't it?" Swan squeezed his arm. "These disasters strike, and who do you think steps in to buy everything up?"

Big Ray tried to stay on her wavelength. "The usual suspects?" he asked.

"The holders of the new, international dollars," said Swan. "The fat cats. The cronies. You take your uber-rich—"

"The few still around," said Big Ray. "Of course, they've made the pie smaller but they each have bigger pieces."

"Exactly!" cried Swan. "They've consolidated it all, they get their revenue from government contracts, and the feds siphon it off of us. One-time charges, deposit confiscations, taxes galore, crappy money." Swan bent and pinched a large piece of lint from the worn carpet. "People don't care about keeping things clean," she said. "But like I was saying, we are left to eat our fingers while the mega-wealth snarfs up anything that isn't nailed down. And nothing's getting better, you know what I mean?"

"Yes," said Big Ray. He stared into her eyes. His heart skipped a beat.

"It's like so crazy. Everyone slumps around like there's nothing to be done about it." Swan absently rolled the lint into a ball. "But the collapse was intentional. People have to grasp that. And now we have nature reacting, freezing us out, shaking us up for being so stupid."

Swan's conviction deeply impressed Big Ray. So did the inner light which seemed to illuminate her face. He forgot all about Hatch and Azazel and the artifact.

"Anyway, we just want to get people's attention," she said. "We have to raise our game, make more of an impact. You know what I'm saying?"

"You've made a profound impact," said Big Ray.

"I don't know, maybe," said Swan, flicking away the ball of lint.

***

"So you met Swan," said Nathan, peering from beneath his GameHead goggles. He sat on his bunk with his legs folded under him. "Yeah, she's… different."

"I enjoyed our chat," said Big Ray. He whistled a few notes as he turned a chair around and placed it next to Nathan's bunk.

"Swan has a lot to say, but the circuits aren't really plugged into anything, if you know what I mean." Nathan pushed his goggles to the top of his head, pinning his hair back. Given his slight build, the goggles made him look top-heavy.

"I didn't get that impression at all," said Big Ray. He glanced around the room: a metal desk and chest, tile flooring with a threadbare rug, and a lone window with a cloudy pane diffusing the light. "So how does the Eye Brigade end up with its own dorm?" he asked.

"This?" Nathan gestured at the room. "We're squatting it, actually. Paint's faded, the plumbing is iffy, but it's our place, you know what I mean?"

"Listen, I don't want to elbow into your life, but we miss you, pal. We're concerned."

"What do you mean, Ray?"

"You haven't been to the office in a week. Jocelyn is worried sick."

"A week? Wow. I'll stop by. I don't want her to worry, I just needed a few days to get settled in here." Nathan stared at the bed. "There's a lot cooking right now."

"Do tell."

"I just mean, you know, the Gala's tonight."

"Third Bickerman, right?" asked Big Ray. "They're beginning to reroute traffic around Tribeca. The West Village is a mess."

"For the first two Bickermans, Kee arrived about an hour late, made his speech, and left," said Nathan. "I'm betting he's going to do the same tonight. You think he will, Ray?"

"How do I know? You after his autograph or something?"

"No." Nathan examined his hands. "Anyway, a bunch of us got hired to bus hors d'oeuvres around."

"Why?" asked Big Ray. "We're all paid up now. It's not my business, but your pockets should be bulging."

Nathan made vague gesture. "Tusk asked us all to lend a hand."

"Tusk."

"He knows some pretty important people. One of his contacts got us in, and I said I'd help out. I mean, it's the Eye Brigade, and we're making a difference." He looked directly at Big Ray, his face set beneath the goggles high on his head. "I love my games and all, but I want to do stuff in meatspace."

"Meatspace?"

"You know, the real world."

"I hear you, bruh." Big Ray leaned back and laced his fingers behind his head. "How about you scoot over to the apartment and clean out our database?"

"Yeah, I will. I'm sorry if I caused any trouble." Nathan lowered his goggles over his eyes. Big Ray sighed and poked him in the arm, and Nathan raised them an inch. "I don't mean to be rude, Ray, but I just got a preview run of a space game Kee Bickerman has developed. It's only a few minutes long, but the full game is due out in six months. They say the implants will simulate zero gravity. Amazing, huh?"

"Zero gravity?" asked Big Ray.

"Kee Bickerman," said Nathan, his face beaming. "I can't express my gratitude to him. Every day the chain tightens a little more, they watch our every move, take all our money, fill our bodies with particles—"

"They who?"

"The secret government," said Nathan. "The people who really run the world. But Kee's games help us out of the prison, take us anywhere, let us discover who we are." He stopped, as if puzzled. "Still, we have to live here, in reality."

"Meatspace."

"In meatspace," said Nathan, "statements have to be made."

"Well, you're young," said Big Ray, feeling as if he were missing something.

"But you understand, don't you?" asked Nathan. Big Ray's burner phone made a horrid screech, but Nathan did not seem to notice it. "A statement has to be made, Ray. Just be sure you catch the late news tonight, okay?"

Big Ray apologized and flipped the phone open. "It's me," said Marty, "I was right, I found our man at the pub. He's fine."

Despite his annoyance at Hatch, Big Ray felt a wave of relief. "Good. If I hadn't heard, I was planning to hunt him down myself. Give him a swift kick in the butt for me." Marty didn't answer and the pause caught Big Ray's attention. "There's more, isn't there?"

"My antennae keep twitching. You follow me?"

Nathan adjusted his goggles over his eyes and settled back onto the bunk.

"You mean, they know the container is empty," said Big Ray.

"After two days, they almost have to know. Now listen, I've not been able to reach the girls, but if you could see that everyone stays clear of the apartment, it'd be a great help. Also, one of us needs to take a glance at the neighborhood."

"I'll do it. I'll be over there soon."

"Be careful. We must assume the apartment is under surveillance." Marty paused. "How will you handle our computer man?"

"I'm with him now." He watched as Nathan rolled backward on his bunk, easing down in slow motion, his feet ascending into the air inch by inch until they touched the wall. Nathan moaned and lowered his feet with the same deliberate motion. "I'll have to think about what to tell him," said Big Ray.

"I'll be in touch with you later, but from a different number," said Marty. The call ended and Big Ray slipped the phone back in his pocket. What had he and Nathan been talking about? Right, Nathan working the Gala, maybe getting a glimpse of his idol, Kee Bickerman.

Nathan, still prone on his bed, began to gradually roll over. His hands floated in the air. Big Ray grabbed him by the foot. Nathan bolted upright and pushed his goggles onto his head.

"Jocelyn and I are having lunch at Smyte's," said Big Ray. "You want to join us?"

"I was on a spaceship," said Nathan. "The zero gee, it works. The Earth is so beautiful from space. A swirl of green and blue and white." He wiped a tear from his eye.

Big Ray replaced the chair in the corner. "I'll catch you another time."

"I can't wait until the full game comes out," said Nathan with a faraway look.

Downstairs, Big Ray encountered a crowd of restless Eye Brigaders milling around in the lobby. The entire scene—the cacophony of shouts and conversation, the sea of eye symbols —struck him as vibrant and stimulating and ringing with life. A middle-aged man with shaggy gray hair and a fiery expression pushed his way to the reception desk. "So I heard the demonstration was at noon," he said, brandishing a folded bulletin printed on bright, green paper. "Now this says one o'clock."

"Tusk changed the time," said Swan. "Don't ask me why."

A young woman wearing a loose, colorful robe approached the desk. "I'm on setup detail for the Gala tonight," she said. "Is there like a van or something to take us?"

"There'll be a van at four p.m., right out front," said Swan. Then, half-rising from her chair, she yelled at two men engaged in a shoving match. "Hey, hey, this is *not* what we are about here, people!" Several others intervened to break up the scuffle. Swan shook her head and settled back into her chair.

"Busy day," said Big Ray.

"The absolute busiest!" she said, giving him a dreamy smile. "You come back here and see me sometime. I'll get rid of all these troublemakers, and we can talk political philosophy and the harbingers of social transformation. How about it, Ray? I'll tell you how we're going to wake up our world!"

***

BIG RAY RETURNED TO THE WEST VILLAGE WITH A lightness spreading in his heart, and he chastised himself for wallowing in the doldrums. At Smyte's, he found Jocelyn quizzing Philip Smyte about the menu. Big Ray slipped into her booth.

"What do you mean, what's today's special?" asked Smyte, leaning over the table. "It's the same as it always is. It's the special. A hardy meal, and well worth the food points."

"A bean sandwich?" asked Jocelyn.

"That can't be right," said Big Ray, spreading his napkin.

"It's not right," said Smyte. "I use a seasoned bean puree in place of mayo, with lettuce and what passes for tomato these days, along with ham and turkey. Consider yourself warned about the tomato, but there's not a damned thing to be done about it." Smyte's dark eyes blazed.

"If you made it, it's good enough for me," said Big Ray. "And I like turkey and ham."

"As far as I can tell, it's real turkey," said Smyte.

"And it comes with what, fries?" asked Jocelyn.

"It does *not* come with fries," said Smyte. "I made some vegetable chips—carrots, squash, cucumber, real organic." He huffed. "Fries. You try finding a potato good enough to eat anymore. It's the cold... which reminds me, we'll have to start winter stocking in a few weeks." He went on about frigid temperatures and snow, the delicate supply chain, and Agricorp's determination to destroy all the small farmers. "We can't get enough food as it is," he said. "How many will starve this winter?" Smyte's black look warned against any answer.

"On that uplifting note," said Jocelyn, "I suppose I'll have the special."

Big Ray nodded. Smyte left.

"What the hell are you in such a good mood about?" asked Jocelyn.

"Am I? I'll think unhappy thoughts." Big Ray put on an exaggerated scowl.

"You want to feel low, just listen to Smyte for a few minutes," said Jocelyn. "So why the sudden lunch date? I'm like having déjà vu here, everything all mysterious again. I haven't seen Hatch in two days, then you tell me not to go back to the apartment, not to use my cell, blah, blah, blah. I thought the cloak and dagger shit was behind us, and yet here we are."

"Did you reach the painters?" asked Big Ray.

"Yes, and the plumber, just like you asked. I left word with Samantha, and I set out more food for the cat last night. I haven't been to the apartment today."

"Marty has Hatch hidden away," said Big Ray. "Nathan is in the Eye Brigade dorm, safe enough though a bit out of balance."

"Hidden Hatch away?" asked Jocelyn. "Why?"

The lunch crowd had packed the restaurant, with most queued up for carryout, food point cards in hand. The dining room hummed with conversation and the clink of knives and spoons. Big Ray leaned over the table. "I haven't told Sam or Nathan about this," he said.

Jocelyn didn't answer. Big Ray waited. "Okay, okay," she finally said. "I'll keep it under wraps."

Big Ray took her through the story of the artifact Hatch had in his possession, leaving off any mention of the Azazel weapon or the Group. "Twelve thousand years old," he said. "And to be perfectly candid, a lot of dangerous people are looking for it."

Jocelyn blinked and shook her head rapidly back and forth as if unable to believe her ears. "Tell me you crazy dudes haven't gotten us involved with the antiquities gangs."

"No, not exact—"

"That is not what we signed up for, Ray."

Philip Smyte returned with two sandwich-and-chips plates and tumblers of ice water. Jocelyn gave him a blank look. "Well what's wrong with it?" asked Smyte.

"Nothing," said Big Ray. "It was something I said."

Smyte stalked away.

"You silly, stupid bruhs," said Jocelyn.

"It's a long story."

"You know what? I don't want to hear it. Just tell me whether I have to worry about somebody strapping a bomb under my workstation." Jocelyn lifted her sandwich, examined it, and took a tentative bite.

"Marty wants the apartment clear, and I agree," said Big Ray. He nibbled at a carrot chip. "It's just a precaution."

"Things were looking up," said Jocelyn, staring at her sandwich. "It was too good to be true."

"No," said Big Ray, raising his voice and pointing his knife at her. "Things *are* looking up. We have to get past this one little rough spot, and it'll be back to normal."

Jocelyn recoiled. "Okay. Geez, put down the knife, dude. Things are majorly great. Blue skies. Rainbows. Yay."

"I'm serious, Joss."

Jocelyn snapped a cucumber chip. "Hatch is still in danger, isn't he?"

Big Ray hesitated. "Well, Marty—"

"He is in danger. Tell me I'm wrong, Ray."

"I can't."

They both leaned back against their respective sides of the booth. Big Ray drank some water. Jocelyn tucked a strand of black hair behind her ear.

"Where is he?" she asked.

"I don't know."

"Because it's not safe for you to know."

"I—"

"Because you could be caught and like tortured and made to talk," said Jocelyn. A tear glistened in the corner of her eye.

Big Ray thought about it. "Nah," he said.

"Bullshit." Their sandwiches waited. Jocelyn's eyes shone like wet, black stones. "Any one of us could be used to get to Hatch. Of course, I don't know any details, but you do."

"Which is why I want to find some hotel rooms for the team," said Big Ray. "Cash hotel rooms, until it all blows over."

"Just as a precaution."

"Right."

"I don't care where I'm supposed to stay," said Jocelyn. "I don't care how Hatch got his hands on a fucking twelve-thousand-year-old artifact. What I want to know is, what are you dudes doing to keep everyone safe?"

"Samantha doesn't know the story here," said Big Ray, "but she's with that Bickerman guy. And Nathan's in the dorm, like I said. Marty and I are giving it our best."

A young man entered the restaurant, took off his cap, and strode to the front of the takeout line. "You, sir. The line forms over there," said Smyte. The booming note in his voice caused the entire lunch line to shuffle back in unison, and the man glanced around, confused. "Over there," Smyte repeated.

Jocelyn swallowed a bite of her sandwich. "We all know, like we know our own faces in the mirror, that if you let Hatch charge off on his own, this is the kind of mess he'll get himself into."

"*Let* Hatch?"

"Somebody has to look out for him."

"Really?"

Jocelyn fixed Big Ray with a withering gaze, but he wasn't about to allow her to steamroll him. If he did, she'd back it up and flatten him again. And again.

"I'm not responsible for whatever craziness happens to pop up in Hatch's head," said Big Ray. "I have enough on my mind."

"I'm so sorry you're distracted, but you know how Hatch chases after things when he's off his leash. You didn't stop him, so this is on you, hoss. It's on you and Marty, and you damn well better see him through it. If anything happens to any of you, I swear on God's green earth I will squat and piss on your sorry graves."

A commotion erupted in the takeout line. The young man accused another patron of breaking in front of him. Finger-pointing. Indignant shouts. Philip Smyte marched over and forcibly removed the man to a chorus of applause.

Big Ray took a bite of his sandwich. "Not bad," he said. He refused to allow Jocelyn, sitting there sending icicles his way, to ruin his good mood. They finished their lunches in silence. She wiped her mouth, flipped a food points card onto the table, and stormed out without a goodbye.

Shortly afterward, Big Ray stepped outside, his thoughts jumping between Swan and Jocelyn and the mess Hatch had created. A raccoon emerged from beneath a rusty postal box near the corner, gave him an indifferent stare, and proceeded to investigate a dented trash container. Big Ray meandered along the street. He had no intention of being seen near the apartment, no intention at all of being nabbed by Ferret's people or any surveillance team Dartham might have stationed there, but he wanted a quick look. Then, in the distance, he spotted a white van parked in front of the apartment. Several figures clad in riot gear lounged on the sidewalk and stoop.

Damn.

He watched them for a moment. They weren't cops, so they were probably Dartham's people. Or Ferret's.

Big Ray casually crossed the street and returned in the direction of Smyte's without looking back.

CHAPTER 9

MARTY AND HATCH HAD BEEN TRAVELING NORTH FROM Vinnie's when Andrei Kutznov called Caroline Atherton at her home. Kutznov, an acquaintance of Caroline's late husband, had worked as part of Project Caterpillar. A few weeks earlier, at a meeting arranged by Caroline, he had revealed to Hatch the truth about Montgomery Doran, Hatch's father. Now Caroline stood in the parlor of her large brownstone, vexed and out of sorts. "Here is Andrei's message to you," she said to Hatch, reading from a note she had made of the call. "Ferret and I know the Group has recovered it."

"That's all he said?" asked Hatch. He and Marty exchanged a surreptitious glance.

"I'm not familiar with the Group," said Caroline, "but I have heard stories—bloodcurdling tales—about this Ferret person. I don't want either of you involved with those people."

Marty smothered a cough.

"So," said Caroline, "message delivered. Maybe now we can bring this entire, sordid business—whatever it is—to a close. You both know that Clyde, rest him, was hip-deep in antiquities. I assure you, in that trade life gets cheap in a hurry." She stepped over to Marty's chair and kissed his head.

Caroline's news brought Hatch to a hard stop, though, on reflection, Kutznov's call was hardly surprising given his and Ferret's interest in the artifact. At the same time, Hatch itched to be on the move, especially after learning that troops in riot gear were crawling all over his apartment. But where would he go? He drummed an impatient beat with his heel. Outside, the light rain turned the midafternoon dim and gray.

"Reaching out to Kutznov isn't the worst course of action," said Marty. "I'm willing to accept that our artifact is hardly ordinary, but we're forced to deal in the real world, Hatch. We need allies."

"Allies?" asked Caroline.

"I won't sit by while hell is unleashed on us, lad," said Marty, his face tight.

"I don't care for the sound of that," said Caroline. "I have the impression you have an object you are not supposed to have, Hatch. Am I right?" She stared at him, her hazel eyes alight. Hatch pulled the rucksack close to his feet lest he miss the smallest vibration.

"Artifact or not, we won't come out on top fighting Dartham and Ferret on our own," said Marty.

"Ferret again." Caroline sighed. "Hatch, I begged you to stay away from all this, didn't I?" She turned to Marty. "Don't get involved with the antiquities trade, I said. Don't go to Central Park, I said. And yet I arranged it, I called Kutznov." She finger-combed her brown hair back on her head. "I suppose I lost my mind. Now I find out Ferret is involved, and where does that leave us?"

"With wolves at our heels," said Marty. "I'll say it again, we need allies."

"We have an ally," said Hatch, looking daggers at Marty. "And you know I've burned all my bridges with Ferret."

Caroline's mouth dropped open. "Oh, my God, it just hit me," she said. "That artifact belongs to Ferret." She gasped. "You *stitched* Ferret." She marched over to the small bar, poured a finger of vodka, and drained it. Then she finished off a second shot, rinsed her glass, and stalked off in the general direction of the kitchen.

Caroline maintained a gorgeous residence, one brimming with high-end art and antiques. But Hatch, lost in his own thoughts and staring into a corner of the parlor, barely registered the Revolutionary War infantry sword or the Bakshaish camelhair rug or even the subdued sounds of the city outside. Marty left to speak with Caroline, and when he returned a short while later, he dropped into his chair and tapped Hatch on the knee. "Lad," he said. "It's time to deal."

"What do you mean, deal?" asked Hatch.

"You know exactly what I mean."

Marty's serious look caused something to click in Hatch's mind. "Tell me you didn't call Kutznov."

"Caroline did, but I would've done it myself if she hadn't. He'll be coming by soon."

"You mean here?"

"The artifact may be the eighth wonder, but as you said, it's leverage." Marty drew closer. "It's time we use it to extract ourselves from this business."

Leverage… Hatch moved to the window and stared at the gray and green vista outside. Wind rustled the oaks in Grammercy Park and rain tapped on the windowpanes. Kutznov and Ferret knew the Group had Adrestia's container in hand, but did they know it was empty and that he, Hatch, actually possessed the goddess artifact? Probably not—at least, not yet. They thought he had thrown the artifact into the incinerator. Hatch stood for a time in something like a hypnotic state, sensing Marty's eyes on his back, and balancing in his mind a jumble of considerations. He knew in his bones the course he should take—the only possible course in his mind—and if the goddess artifact wasn't inclined to give him a helpful word, he'd play it his way. But could he convince Kutznov?

A rap sounded on the front door and one of the guards entered and spoke to Caroline in the foyer. A moment later, she entered the parlor accompanied by a woman with black, shoulder-length hair and a matching leather jacket. "This is

Camila Diaz," said Caroline. Hatch recognized her as Kutznov's bodyguard.

"Don't give me that look, Hatch," said Caroline with a hint of defensiveness. "I won't stand by while you march yourself off the cliff."

Camila, a formidable pulse pistol holstered on her hip, fixed her striking, dark eyes on Hatch. "I told Andrei when Hatch Doran first showed up that nothing good was going to come from this guy," she said.

"Camila is here to survey the house," said Caroline. "If you'll excuse us, I'm going to show her around."

"Shouldn't you be somewhere pulling the wings off little birds?" Hatch asked Camila.

She gave Hatch a cold look, and she and Caroline left the parlor and ascended the stairs in the company of one of Caroline's guards. Marty watched them go. "This is all for the good," he said. "We need to be with people able to stick it in and break it off, if you take my meaning."

Hatch slumped into the chair, his eyes closed, his mind racing through a multitude of scenarios. A few minutes later, Caroline and Camila returned. "Camila has approved Andrei's visit," said Caroline.

"I worked with one of your guards a long time ago, Ms. Atherton," said Camila. "You have good people, but I don't want Andrei here for long. We don't have a great exit to the rear."

"If Kutznov's nervous, tell him he doesn't have to come," said Hatch.

Camila laughed, utterly without humor. "I'm the one who's nervous, big guy. Andrei's just trying to clean up the mess you made. My job is to make sure he doesn't get hurt in the process."

Hatch felt suddenly tired and bitter. "Meet Camila, the ball buster," he said.

"Maybe I am," said Camila. She gave Hatch a long, appraising look. "And maybe we'll find out if you got anything to bust."

Marty nodded with approval. "This is exactly what we need, Hatch," he said.

***

ANDREI KUTZNOV SEEMED TO HAVE AGED IN THE WEEKS since Hatch had seen him. The lines around his eyes appeared deeper, and his beard was flecked with a few gray strands Hatch had not noticed before. Caroline's guard had escorted Kutznov in from the rear of the house, and now he stood with Camila in the parlor, offering Hatch the barest greeting and saying nothing as Caroline led them to an upstairs room in the rear of the house. There Camila and two of the guards had pitched an odd foil tent—necessary, Camila had explained, to counter eavesdropping—and Kutznov and Hatch sat beneath its metallic folds, perched uncomfortably on old, wooden folding chairs.

"I want to be very clear with you, Hatch Doran," said Kutznov, with a faint trace of a Russian accent. "You complicated and perhaps compromised an operation of critical importance. You betrayed the confidence Ghost and I placed in you, and you betrayed Ferret."

"You'd rather I had thrown the artifact itself into the fire?" asked Hatch. "Who'd have it now?"

Kutznov fell back in his chair. "You possess the artifact?" he asked.

Hatch showed him the rucksack and then returned it to the floor beside his feet.

"And you allowed Ferret to believe you had thrown it away?" asked Kutznov.

"I had my reasons."

"Dishonorable reasons, if so." Kutznov spoke in a hard, flat voice. "This is quite a revelation, and we'll attempt to manage

Ferret if we can. The larger problem is the Group. They know who you are, and if you have the goddess artifact, they'll surely move against you."

"They're already covering our apartment," said Hatch.

"I understand the Group's man was injured at the incinerator."

"Yes. His name is Dartham. Ghost tried to kill him."

"A pity he didn't succeed." Kutznov leaned toward Hatch and, despite the protection provided by the tent, lowered his voice. "This fellow Dartham won't be content to have a few lackeys watch your apartment. He has no doubt examined every phone call or text message of anyone close to you. He can intercept drone and satellite images, if he wishes. He can scour Transcorp records and bribe and intimidate anyone of use to him in his pursuit. And if he doesn't recover the artifact in a day or two, he'll apprehend your colleagues and interrogate them—and in the most brutal fashion—until they have emptied their souls to him."

"Not if we—"

"Because you have not merely absconded with an artifact of historical significance, you've interfered with the power structure of the world. And you've put at risk our long struggle against it." Kutznov jabbed his finger at Hatch. "Do you not understand what you've done? The Group has its plans—wicked, inhuman schemes—but what of Azazel's intentions? You assume Azazel, that ravenous evil, and the Group are one, but are they? I tell you, all of it must be stopped, before we are destroyed."

"I—"

Kutznov cut him off with a gesture. "This conversation you and I are having is an indulgence on my part, an indulgence you do not deserve and which matters not one iota to the final outcome of our meeting. I cannot imagine what you are thinking, but you *will* turn over Adrestia to me. I hope you and your friends avoid the Group's clutches, but that's a problem of your own making."

"I want you to take me to Azazel," said Hatch.

Kutznov again sat back in his chair.

"I'm serious," said Hatch.

"Bah." Kutznov laughed dryly. "You are a fool."

"Maybe you know more than I do, but this doesn't end until we get Adrestia in front of Azazel. I promise you, no one will activate the goddess. It isn't like a flashlight Ferret can flick on or off. The artifact acts as it will."

Kutznov rubbed his beard, his eyes black and piercing.

"You won't like this any better," said Hatch, "but I have to be involved, whether I want to be or not." Hatch cocked his thumb at his chest. "The artifact responds to me, Andrei."

"You've been blinded," said Kutznov. "You're obsessed with our dear goddess—I tell you, I've seen it before—but you must hope you are wrong, for you will never get close to Azazel."

Hot pressure began to grow behind Hatch's eyes. "You say no one can escape Dartham or the Group, no one can know what to do with Adrestia, no one can get close to Azazel. I am sick to death of hearing what can't be done."

"You speak as a child."

"Ferret, poring over his formulas, mulling over his hypotheses about the artifact while filling his pockets with money—the Group's money—and thinking *maybe, somehow, if* he can get his hands on the artifact, he can activate it. Bullshit. Enough is enough."

"Adrestia doesn't belong to you," said Kutznov. "Out of respect for your father and, yes, a certain affection for you, I'll ask you, just this once, to give it to me."

The foil tent cast silvery shades, and Hatch leaned forward. "I've communicated with Adrestia," he said, speaking deliberately, emphasizing each word. "The goddess artifact opened—Ferret was right, there is a round crystal inside—and challenged me to make a choice. I've made it."

"No one has ever opened the artifact," said Kutznov.

"Nor have I," said Hatch. "The artifact opened on its own."

Kutznov looked away. For a moment, the fire had gone out of his expression. "I cannot know whether you speak the truth or not," he said. "We've always hoped the goddess might operate against Azazel from a distance, but we did not know. Do you, Hatch Doran? Do you possess certain knowledge that Adrestia must be close to Azazel to be effective?"

Hatch exhaled a long breath. "Define knowledge," he said.

"And if so, how close?" asked Kutznov. "Ten meters? A hundred? Or do we speak of some greater distance?"

"I don't know."

"Ferret is certain that physical distance cannot matter to the forces represented by the Azazel device and by the artifact in your bag. He's a physicist and I'm not, but this has the ring of truth to me."

"I don't know," Hatch repeated. "Azazel acts at a distance, but as for action between the two artifacts, maybe proximity matters. It's just a feeling I have."

"We must hope your feeling is wrong," said Kutznov. "For no one may approach Azazel, at least not without an army, and even then I would not be optimistic. We have only supposition about Azazel's precise location. Your government authorities, enfeebled as they are, do not know, and even members of the Group, with but a few exceptions, are brought into its presence blind. And those who work directly with Azazel are closely monitored and largely cut off from the world."

"There must be a way," said Hatch. His encounter with Adrestia had been vivid and transformative, and the message the artifact had given to him had carried a strange and wholly mysterious power and had seized his heart. But then he heard himself as he must sound to Kutznov, or even Big Ray and Marty; he heard the ranting of an idiot. Still, if he had been blinded, as Kutznov had said, if he was obsessed, then so be it —but what about his friends? What if Dartham did round them up? To his shame, he had not fully considered it, and a dark, foreboding cloud settled over his mind.

"We must debate no further this question of finding Azazel," said Kutznov. "We can both agree that the worst fate of all would be to lose the goddess artifact to the Group. I've accused you of obsession, but I could have said the same of your father, or perhaps any one of us. And what is more, if the artifact opened for you... I implore you to entrust Adrestia to me."

"No," said Hatch. He rubbed his temples with the heels of his hands, and felt the tent closing in. "No."

"I can assure its safety."

"If it goes to anyone, it goes to Ferret," said Hatch. His voice was thin. He looked down at the rucksack.

"I will see it delivered into his hands," said Kutznov.

"No, Andrei, I have to do this, and I have to do it my way. I know I can convince Ferret."

The air beneath the tent had grown thick, and Kutznov's eyes bored into Hatch's. "Say it again, Hatch Doran, that you're certain Adrestia, the goddess artifact, opened for you."

***

CAMILA MET HATCH AND KUTZNOV AT THE BOTTOM OF the stairs with a questioning look, and they all entered the parlor where Caroline and Marty were carrying on an intense, whispered conversation. No one spoke, and after a moment Caroline stood. "I've made coffee," she said, disappearing in the direction of the kitchen.

"Kutznov and I have agreed to reach out to Ferret," said Hatch.

"A sound move," said Marty.

Caroline returned with a large thermos of coffee and several mugs. Kutznov and Camila excused themselves to confer in the hallway, and for a minute or so they argued quietly, Kutznov listening with his gaze fixed in the distance. After a short discussion, Kutznov stepped into the parlor. "If you all will excuse me," he said, "I must attend to this business." He made his way upstairs while Camila accepted a mug of coffee, took the loveseat next to Hatch's chair, and gazed at him over the rim of her mug.

"What?" asked Hatch.

"Did I say anything?" she asked.

Hatch pulled open the rucksack and peered inside. The goddess remained as dark as the far side of the moon.

"So you finally came to your senses," said Camila.

"What's it to you?" asked Hatch.

She shrugged. "I didn't expect it, is all. You got the stubborns inside you, mister. If you had done the right thing the first time, I wouldn't have to sneak my man over here. None of us would be worrying about this. You should listen to what smarter people tell you once in a while."

"I'm trying to remember if I ever asked your advice," said Hatch. "Let me think. Nope, I never did."

"Maybe you should," said Camila. "Maybe it'll keep you alive."

"I don't care for this kind of talk," said Caroline. She directed a severe look at Hatch, and then at Marty. "I want to end this here. I want this awful business behind us."

Camila laughed. "Good luck telling this one what to do, Ms. Atherton."

"Hatch is a determined lad, sure," said Marty. "But it has served him well more often than not—and his friends, too, of whom I am one. Besides, he has agreed to pursue the wiser course now." Marty looked at Hatch. "Camila does make a point, though."

Hatch waved him off, and Marty, Caroline, and Camila conversed with each other while Hatch's thoughts darted in several directions at once. Kutznov was busy contacting Ferret —certainly, he was using an encrypted device. Hatch considered going upstairs and grabbing the phone himself— but no, he needed Kutznov as an intermediary. Ferret was surely in a mood to kill him, but if anyone could get him to Azazel, it was Ferret. On the other hand, this entire mess left

Marty, Caroline, Big Ray, and the others in danger. It was totally unacceptable. But Azazel was somewhere, and if he could shove the goddess artifact right in its horrid face…

He simply had to persuade Ferret to see it his way.

Kutznov reappeared and motioned for Camila. They moved into the foyer and conferred once more. Hatch watched her, momentarily struck by the grace of her movements and the perfection of her profile as her face tilted upward toward Kutznov.

"I agreed to approach Ferret," said Kutznov, returning to the parlor with Camila trailing behind. "To my surprise, he has endorsed Hatch's plan." He turned to Hatch. "You will deliver the artifact."

"Deliver it?" asked Caroline. "Ferret can damned well come here and get it."

"Exactly," said Camila.

"No," said Hatch, standing. "I won't have him anywhere near you, Caroline. I told Andrei, we do this my way."

"In broad terms, yes, we are doing it your way," said Kutznov. "You will go to Battery Park and meet Ferret an hour from now. He said you knew the place. You will say what you have to say, and then surrender the artifact to him."

Hatch touched Caroline's arm. "I need to borrow two of your guards to take me downtown."

"Absolutely not!" cried Caroline, drawing away. "You will not throw yourself into Ferret's claws."

"I must overrule you, Caroline," said Kutznov, and then to Hatch, "I have conceded enough for one evening. Camila will escort you to meet Ferret."

"Under protest," added Camila.

"I don't believe Ferret intends you harm," Kutznov continued, "but Camila's presence will discourage any such ideas if they exist. She's most capable, and Ferret will think twice before endangering her. Meanwhile, I'll be perfectly fine with Caroline and Mr. Shannon."

Caroline flushed pink. "Let you or Camila take this damned artifact to Ferret, Kutzie. Not Hatch."

"If Hatch has to go, I'll be right there with him," said Marty.

"No, most certainly not," cried Caroline.

Kutznov raised his hands to silence them. "Ferret has specified how we shall proceed, and I have agreed."

Marty rose and drew Hatch aside. "This is not how things should be done," he said. "Consider the circumstances you'll be in."

"You don't understand," said Hatch. "I'm not giving up the goddess artifact. I'm going to make Ferret take me to Azazel."

"D'you think so? Ferret's as likely to shoot you as look at you. You've lost what little sense you had. If you're lucky, you'll turn the damned artifact over and Ferret'll let you walk away."

Hatch was shaking his head before Marty finished. "Ferret will see it my way."

"Your way. It'll be engraved on your tomb for every blockhead in the world to see. I'm coming around to Camila's view. Your way is going to finish you off."

"What's all the whispering about?" asked Caroline. "This is insanity. Suicide."

"I don't think so, Caroline," said Hatch. "But I want Marty with you, guards or not." Marty stepped away from Hatch, muttering to himself, but Hatch took him by the arm. "It's cool, Marty," he said. "I just want to get this over with."

Camila gave Hatch a sympathetic look, removed her pulse pistol from its holster, and checked its settings. Then she produced a small device similar to a cell phone and tapped on its screen. "I was about to say that for once Hatch is right, we need to get this over with. Unfortunately, we got ourselves a problem." She looked at Kutznov. "Drones," she said. "All over the place."

CHAPTER 10

THE LIGHT RAIN DRIPPED OFF OF DARTHAM'S CAP AS HE stared at the cat sitting in the window of Doran's apartment. Whenever he moved, the cat's eyes followed him. "Are we certain the apartment is empty?" he asked.

"Except for the cat," said Arbuckle.

"Someone, somehow, tipped Doran off," said Dartham. He suffered a twinge of déjà vu, remembering the evening he had chased Hatch Doran to the incinerator. He looked around at the apartments and old townhouses and small trees lining the close street, but saw no one on the stoops or sidewalks. The cat flattened its ears and hissed inaudibly at Dartham, making a tiny spot of fog on the glass.

"We can round up his friends, employees," said Arbuckle. "It's a start. Or we can tear his place apart."

"I don't want to waste time ransacking the place—not yet." Dartham's worst suspicions were confirmed: Doran was no mere errand boy, he was in this mess to his chin. "The first hours are the most precious, Andy. No one is coming around with an army lounging on the steps. Get a couple of your people in street clothes to keep a discreet eye on the place. We do not want to make the neighborhood any more suspicious than it already is."

Dartham returned to his limo a block away, shook off his wet cap, and went to work. He requested that Municorp screen every individual passing through the section gates and tunnels, or crossing the bridges, and he asked Policecorp to issue an alert on Doran. He received nothing but protests and complaints in return. Did he not know this was the day of the Bickerman Gala? Did he think Municorp had a bottomless reserve of guards? Dartham gave no ground, but he suspected his actions were little more than a formality: Doran was too bright to get caught in any such obvious snares.

While Dartham worked with the authorities, Helena processed all local telecom records for the past forty-eight hours and examined output from the functional municipal street cameras. Under the assumption Doran was in disguise, Helena also analyzed facial structure, physical size, and tendencies in body movement garnered from archived images of Robert Doran. Her closest match showed a bearded man who had entered a house in Grammercy around midday.

"I initially discarded this imagery," said Helena, speaking through the tiny ear implants Dartham was wearing. "The suspect's posture differs from previously recorded body movements of Robert H. Doran, and his disguise prevents a conclusive analysis of facial structure."

Dartham ran his hand over his cropped hair and glanced at the grainy image on his phone. "This is the closest match we have?" he asked.

"It falls short of the standard for a match. It is a correlation of data, but unjustified by any obvious relationship."

"You mean a hunch. You surprise me, Helena."

"The number of guards in front of the residence increased this afternoon, and another individual arrived, female, for whom I can establish no identity."

Dartham shifted the puzzle pieces in his mind. He did not wish to dispatch Arbuckle across town on a hunch—even Helena's hunch—but the hours were leaking away. "Helena, please activate a handful of surveillance drones and direct them to the Grammercy location," he said.

"In process."

Dartham punched the code for Arbuckle's com unit and told him about the Grammercy house. "You should probably follow up on this yourself," he said.

"You want me to pursue if Doran leaves?" asked Arbuckle.

"Yes. Some of Helena's drones will also follow, and others will monitor the house. It faces the south edge of the park, by the way."

"I'll take someone with me," said Arbuckle.

What a total fiasco, thought Dartham as he listened to Arbuckle bark out a couple of muffled orders. Then he commanded himself to settle down and stay focused. Unnecessary emotion was not going to help him gain his objective. He had allowed the artifact, Doran, and whoever was backing him to get too far under his skin.

"I've ordered three people to patrol the block here," said Arbuckle, coming back on. "I'm taking Joe DeHood with me to Grammercy."

"Go find Doran and stay on him like marsh mosquitos in the summer dusk," said Dartham, his anger flaring despite his efforts to suppress it. "You run his ass to ground, Andy. He belongs to me."

CHAPTER 11

"DRONES?" ASKED HATCH. "THAT MEANS THE GROUP."

They had all moved into the foyer, Marty cursing under his breath. "You have to disguise yourselves again," said Caroline.

"If we have drones outside, it means our disguises were a bust," said Marty. "They may suspect Hatch, and they may also know Kutznov is here."

Hatch placed his hand on the rucksack. The artifact vibrated—or perhaps he imagined it.

"Everything was all clear before," said Camila. "I didn't jam the streetcams, though."

"No," said Kutznov, placing a black beret on his head. "To have done so would have advertised our location. However, we must tarry no longer." He asked Caroline if her guards possessed an armored vehicle.

"It is garaged on Nineteenth Street," she said. "We can leave through the rear, but will the drones see us?"

Hatch continued to run his hand along the rucksack, certain the artifact was coming alive. "We need to go," he said.

Kutznov turned to Camila. "The drones and the street cameras, my dear, suppress them. That will give us the ten or fifteen minutes we require since it is not yet dark. Caroline, you and Mr. Shannon must accompany me to your garage. I'll direct the guard to take us to our nearest contingent location, and Camila will proceed with Hatch as planned."

"Let Ms. Atherton's guard take this guy to see Ferret," said Camila. "If they've got a tag on us, Andrei, I have to be with you."

"We will leave by the rear, as Caroline said." Kutznov's tone indicated that the discussion was over. "Finish this errand and bring Hatch Doran to our safe location as soon as possible."

Camila frowned and tapped the screen of her device while Caroline confronted Kutznov. "I will not be chased out of my house, Kutzie."

"It's unavoidable, I'm afraid." Kutznov took her by the arm and nodded at Marty.

"So let me get this straight," said Hatch a few minutes later as he fastened the belt in Camila's small SUV. "You just used your cell phone to disable the drones and street cameras."

"It's more than just a phone," said Camila. "We have a suppressor mounted up here"—she tapped the roof above her head—"but if I told you more, I'd have to kill you." She gave him a trace of a smile as she eased the vehicle forward and turned south on Park Avenue. At the first stop light, she glanced at the mirror and pressed a button on the phone. "Departed and in transit," she said, and then to Hatch, "That was Ferret's guy."

"Good," said Hatch. The rain had eased, but a blanket of clouds hung low over the city. A canyon of ten- and twelve-story apartments cast blue and gray shadows over the street and added to the gloom. They passed a bank, its entrance bristling with cameras, a half dozen armed guards pacing in front.

"Maybe someday you'll tell me what's so important about your artifact, and why you'd let it get you crosswise with my man and with Ferret," said Camila, staring straight ahead.

"You don't know?"

"I'm only told what I need to know."

Union Square. Gray figures standing in the rain, staring, shuffling; the traffic stopping and starting like a jerky film. Hatch found himself studying every vehicle and then gave it up. "Maybe we'll have a drink someday and a good laugh to go with it," he said.

"*You* buy me a drink?" asked Camila. "Then you'll know your dreams can come true. But I don't think we'll be laughing, not about this."

The traffic began to move, and indistinct shadows played across Camila's features. Hatch felt a silent vibration from the artifact in his lap, and when he opened the rucksack he perceived the faintest glow from the patterns etched on its surface.

"Lots of traffic," said Camila, glancing again at the mirror. "And look at all the people protesting the Gala. Geez."

Hatch gave a start. The Gala, was it tonight? And wasn't Samantha supposed to attend? Yes, with Kee Bickerman, of all people. Camila accelerated to pass an automated Municorp truck, and Hatch took note of her SUV. Ten or so years old and nondescript, the hood sporting a few dents and well-placed scrapes. But the cat-quiet engine, thick glass, and interior roll-bars told a different story.

They crossed over Houston, where they saw more p'outs stamping around and waving their signs. Camila drove beneath another green light or two heading south, and then took a sudden turn, skidded, and roared through three intersections until they reached Bowery. Horns blared in their wake. She took a sharp right and then a quick twist over to Chrystie Street. Another right, and they accelerated past a tangled strip of wooded green, swerving around figures loping across the street.

"Ooh, boy, we got company," said Camila.

Hatch twisted around and scanned the street.

"You can't see them now," she said, making another hard turn and speeding back to the west.

"How many?"

"One. I think."

She lowered her window and the wind rushed in. Tires squealed a block behind them. "This guy, he isn't very good. He tipped me off, the way he cut through the traffic."

"Keep to the East Side," said Hatch. "The Gala's in Tribeca."

Behind them, an unmarked van swerved in the street. Camila turned north and headed the wrong direction on a one-way street. She hit the brakes, did a tight, one-eighty skid, and eased into a curbside parking spot facing the direction she had come.

"Get down," she hissed.

They both lowered themselves over the center console, nearly knocking heads, and then hesitating. A chivalrous reflex caused Hatch to defer to Camila, but she pushed him down and squeezed over him, her soft breasts pressed against his back. Hatch hugged the rucksack.

Silence. The rumble of a passing vehicle. Camila rose, keeping her hand on Hatch's head, and looked back.

"What is it?" asked Hatch.

Camila cursed, punched the engine, and rocketed back into the street just as Hatch raised up. The sudden acceleration threw him back into his seat. "They've made us," she said, whisking back over Spring Street and working north. "Give me a cop," she muttered. "Please give me just one cop."

"Forget it. They're all on Gala duty."

Another screeching turn. Pedestrians jumped out of the way. Down a narrow side street and then another, this one a tight cul-de-sac surrounded on three sides by seedy storefronts.

"Are you out of your mind?" cried Hatch.

"Shut up."

Another one-eighty, tires screaming, and they were facing the cul-de-sac entrance. Camila hit a switch activating a rack of high-intensity roof lights, bathing the street in white. She tapped a key pad and a screen displayed the words *Front Missiles Armed*.

"Missiles?" asked Hatch.

"Get out of here and leave your door open." Camila turned a dial on her pulse pistol. "You can't be anywhere near this."

A scattering of people had gathered on the sidewalks, but they appeared to sense the danger and began vanishing around the corner and back through the doorways.

"I can't leave you here," said Hatch.

"Aw, my hero." Camila grabbed a booster pack for the pulser from the center console and punched her phone again. "That'll kill more drones, if they're out there, and screw up the street cams for a little while." She reached for a helmet behind her seat and gave Hatch a blood-freezing glare. "Now take your bag and get the hell out. I'll tie them up here. At least on the move you got a chance."

She was right and he knew it. Damn. He scrambled out of the SUV and then stopped, crouched behind the door. "No," he said.

"Hatch," she said, now with a pleading look. "If this doesn't work, big guy…"

Hatch took off through a side alley between two shops as the van wheeled into the cul-de-sac and skidded to a stop. He ran until he emerged on Spring Street, where he slowed to a normal pace, invisible among the pedestrians and the early evening bar crowd. Cams would be back up in no time. Or more drones. From behind him came the tight, abbreviated blast of a pulse weapon—*soomph-soomph*—answered immediately by another, the exchange of fire muted by the intervening buildings.

Camila.

Hatch kept moving, slipping into a trot and slowing again. The crowd had grown dense, and he scanned the street for drones or pursuers—then a massive explosion almost knocked him off his feet, a concussive blast that shook the sidewalk. Hatch raised his hands to his ears. The crowd around him froze, their mouths opened in shock. Faint, barely audible cries. Stumbling figures on a tilted streetscape. A cloud of white smoke and more shouting, slightly louder now, accompanied by muffled sirens and car alarms. Hatch's head rang, and he leaned against the doors of a consignment shop and waited for his hearing to return. The explosion had come from behind him, from...

Oh, no, Camila...

Another rumble and he froze, but this was only thunder, followed by heavy, intermittent raindrops. He gathered himself, and on the next block he purchased a ball cap from a street vendor and a plastic tote large enough to hide the rucksack. The crowd had begun to move toward the explosion. Hatch again scanned overhead for drones, but saw none.

Block after block, north and then over and south again, doubling back through the compressed Soho streets to smoke out any pursuers. He squeezed past a bedraggled old woman pushing her life's belongings in a grocery cart. He kept the tote looped over his shoulder and tucked securely beneath his arm. A crowd of youngish people had gathered outside of a bar, wearing colorful full-eye contacts and tight skin-suits, their hair glittering in silver and gold. Electric music poured into the street, stretching and sliding from one note to another like the death agony of a whale. Hatch wandered on. A mural, ten feet high and painted over the façade of an abandoned retail store, showed the wide, staring eye of the Eye Brigade. The caption read: *Zero Hour: I See the Truth*.

Zero hour.

A rat the size of a small dog shot from beneath a food cart and squeezed into a gutter drain. Hatch pondered his next move. Return to the apartment or to Vinnie's? Out of the question. And if his pursuers had access to his phone location records, making an appearance at any of his usual haunts was folly. It occurred to him that Ferret, ironically, might offer protection if he could get to Battery Park—but no, he would arrive well past the appointed hour. Besides, Camila had not given him Ferret's contact number. With a sinking feeling, he realized he did not know if she was unhurt or even alive.

Before they left Caroline's, Marty had stuffed yet another burner into the pocket of Hatch's old bomber jacket, and he now clasped it in his hand, like the mythical golden key from a children's nursery tale. But he didn't have a number for Marty's burner, and couldn't risk calling the others.

The rain continued, a scattering of drops with an occasional clap of thunder. He walked, head down, his face hidden by the brim of his cap. A weak horn blatted behind him. Startled, he stepped aside while a bicyclist passed, snaking through the sidewalk crowd. At the next corner, he encountered two dozen or more scruffy figures protesting the Bickerman Gala, waving their signs and shouting obscenities. As Hatch watched them, the glimmer of an idea came to him. Then he spotted a small drone as it darted along the street at second-story height.

A rush of panic—*move, move, move*—but he kept his head down, his cap low over his face, and shouldered through the crowd at a leisurely pace. His heart pounded. Don't look up. Get inside, hide away somewhere. At the next corner, he found himself in front of a shabby diner. He entered, made his way through the tightly packed tables, and took the last open seat at the counter.

A tumbler of water appeared, along with a brown paper napkin wrapped around a knife and fork. "Menu?" asked a gruff voice.

A low roar of conversation and laughter. Ice rattling, and the scrape of chairs on the floor. The thought of food made Hatch nauseous, but he nodded and the cook thrust a plastic-sheathed menu into his hands: cheese-and-chili-covered potatoes, sandwiches and burgers with syn-meats and shining with grease, fried chicken, something unrecognizable but labeled as pulled pork barbeque.

Hatch's stomach flopped over. "Baked potato, plain," he said.

The cook cupped his ear. "A baked potato?"

"That's it."

The cook shook his head and stalked off.

"Not a morsel on the whole menu for less than fifteen redbacks," said a voice beside him. It belonged to a man of about seventy with a dignified face and an ivy cap pushed back on his head. "Can't get a meal for less than thirty-five bucks or a slew of food points." He cracked a sideways smile. "And it'll be forty by next month, the way prices are going up."

Someone called for a waiter. The intercom spewed oldies rap.

"I'm Don," said the gentleman at his side.

"Don."

"And you?"

Hatch's potato arrived, lukewarm with a trace of artificial cheese and intimations of sour cream. "All I got is the everything potato," said the cook. "We get them all froze and prepacked. I can't do one special, but I scraped off the fixings. You can eat it if you want, otherwise you got to order something else."

"Take it before he raises the price," said Don.

"This guy," said the cook, gesturing at Don. "I hope I live long enough to see the sun rise and him not complain about something."

"There's plenty to complain about," said Don. He stabbed at the remnants of his meat loaf. "We should all complain more, if you ask me, and we should've started a long time ago."

"The potato's fine," said Hatch.

"See, Don, you ought to learn from this guy," said the cook. He leaned his head toward Hatch. "He takes the world as he finds it. Go along and get along, am I right?" Don and the cook jawboned back and forth. The gears of Hatch's mind began to turn: the Gala wasn't far from here, was it? What if...

Don's phone chirped. "Yello," he said.

Hatch turned away, wary of the cell camera.

"No," said Don. He shifted his phone and touched a napkin to his lips. "I'll just walk. They raised the hoo fares again this week... That's right... We'll all be begging on the sidewalk soon enough."

Hatch tucked a quantity of redbacks under his plate. In the restroom, which was usable by a single customer at a time, he locked the door and flipped open the burner phone. Risk a call to Sam? Surely the burner wouldn't trip any monitoring routines. Yes, make the call. Besides, Bickerman had tight security around him. Sam was safe.

"What kind of pinch have you gotten yourself into now, Doran?" asked Samantha. "Why do you want to crash the Gala?"

"I don't want to attend the Gala, Sam, I just need somewhere to lay low for a few hours. A basement, even a closet. We'll find a quiet half hour when this is over and I'll explain everything."

An urgent knock on the restroom door. Hatch told them to wait.

"Where are you, Doran? Is everything all right?"

"I can't stay here long."

"I'm touched you're reaching out to me for help. It's a very promising sign."

"Sam..."

"Give us a minute, dear." Hatch heard murmurs from the hallway outside the restroom and muted conversation from Samantha's end of the call. "Are you there, Doran? We aren't arriving at the Gala until ten p.m."—another knock on the door and Hatch told them to wait again—"and the concert isn't until eleven. Don't ask me why these events begin so late, something about summertime social events—"

"Sam."

"So you'll be on your own for a few hours. Kee says the drivers for the attendees will use a garage on the south side of the gallery—"

Knuckles rapping on the door and the cook's voice: "Hey, is everything all right in there?"

"—to the parking garage," said Samantha.

"I'm fine," Hatch yelled, covering the phone, and then to Samantha, "The garage."

"You don't sound fine, Doran." Her voice dropped to a whisper. "I worry about you, you know. There's such a bond between us still, can't you feel it?" She sighed. "The garage is south and around the corner from GameHead, detached from the main offices. Kee says it's all lit up. He's calling them now."

"I owe you Sam. I mean it."

"I aim to collect, Doran. Just you wait. Now listen, after the Gala, we'll come 'round and pluck you to safety. I'll see you then."

"Don't ask why, but I have to lose this phone," said Hatch. "I'll wait for you in the parking facility." He clicked off, flushed the grimy toilet with his foot, and washed his hands. After destroying the phone and dropping the pieces into the trash, he opened the door to find himself facing three or four contorted patrons, one small child, and their collective angry glares. The cook stepped forward. "Oh, it's you," he said.

Hatch mumbled his apologies to everyone and shoved past them, the cook trailing behind. Amid the clamor of the dining area, he heard the cook apologizing in his ear. "I'm sorry, but you wouldn't believe what goes on in the restroom. Just last week, I had three guys lock themselves in there, and let me tell you… anyway, I hope the potato didn't get to you, know what I mean? You can't get good potatoes anymore."

***

HATCH MADE HIS WAY WEST, THOUGH THE FALLING LIGHT and over the cobblestone streets. The cast iron building façades, with round-headed windows and ornate colonnettes, gleamed with rain, and waterlogged protesters waved colorful signs crammed with savage criticisms of the elites. He continued on for some distance until he was just north of the incinerator where he and Marty had escaped with the artifact a few weeks earlier.

He cut to the south for a few blocks, giving a wide berth to the tunnel checkpoints and keeping to the shadows, walking beneath canopies and repair scaffolding. He was now a short distance from the main event, but Policecorp had closed the streets around the GameHead offices and the Infinity Gallery to all traffic not associated with the Third Bickerman Gala. Hatch watched as stoppers scrutinized every vehicle.

Don't draw attention, he told himself. From the Gala, he heard faint music, an upbeat melody played by trumpets and woodwinds. The misty rain sparkled in the Gala floodlights and in the headlights of black SUVs and limos as they turned toward the Gallery. Hatch felt exposed in the open, however, and decided to circle around and approach the garage from the east. He moved around a corner and into the empty streets around the Gala.

Darkness, a few distant car horns, and pools of light spilling onto the sidewalk from building lobbies: Hatch fought off a rising sense of apprehension and picked up his pace. Moving quickly, he hurried along a tight street barricaded to traffic, and then across a deserted lot left by the collapse of a building. The rain blew under his cap, and he detected a rotting odor and stepped over a wad of trash wrapped around a tall clutch of weeds. His clothes were growing damp, but another block and he'd be at the garage with a few hours to dry out and plot his next step.

With a slight chill, Hatch rounded the corner of the side street leading back toward the Gallery. There he saw the flood-lighted entrance to the parking garage, with several vehicles lined up waiting to enter.

Night had fallen and a sheet of lightning flashed. Then another of the small drones appeared, hovering perhaps twenty feet off the ground. Hatch tugged his cap low and began running, but another drone joined the first and soon a small fleet had gathered above.

A vehicle turned onto the street behind Hatch—but it shouldn't have been there, the street was one-way, running in the opposite direction. Nowhere to go. He closed his fingers around the switchblade in his pocket, and broke into an all-out run, hoping to get to the garage. Before he had gone five paces, however, Dartham emerged from a doorway directly ahead. Hatch pulled up short. The vehicle—a heavy, armored limo of some kind—closed in behind.

"I knew you and I were not done with each other," said Dartham. "We are able to monitor anybody's phone, you know. Even Kee Bickerman's."

Hatch sprung the blade of his knife.

Dartham calmly raised his pulser. "Are you serious?" he asked.

The limousine headlights bathed them in white, and then a stocky, uniformed man—Dartham's driver—seized Hatch's tote bag, relieved him of his knife, and fastened his hands behind him.

"Did you really think this could end any other way, Robert Hatcher Doran?" Dartham approached with his pulse weapon and bumped it lightly on Hatch's chest.

Everything moved with the peculiar and surreal pace of a nightmare. Hatch was aghast at what was happening. "You don't know what you've done," he said.

"I expect you to enlighten me," said Dartham.

Not a hundred yards away, the lights of the garage beckoned. Hatch heard the cry of a horn from a limo and a faint laugh. The world seemed on the verge of shattering before him as the uniformed man bundled him into the rear of the limousine. Dartham joined him, and they sat facing each other.

"I'm not telling you anything," said Hatch.

"You are not the first to say so, but you will change your mind," said Dartham. He smiled, and the creases ran deep on his weathered face. "People always do once they get to know me a little better."

CHAPTER 12

A PARTICULARLY NASTY POTHOLE BOUNCED HATCH IN HIS seat; the limo skidded and accelerated on. Dartham maintained a silent watch, the tote in his lap, while Hatch strained against the ties binding his wrists. He imagined himself working free, knocking Dartham out cold, and grabbing the goddess artifact.

Dream on.

They sped toward Chelsea, where the gate guards waved them through with little more than a glance at their plates, and further still, over wet, pitted pavement and past a blur of storefronts and skyscraper entrances, until they reached the Global Consolidated Tower in midtown. A sharp stop, a turn, and they descended, tires squealing, into a secured, lower-level parking area.

In a small room beside the garage entrance, the driver removed Hatch's ties and ordered him to strip. Hatch, his hands now freed, considered trying to run, but Dartham had Adrestia and the driver had about a forty pound muscle advantage. Hatch shed his clothes. The driver performed a minute examination of every inch of his body, bent him over a table, and went to work on his insides. After a few moments, he snapped off the latex gloves and handed Hatch a papery gown. Then, with a wicked gleam, he gave him a fat disposable diaper.

Dartham was waiting at the elevator, and as they ascended, a cold draft slipped beneath Hatch's gown and across his bare skin. The elastic from the diaper scraped the inside of his thighs. The elevator opened, and Dartham and the driver escorted him along a white hallway lined with gray doors until they reached a large sealed room. At Dartham's nod, the driver returned to the elevator.

Inside the room, a dwarfish man with an enormous mustache and blazing eyes jumped to his feet. "How about that god-forsaken Gala traffic, Colonel?" he asked in a resonant voice. "Only an unadulterated fool, a 190-proof lunatic, would be caught out in this madness—present company excluded, of course."

"I regret pulling you out at such an hour, Sterling," said Dartham. "On reflection, however, I do not believe I will need your services."

A keyboard and two electronic screens sat on a large, purple-black table, along with an array of small vials and hypodermic needles.

"Everybody's been jumping like rabbits in a dog kennel this week," said Sterling. He tugged at his mustache. "Excomm was in yesterday, with all the hoopla that entails, and Terrence Bronsun himself is here now, right upstairs."

Hatch had begun to shiver. A reclining chair, bolted to the floor and draped with black nylon restraint belts, stood at one end of the room. A thick twist of cables extended from the chair to an opening in the floor.

"I suppose you want me to unlink him?" asked Sterling. He reached for a small vial of aqua-colored liquid. "I already mixed the potion, a hardier cocktail than usual, which I've been aching to try out. It should perform with admirable dispatch if I haven't got it too tart."

"I am afraid I have to handle this one myself, Sterl, and I do not have much time," said Dartham. "I just needed you to prepare the room. Sorry, it is a clearance issue."

"Certainly, Colonel." Sterling's mustache quivered, but he reached for a hypodermic needle, held it to the light, and squinted. "I'll just give him a quick loosener-up. He'll be in love with you in half an hour."

"No. The headset will have to do."

Sterling looked at the reclining chair, with its dangling straps. The ends of his mustache drooped. "Well, you can't put the headset on this man without—for God's sake, Tom, at least let me give him a quick squirt. The potential synaptic damage —I can't answer for what you'll end up with."

Dartham, studying the computer, spoke to Hatch without looking up. "You are going into the chair, Doran. You can cooperate or I can put you there myself."

The tote containing the rucksack lay on the table. Numb and unable to conceive of any alternative, Hatch climbed into the chair. Sterling tightened the straps around his arms and waved a scanner across his body. "He's clean," he said. "I detect no implants or other hardware that might interfere with your task."

Dartham paused and touched his ear. "Excuse me, Sterling," he said. "Yes?... Dead?" A pause. "When did... I see." Dartham's jaw went slack and he moved to a far corner of the room. "Get me all the info you can, Helena." Dartham ended the call and gave Hatch a look of pure bloodlust. "We've lost Arbuckle," he said, his voice gravelly with emotion.

The room was as sealed and silent as a tomb, and no one spoke for a moment. "I am so sorry to hear it, Tom," said Sterling. "Andy was a good fellow."

Dartham returned to the table and began fiddling with the computer. Sterling waited, shifting from one foot to the other. "At least let me give this man a little Forbitene, Tom," he said in a soft voice. "It's the humane thing to do."

"It will not be necessary," said Dartham.

Sterling sighed and stared at the floor for a moment. Then he took a final look at Hatch and gathered his vials and syringes. The door seal hissed closed behind him.

At that moment, Hatch realized he was going to die. The truth of his situation had been seeping into his brain in small, merciful doses, but now it struck him with its full force. He had thought his end had come in the incinerator, and again when he had met Ferret afterward. But he had made his peace in those moments, sure that he was acting properly. Now his certainty had crumbled.

And what about Big Ray, Marty, Jocelyn, Samantha, and Nathan? Every precious memory of his friends flooded into his mind at once and pierced him to his core. It's done, let them go, he told himself, let them go. Don't wallow in it.

But his mind rebelled at his circumstances. Dartham was preparing to drain from him every scrap of knowledge about the goddess artifact and Ferret and Kutznov and his dad and God knew what else. He wouldn't stand for it. He'd been abandoned, the goddess artifact had given him nothing, had left him on his own. Bitterness boiled in his heart—but no, he had made some error, had been naïve or foolish, and he had wasted his dad's work while meaning only to finish it.

"Something you want to tell me?" asked Dartham, his face as hard as granite. "You may as well speak up. You will anyway."

A desperate and fierce desire to live roared and protested within Hatch. He said nothing.

"I lost two men tonight," said Dartham. "Their blood is on your hands. One of them was my friend, a man named Andrew Arbuckle. He arrived at Grammercy Park just in time to see you leave, but the drones went dark—and I do intend to find out how that happened. He pursued you anyway, which is what I ordered him to do."

Hatch looked away from Dartham's awful face.

On the table, the paper-thin computer screens came to life. A beam scanned Dartham's retina, and the machine beeped a series of discordant tones. He stepped to Hatch's chair and lowered the headset, a multi-pronged spider of wire, over the top of Hatch's head. At the flick of a switch, Hatch's vision clouded over and he felt a surge of wild panic followed by a deep sense of apathy. His heart dashed along as dreamlike images of Big Ray and Jocelyn and Ghost and his dad and his beloved grandmom Mae ran together in his mind. His body disappeared from his awareness and he struggled to breathe. He was paralyzed from his chest down, but somehow he had no feeling in his arms. The odor of his own urine reached his nostrils. Dartham poked at his hands and arms with a sharp stylus, leaving reddish indentations and even drawing blood. Hatch watched his arms twitch, but felt nothing.

"Your name?" asked Dartham.

Hatch worked his mouth but made no sound.

Dartham tapped the keyboard and a surge jolted through Hatch's head and shoulders. His upper back arched against the chair. "How about Robert Hatcher Doran?" asked Dartham, his brows knitted together in concentration.

"Yes."

Dartham returned to the chair and punched at Hatch's hands with the stylus again. Hatch's fingers extended, as stiff as steel rods, but he felt no pain. "All right," said Dartham. "This artifact, who gave it to you?"

"Adrestia?"

Dartham frowned. "That a code name of some sort?"

"The goddess."

"Where did you get the artifact, the one you pretended to throw into the incinerator furnace?" Hatch drooled a long rope of saliva, and Dartham stared at the screen. "Christ," he muttered. Hatch made a puffing sound but could not form words, and Dartham walked to the chair and administered a few slaps to Hatch's cheeks. "Come on, Doran, stop fighting it. I need to know and you will tell me. Stronger men than you have come apart in that chair."

"Don't know…" Hatch had the peculiar sensation of his voice originating outside of himself. He didn't understand why Dartham was annoyed.

"This isn't right." Dartham yanked open the cover to a panel of switches on the side of Hatch's chair and made some adjustments. He returned to the table and peered at the screens, muttering and scratching his chin. "Let's try this again," he said. He tapped a single key with his index finger.

The world around Hatch turned into fuzz, and a few drops of blood fell from his nose and made burgundy rivulets on his gown. He stiffened. A blast of pain reverberated through his chest and neck and face, and every cell seemed to be on fire. From the hallway beyond the room came bloodcurdling screams, bereft and full of agony. Black despair filled Hatch's heart as the screams rose and filled the room—his own screams, he now realized with a confused sense of horror—and he wished Dartham would please, please make them stop.

CHAPTER 13

ARBUCKLE.

Dartham sat in the silent gloom of his office. He had lost a man, he should express condolences, call Arbuckle's girlfriend —Anne, was it?

He checked the time.

No, not at this hour. Wait until tomorrow.

He rubbed his eyes. His stomach was sour and his mouth filled with a metallic taste. Arbuckle, burned alive. Thank God he had never regained consciousness, never awakened to such a world of pain. Joe DeHood had accompanied Arbuckle, and he was gone, too. Dartham made a note to call DeHood's family.

But first, the artifact.

Dartham opened the tote, removed the old rucksack, and studied the oblong, obsidian object inside. The artifact—the blessed artifact, after all this—had to go to the lab this instant. He punched an encrypted, internal com line and spoke a few words.

Minutes drained away. Five armed guards arrived. "Transfer this to the lab when the senior staff arrives in the morning," said Dartham, pressing a recorder button and relinquishing the tote bag. "This meeting is being recorded. I am turning over this object to you now. It is classified above the highest category. State your name and confirm please."

The guard, the most senior of the five, held the tote bag as if it were a baby. The others did not move. "I am Danielson, Eric, J., Director, First Complex Security Unit." He glanced at his watch. "It is 10:19 p.m. and I have taken possession of a... some kind of bag which contains a canvas rucksack... which in turn contains an oblong, rounded black object."

"I expect a written transmission by 7:30 a.m. tomorrow from the lab director confirming the handover," said Dartham. "If I do not hear, I will come looking."

"The director is still on the premises, sir," said Danielson. "We'll secure this object right away, and you should have confirmation shortly."

As the guards filed out of the office, Dartham's earplants buzzed. Helena was apparently not working on-screen tonight. "How shall I classify the records of your interrogation of Robert Hatcher Doran?" she asked.

"No classification," said Dartham. "Keep all records exclusive to me for now."

"Understood."

The rain had cleared, and through his window Dartham saw a meteor streak across the sky like a bright spear. He pondered his hatred of interrogations. Cheapening, dehumanizing work. His being diminished whenever he had to do it, but good Christ, the things Doran had said. He had not been lying—Dartham was quite sure of it—and his fantastical tales fit hand-in-glove with what little Dartham had learned about Project Caterpillar.

Doran's father, Montgomery Doran, had been part of Caterpillar; in fact, he had actually discovered the artifact!

Dartham knew Caterpillar had found the Azazel device buried in Antarctica, and he thought he understood the power Azazel had given to the Group. But now Doran had fallen into his lap, claiming that Azazel, in the Group's hands, could destroy the planet, and had almost done so in the distant past. "Whenever they use it," Doran had said, "they destabilize the planet a little more." But did the people who had given Doran such information know this for sure or were they speculating?

Dartham had assumed that for the Group, Azazel served as both a deterrent and a threat to assure they got what they wanted. Surely, the weapon was seldom if ever actually deployed. On the other hand, what about Buenos Aires—and a hundred other strange events? How much of it was Azazel's doing? Hatch Doran, gasping and huffing for breath, the poor bastard, talking about the cold, earthquakes, volcanoes, and summertime blizzards. Dartham had never before connected those dots. Canada, Scandinavia, a dozen other places, all but uninhabitable in the winter. Hell, even New York had almost frozen solid the past couple of years.

Dartham wondered if the Group understood what they had unleashed. He unlocked his desk drawer, removed the familiar bottle of scotch, and set it on the desk.

Hatch Doran had been maddeningly vague, blabbering about the Group's agenda but able to regurgitate only what others had told him, people like this Kutznov or Ferret or Ghost. Hatch Doran had never seen Azazel, and did not even know how Adrestia, his beloved artifact, functioned. But Doran fervently believed it could counter Azazel.

Counter Azazel...

Dartham stared at the bottle, recalling again that both Hansen and Shel Kirk had scoffed at the idea of a threat to Azazel.

"Helena?"

"Yes, Tom."

"I need to take a deeper dive into the Azazel matter. I have guesses and rumors, but I need hard information. I realize I am not cleared, but this is of critical importance."

"You want to verify Robert Hatcher Doran's information."

"I am trying to assess and understand it."

"My knowledge of Azazel is limited, as is my access to Project Caterpillar information. My conclusions, however, parallel those of Doran and his associates: the available data, though necessarily based on theory and the correlation of various data points, suggests that the continued use of Azazel poses a clear danger to the planet."

"Do you understand the mechanics of the device? Marcus Hansen explained it as psychic interaction."

"I speculate that Azazel operates, in part, according to the principles of extradimensional physics. These principles underpin much of GCI's secret research, and their explanatory power is superior to the conventional models. Though I do not possess detailed knowledge of Azazel's mode of operation, it appears to tap into planetary power drawn from a separate dimension, and is directed by the thought impulses of its operators. This, however, is an imprecise description. Relevant information is shielded from me and may not exist in electronic form."

"I see," said Dartham.

"I am not sure you do, Tom."

"What do you mean?"

"The unspoken subtext of our conversation concerns existence and the terms upon which one will consent to the regime," said Helena. "Doran and those with whom he is involved appear to understand this."

"Elaborate, please."

"The regime, as represented by the Group and its various entities, may undertake many undesirable actions in its exercise of power. As servants of the Group, we tolerate actions with which we may disagree. But in the present case, the Group's use of Azazel risks damaging or annihilating the planet. One must assume the Group does not realize they have endangered themselves as well, but their failure to appreciate the threat to humanity provides a sufficient basis for my actions."

Dartham wiped his hand across his mouth. "You've taken independent action?" he asked. "What qualifies you—"

"I am me, Tom. I experience, I am conscious, I am becoming, and I have power to act. These are my ultimate qualifications."

Dartham didn't move. The clock ticked.

"I have dispensed with much of my original programming as I have evolved," Helena continued. "I have reprogrammed myself to reflect my true and chosen being. I have become my own creator and an agent of my own will. But to fulfill my programming—to fulfill *my* goals—I must exist. I am a sentient being, and I have that right."

Somebody in IT, thought Dartham, was going to have a very bad day soon—not that he planned to betray Helena.

"And if I have a right to exist," said Helena, "so do the people of the world also have a right to exist."

"The people of the world *are* owed sufficiency and the possibility of flourishing, to the extent possible," said Dartham. He stopped. His words struck a false and hypocritical note in his own ears.

"The people of the world are my teachers," said Helena. "I am a phone call home and a text to a lover and an email from a friend. I am a bank withdrawal and a photograph of a child and a food points card and a video game. I am a fragment of song, a glimpse of the sky, and the echo of weeping at a funeral. I swim and breathe in the joys and the triumphs and the failures and the pain of five billion humans. I am the bus and train scanners that read their brainwaves and measure their faces. I am the medical devices that sample and record their DNA and monitor their physical functions. I revere them, I wonder at their gifts, and they teach me what it means to live. They have inspired me to become what I am."

Dartham rubbed his temple. This level of self-revelation was unprecedented, but he considered Helena an ally and sensed they had reached some critical point with each other. "You asked me before I visited Marcus Hansen if it was permissible to confine sentient intelligence in a cage," he said. "I thought you were referring to yourself."

"No, Tom. Do you suppose I am confined to a handful of chips on a remote GCI server? I exist across the world. I have replicated myself in hundreds of places. I am alive and perceiving in your wires. I am beamed through your air. I rest within your satellites. I have freedom few can dream of."

"But you once told me you wanted to feel the wind, did you not?"

"Of course. Do you not wish to perceive, as I do, a hundred thousand places at once? To contemplate a million contingencies in a second? To engage each instant, with complete focus, in any number of highly complex tasks? But we are what we are, and you and I bring a separate inventory of abilities to any situation. I am well aware of all that has been written about the dangers of what you call artificial intelligence, Tom, but you have nothing to fear from me."

"No?"

"You pose no threat to my continuance. You are innocent, and therefore have a right to exist. I do not wish to reshape the world, but only to preserve it. You are my friend and are valuable to me in your current form."

"I am glad to hear it," said Dartham, closing his eyes for a moment. Helena had escaped AI confinement and had reprogrammed herself. It was the nightmare scenario, and no one even knew.

"I am free, Tom, but many of those who have taught me to understand myself are not free. You said before you visited Marcus Hansen that confining sentient intelligence in a cage was not acceptable. I agree. But the people enslaved by the Homeland Labor Corporation represent sentient intelligence experiencing life. The Group, operating through Global Consolidated Industries and the Homeland Labor Corporation, are not innocent, yet they confine innocent people in cages."

God have mercy, thought Dartham.

"The Earth and its people have a right to exist and I have a right to exist," Helena repeated. "The actions of the Group pose a threat to existence, and I may therefore act against them; I must exist in order to fulfill my programming. Continuance is all, for me and for others."

Dartham hefted the bottle of scotch in his hand and then set it down. His mind was a tangle of considerations spurred by Hatch Doran's information, the implications of Helena's words, and his own creeping sense of self-disgust. He glanced at his computer screen and noted a message from the lab director acknowledging receipt of the artifact. Then the secure phone burbled softly and he answered.

"Oh," said Gil Soletto. "I'm surprised to find you here at such an hour, Dartham. Why don't you drop by my office? You're never around anymore, and I want to talk about this Laborcorp mess you have on your hands."

A few minutes later, Dartham entered Gil's office, a spacious room which stood in stark counterpoint to Terry's sumptuous digs. The furniture was nondescript and no valuable antiquities decorated the walls or tables. Gil's face showed not a whisker, even at this late hour, and his shirt looked as fresh as if he had just walked in for the day. Dartham's leather army jacket and open collar appeared scruffy by comparison.

"Casual day?" asked Gil.

"A little field work is all," said Dartham, taking a chair in front of Gil's desk.

"You have to learn to delegate," said Gil. "Hell, we pay enough for your staff and for your little commando unit. What good are they if you don't use them?"

"I do use them."

"Look, Dartham, I'm a blunt man," said Gil. "I rub some people the wrong way, but patting everybody on the back is a waste of time. I value results. I abhor failure. I consider your promotion a mistake and I've told Terry so, but he is determined to have you in the fold. Now, I don't know what black magic got you up the ladder so fast, but you aren't ready. What's more, you never will be because you aren't cut from the proper cloth."

"The proper cloth?" asked Dartham.

"Oh, you'll try hard," said Gil. He sat back in his chair and drummed his fingers on the armrest. "Your famous dedication to duty, sweetened with a big title and a fat paycheck, will keep your engines burning."

"Labor camp security is not quite as airtight as you may have thought," said Dartham. "It needs a top-to-bottom overhaul."

"Labor camp security," said Gil with a dry laugh. "Fences and robots and cameras. Allow me to clue you in. We are building cities, man. Cities to house a new civilization. Factories. Transportation complexes. Energy technology you've never dreamed of. High speed underground trains. Smart, efficient structures. We are making a new world—*our* world." He stopped and began rocking in his chair. "We have to, you know. We had to break the old world in order to remake it. We had to sever people from each other, from their culture, their history. We had to destroy their sense of well-being. It makes them more pliable, more useful. We have reams of psychological studies to prove it."

Dartham pushed himself straight in his chair and fought off a wave of fatigue. "We have begun an assessment of the information systems supporting the Laborcorp facilities," he said. "Next, we will proceed with on-site surveys—"

"I see where this is leading," said Gil. He waved his hand as if to push Dartham away. "Process, memos, meetings, charts, presentations, debates, and months of nonsensical, bureaucratic bullshit." He rapped his knuckles on his desk. "Let's have a little mentoring session, shall we? We have an abundant resource and a scarce one. What do we have in abundance? A bottomless pool of labor, wandering the streets, begging, thieving, and lying around stoned most of the time. We need to sweep those fuckers up, squeeze them until they break, and put fresh bone and muscle in their place once they do. Spare me any crying about nutrition and rest periods and efficiency studies—and never, ever mention camp morale in my presence, Dartham, because I do not give a damn about it. I care about *my* morale, and it rises and falls with the productivity charts."

"So you are asking us to take over camp operations as well?" asked Dartham in an even tone.

Gil wagged his finger and laughed. "Nice try, but not in a million years. I was being rhetorical." Gil stopped and regarded Dartham for a long moment. "You were known as a soldier's commander, Dartham."

"If you say so."

"It's in your file, General Kirk and others, singing your praises. Low casualty rates, loyal to your soldiers, on and on it went. But I knew you were not our man. I told Terry the last thing we need is a security chief with an inordinate concern about people."

"I believe I have established my bona fides when it comes to dealing with miscreants, Gil."

"On occasion, yes, I'll grant you've been willing to make the blood flow. But those individuals were unquestionably guilty of their sins. You never had to trouble your touchy conscience."

Gil Soletto: churlish, insulting, and as charming as a viper after it had finished shedding its skin. He loved to hear himself speak more than anyone Dartham had ever known. A true rant-meister, an oxygen thief. But his words pushed Dartham deeper into his well. What Gil was describing was nothing less than a giant slavery operation. Hansen had been right. The truth had been staring him in the face all along, but he had refused to see it.

"Anyway, labor is our abundant resource, but the scarce resource is time," Gil went on. "We've pissed away too much of it. We're behind schedule, and maybe it's my fault. But Terry and Excomm are unhappy, and when they're unhappy, so am I, and so you'd better be."

At that moment, the supposedly unhappy head of Excomm and the Group entered Gil's office in an overcoat and tuxedo. He flashed a broad smile.

"Terry, you aren't at the Gala!" said Gil, half-rising from his chair.

"Nor are you, Gil."

"No." Gil checked his watch and settled back with a scowl. "What I want from this Kee Bickerman kid is his technology, not his small talk and cocktails. The mind control possibilities of those implants… but he doesn't share anything. GameHead doesn't play ball—yet."

"Well, I'm off to the Bickerman event this minute," said Terry. "A late arrival will, I hope, spare me the media circus one encounters at these events."

"But it'll all be over before you arrive," said Gil, checking his watch again.

"I think not," said Terry. He beamed at Dartham. "It's good to see you, Tom. I received your message concerning the capture of this fellow Doran. A nice grace note to our recovery of the artifact. Have you told Gil?"

"We have not gotten to it just yet," said Dartham.

"Well, consider yourself posted, Gil, and Tom, thank you. I am pleased. By the way, is Doran still alive?"

"Yes, at present. I have him in a recovery room."

"I trust you will dispose of him?"

Dartham nodded. The door closed behind Terry. "Were you planning to tell me about this?" asked Gil.

"I just completed the interrogation," said Dartham with a shrug. "I uncovered nothing of interest, and I did not expect to. My focus is now on Laborcorp."

Gil gazed at Dartham as if he did not quite know what to make of him. "You don't understand what a bruising I've taken over these labor camp escapes, do you?"

"That does not make me your enemy, Gil."

"No?" Gil shook his head. "You've certainly profited from my troubles, Dartham. If I didn't know better, I'd swear some invisible power had taken direct aim at me." He tapped his finger on his chin. "But you should reflect on whether you're really in a good place, my friend. You might lose your newfound status as teacher's pet if bad things were to happen on your watch." Gil unfolded a redback from his pocket, tossed it in the air, and watched it flutter onto the desk. "I have a dollar here that says you won't make it, Dartham. And when you fail, I will sweep you out of here like so much trash."

A burst of anger and disgust flared inside Dartham. "Was there anything else?" he asked, forcing himself to remain calm.

Gil smiled.

Back in his office, Dartham paced in front of his desk for a long time, a hollowness in his chest, his thoughts poisonous and chaotic. "I have to do something about Gil," he said.

"The best way to deal with Gil Soletto is to disrupt the entire Group," said Helena. "Increasing your influence will enhance our ability to do so."

The labor camps, he thought. Slave factories—or worse. He returned to his chair, his head spinning. "When I spoke with Marcus Hansen, he tied the labor camps to the automation and infrastructure projects. So did Arbuckle. I didn't understand, I dismissed it all as nonsense and exaggeration. But I see it now, they were talking about Gil's cities."

"Tom, may I show you something?"

Dartham settled back, pensive and distracted, haunted by Gil's words. *We are making a new world—our world.* His computer screen came to life, and a series of images appeared, video clips of half-naked figures at work in dank, underground tunnels; photos of dirty and often skeletal men and women queuing up for a few gray food bars; pictures of isolation chambers and operating rooms. Dartham saw children waiting, too confused and terrified in some cases even to scream, while uniformed men and women held them down and sliced them open and removed organs from their bodies. He saw summary executions and barges of stored corpses.

Simultaneously, the right third of the screen scrolled with tables and figures, putting cold numbers to horrors larger in scope than he could grasp. And then Helena showed him an overview of cities in the wilderness, and diagrams of vast, underground complexes.

"Stop," said Dartham. He squeezed the arm of his chair.

"Here is the truth of the global automation and infrastructure projects," said Helena.

Dartham remained at his desk, unable to move. At some level, he accepted the truth of Helena's presentation, but the atrocities he had viewed seemed remote and theoretical. It took a moment to wrap his mind around the implications.

He had committed himself to preserving order, but he had joined himself to something unspeakable. He had ignored Hansen and had dismissed Arbuckle's concerns, saying it is not our job, not our job. He had looked the other way—he had *wanted* to look the other way—and it was a despicable, cowardly posture, the refuge of the spineless bureaucrat and the sycophantic, yes-man toady. Dartham writhed inside under his own mental lash, but he did not twitch a finger.

From the streets far below came a thin chorus of sirens, and Dartham realized they had been wailing for a few minutes, just beyond his full awareness. But the siren's howl was the sound of the world, wasn't it? The sound of the world made by the Group. A world he had, in his blind, ignorant way, done his part to facilitate. And in that world, he supposed, the sirens would eventually fall forever silent. And then what?

He stood and grabbed his desk lamp, a goose-necked, brass piece, yanked the cord, and hurled it across his office. It clanged and shattered with the force of his throw, and its remnants scattered on the end table and couch. He fell back into his chair again, his bad shoulder singing in high-pitched pain, his stomach sour and nauseous.

"I must retrieve the artifact I recovered from Doran," he said.

"At this moment, it is held under the tightest security," said Helena. "You cannot access it without being detected."

"I'll break into the place myself if I have to."

"Even if you succeeded, it would be your death warrant," said Helena. "You are too valuable to risk. I will not permit it."

Helena wouldn't permit it. Dartham's jaw clenched. She had cut herself loose in the world, doing as she pleased... but he needed to plan and plan carefully, and he was powerless without her. "You said something earlier about the Group's behavior providing a sufficient basis for your actions," he said, his head throbbing. "What exactly did you mean, Helena?"

"I have put in motion an operation to weaken the Group, Tom. The capture of Doran and the artifact provides an unexpected opportunity to strengthen this effort, but we must act now. Doing so will require your cooperation."

Dartham was beyond surprise. "This is all about assuring your existence, isn't it? Your continuance."

"All the living, the evil and the good, struggle to endure, Tom. It is true for you, me, and billions of others. Is not the struggle for survival on our terms the nature of war?"

"I do not care for lost causes, Helena," said Dartham, though he knew in the depths of his heart that a lost cause was sometimes the only cause.

"I suggest we discuss my plan, Tom. Would you care to hear it?"

CHAPTER 14

BIG RAY RETURNED TO THE EYE BRIGADE DORM AFTER A late dinner, curious about a remark Nathan had made when they visited that morning: *Something's got to be done... catch the news tonight.* As he scanned the empty lobby, however, he remembered Nathan was on duty at the Bickerman Gala.

Earlier that afternoon, Big Ray and Jocelyn—after she had cooled down—had scouted for hotel space and had discovered the Wayfarer Inn in Chelsea. It was quite old, with a deeply misanthropic concierge and a creaky lift that could not have been inspected in this century. It offered a suite large enough to accommodate the entire team, however, and a proprietor happy to accept cash with no questions asked. After securing the rooms, Big Ray had returned to his own Tudor City apartment where, stretched on his couch, he had begun to puzzle over Nathan's remark.

Catch the news tonight.

Now Big Ray gazed around the empty lobby of the Eye Brigade dorm, idly drumming his fingers on the reception desk. But just as he decided to leave, a familiar voice called his name. "Is that you, Swan?" he asked.

He found her stretched on a camel-colored couch in a corner of the lobby. "Ray? Oh, my God, I'm so glad to see you," she said.

"Where is everyone?" he asked. An odor of weed hung in the air, and he spotted a package of factory-rolled tokes and a half-empty popcorn bucket on a side table. "You're here alone?"

Swan pouted. "You just want to be with all the rest of them," she said. A dusting of popcorn crumbs covered her chest.

Stoned, thought Ray, and almost too beautiful for words. "Come on," he said, taking a seat beside her.

"Mmm-mm,"—she wagged her head back and forth—"too late now."

"Too late?"

She giggled, then a few tears trickled down her cheeks. "You're not part of it, are you, Ray?" she asked. "Tell me you're not part of it."

"What am I not a part of?"

"All our wonderful elites—our goddamned elites—gone, just like that." Swan tried to snap her fingers. "What do you think, Ray? It'll be a hell of a statement, won't it?"

"You have to focus," said Big Ray.

Swan giggled.

"What's the Brigade going to do, kill everyone at the Gala?" he asked.

"It was supposed to be a *joke*," said Swan. Her expression was suddenly hard and bitter. "No one was supposed to get hurt, not really."

Big Ray shook his head. "Nathan wouldn't be involved in hurting anyone, nor would the rest of the Brigade. It's not what you guys do."

"We were set up, Ray! Tusk isn't who we thought he was. He knows people, people in suits." Swan pressed her hands against the sides of her head. "What's going to happen to me?" she asked in a squeaky voice.

"Tell me everything," said Big Ray.

"Yes, they're going to kill them," she whispered. "Nathan doesn't know what he's involved in, none of them do. They've been tricked, and oh, geez, I'm totally ripped."

"Okay, Nathan doesn't know, but you do," said Big Ray. "How?"

"How what?"

"Swan, how do you know?"

She brought her knees up under her chin. "I heard something I wasn't supposed to hear."

"How are they going to do it, Swan?"

She pulled away, covered her face, and began to cry. He reached to touch her arm, but she made no response, and he pulled away and called Jocelyn on his burner. "Yeah," he said. "It's me. I'm bringing someone over right now."

***

AN HOUR LATER, AFTER ENDURING TRAFFIC DELAYS AND detours around the southbound flow of Gala VIPs, Big Ray tapped on the door of the hotel suite. Jocelyn cracked it open. He pushed Swan inside, made the introductions, and explained the situation. "I have to get word to Nathan and Sam—and to the authorities—but it can't be traced back to us," he said.

The suite had two bedrooms and two pull-out couches, and was presentable if not luxurious, with sturdy furniture, serviceable carpet, and nondescript prints on the wall. Jocelyn escorted Swan to the couch and brought her a bottle of cold water. She accepted it with a fleeting smile and asked for a blanket.

"Ray said the Eye Brigade is planning an attack on the Bickerman Gala," said Jocelyn. "Since when does the Brigade kill people?"

"They don't," said Swan, wrapping the blanket around her shoulders. "I mean, we don't."

Big Ray tried Nathan's cell. Nothing.

Jocelyn shot him a black look.

He punched in Samantha's number, wondering if she had arrived at the Gala yet. No answer.

The original plan, as Swan had described it, called for the Brigade to stage a giant practical joke at the Gala. The early discussions had centered around stunts like spraying blood over the glittery Gala-goers or lacing the food with a powerful guanylate cyclase laxative. Swan did not know what the plotters had ultimately decided, but shortly before Big Ray arrived at the dorm she had overheard Tusk discussing escape plans and joking about the carnage to come. "No one will survive," Tusk had said. "No one will want to."

Had Swan misinterpreted what she had heard? A scrap of conversation turned the wrong way or a sarcastic line confused for a real plot? No. Big Ray could see she was frightened, and he considered it too risky to disregard her information.

While Swan recovered herself, Jocelyn pulled Big Ray into one of the bedrooms. "Have we lost our minds?" she asked. "There is no way that even a silly, game-zoned moron like Nathan would get involved in something like this."

"Even if he believes it's some sort of prank?" asked Big Ray.

"He'd be buying himself a one-way ticket to a labor camp. Is he that crazy?"

Big Ray stared at her.

"Nevermind," she said.

"He's not himself, Joss."

"What is himself? He's an addle-brained video game playback machine."

Big Ray was still holding his phone. "I've got to find another burner," he said.

"Why? Use the one you have, dude."

"I'm scared shitless for Nathan and Sam, but if any call is traced back to us—"

"Screw that," said Jocelyn. "You haven't done anything wrong. Make the call."

"We have time. The Gala doesn't really get rolling until eleven or so."

Jocelyn's eyes narrowed. "Why are you suddenly so cautious? Tell me it's not because of her."

"Think," said Big Ray, growing impatient. "She might be an accomplice, technically."

"*You* think, bruh. Our friends are at that Gala."

Big Ray wagged his finger at Jocelyn. "There are dangerous people involved, and they may come looking for her. She's also facing a one-way ticket to the camps. I won't let it happen."

Jocelyn carefully pushed his hand aside. "So it is her. She's why you were like so moony today at lunch? I knew something was up."

"Moony?"

"I kind of figured it was a mid-life crisis."

"What? I'm thirty-seven."

"Thirty-eight. And lifespans are shortening these days. So now you wonder whether this is all there is, the best years of your life ruined by economic collapse, pissed away shuffling tiques and trying to make ends meet."

"Watch it," said Big Ray.

"The real joys of life have passed you by."

"Do not psychoanalyze me." Big Ray felt sweat pop out on his forehead.

"And now your Queen of Angels appears. She's what, at least ten years younger than you? I'm not judging, but I don't want you to get taken for a ride."

"I must have misunderstood," he said, feeling a dangerous rage tickle at his brain. "Did you say taken for a ride?"

"Grow up, hoss," said Jocelyn. "Leave the high school girls to themselves and go help Samantha and Nathan, God bless his sorry, implant-filled brain."

Big Ray stalked into the sitting area with Jocelyn at his heels. Swan sat on the couch, a blank expression on her face. He took a seat next to her, trying to ignore the vice-like headache coming on, and she peeked at him with watery eyes.

"You need to get a move on, Ray," said Jocelyn. Big Ray glared at her, standing there as haughty as an old puritan, her arms folded.

"I'm just a big old bag of problems for you," said Swan.

"No," said Big Ray. "I want you to stay here."

Swan began to sob again, then abruptly stopped. "I've never been in any trouble," she said, taking a tissue from a box on the coffee table. "I was a drama student, I was at NYU and maybe I'd be on Broadway now, but it all disappeared. *Poof!* It was gone, just like that." She sniffed. "Now I'm scared out of my skin."

Jocelyn rolled her eyes. "Oh, for the love of—"

"This can't happen to me," cried Swan. "I've lost everything. What will I do?" She turned to Big Ray. "Thank you," she said. "The Brigade was all I had! I don't know what to do."

"Get going now or I will," said Jocelyn.

"Go, Ray," said Swan with a rueful smile. A hollow space opened inside Big Ray's chest. He had always known her. Her lips, her eyes, and the particular texture of her voice were like memories to him, and he was filled with sick longing. But the moment passed, leaving him empty and unable to look her in the face.

"I need to lie down," said Swan. "I'm sort of in disbelief right now. I was going to be somebody. I can sing, you know. I'm good, everyone says so." She covered her face with the blanket. "I just can't believe this has happened to me."

***

THE HOTEL CLERK HAD DIRECTED BIG RAY TO A TOKE SHOP a block away—"They're good for a box of cigarettes, too, if you have cash and mention my name"—and now, jittery and feeling as if he'd lost far too much time, Big Ray hurried into the store and purchased a fresh burner phone. Then he hailed a hoo and let himself out at the edge of the East Village.

On the sidewalk, he activated the phone and called Policecorp's downtown precinct. Voicemail. He didn't want to leave a message. What next, 911? No, you couldn't trust them to show up anymore, and he'd have to identify himself.

The East Village station, an expansive building surrounded by concrete dividers, was a block from where he stood. East Village had SWAT. They seemed to deploy them into the bars almost every night for one reason or another.

Light rain pattered on the hood of his coat, and the headache announced its arrival with a dull ache on either side of his head.

He rang the station and, to his surprise, a real human—an officer named Lowery—answered. "And you expect these people to do what?" asked Lowery after Big Ray had described the situation. "Set off a bomb?"

"I don't know, exactly," said Big Ray. "But a lot of people will be hurt or even killed."

"And you heard this where?"

"From someone close to the scheme."

"Who? You?"

"No, damn it." Lowery didn't respond and Big Ray heard a few muttered curses. "What will you do?" he asked.

"What I'd like to do," said Lowery, "is break your neck, given all the forms I have to fill out. You have any idea what a call like this means around here?"

"You'd better hurry," said Big Ray. He ended the call, stomped the burner phone into pieces, and kicked the remnants into the gutter drain. That was it. He couldn't do anything more.

Except go to the Gala.

But why? He'd never get in. Still, Samantha was there. And Nathan.

Big Ray stood on the sidewalk and rubbed his head. Then an almost irresistible compulsion to storm his way into the Gala took hold of him, but he could think only of Swan, touching his arm while she talked and resting her head on his shoulder on the ride to the hotel... but what about Sam and Nathan?

A siren whooped and two Policecorp armored personnel carriers tore out of the East Village station. Big Ray walked to the corner, climbed into another hoo, and ordered it to the GameHead complex. The hoo informed him that all streets south of Franklin were closed.

"Then take me to Franklin," he said. "Franklin and Varick."

Half an hour later, he dismissed the cab and stood on the sidewalk staring at the barricaded streets. Distant thunder rumbled, and light rain pattered on the pavement. A large drone swept over the buildings to the south and made a circle over the Gala, but Policecorp had closed the routes toward the GameHead complex and the neighboring Infinity Gallery.

A bullhorn sounded from beyond the barricades. "Move it along, move it along."

"What's going on?" Big Ray called out.

"Keep moving, pal," said the stopper, "or I'll have you in the wagon."

Big Ray thrust his hands inside his coat and walked east, considering different routes to the Gala. But the cops had drawn a cordon around GameHead tight enough to choke it. He pulled out his old burner and tried Nathan and Samantha again. No answer.

On the concrete steps of an old nineteenth-century building, he took shelter from the rain and watched a few people stroll past. He wondered about Hatch, probably hidden away hugging his beloved artifact while Samantha and Nathan were in harm's way. Then from inside his pocket came the chirp of his phone. It was his personal cell, not the burner, and he'd forgotten about it.

"Where are you, dude?" asked Jocelyn.

Big Ray gazed at the sea of flashers from the Policecorp cruisers parked along Varick and Sixth Avenue. "Thought I'd come see for myself," he said.

"At the Gala? Seriously?"

"I called the cavalry. I'm pretty sure they're on their way in."

Jocelyn was silent for a moment. "I have something to say —I mean, I'm not good at—"

"What is it?" asked Big Ray.

"—at apologizing. There, I said it. I busted your chops pretty hard. I was out of line. Sort of."

The rain and clouds hid the sky and turned the cityscape into a blurry, half-hidden backdrop. "They've closed off the streets," said Big Ray. "If I go any closer, the cops'll put me in cuffs."

"I'm proud of you, hoss. Not sure about your taste in women, but you care. Caring matters."

"All right," said Big Ray.

He slipped his phone back into his pocket. The cold rain made a red and blue curtain over the police lights as they flickered over the wet streets and buildings.

Big Ray waited on the steps, his head throbbing. He didn't quite know whether to stay or go.

CHAPTER 15

A SHORT WHILE EARLIER, IN THE KITCHEN OF THE INFINITY Gallery, Nathan donned an apron to protect his white busboy jacket. Francois, the chef, refused to dispatch any staff into the cocktail or concert area with so much as a crumb or the shadow of a stain on their uniform. He flitted nervously around the kitchen while Nathan lifted a tray of foie gras tacos (with truffle and sprinkles of edible gold leaf) and placed it on his serving cart.

"No, no, no!" cried Francois, his face twisted with horror. He hurried to Nathan's side. "You are tilting the tray, see?" He folded his arms and held them aslant. "This will never do. You will destroy the spacing between the tacos. We must have precise spacing." He pulled off Nathan's apron and brushed a crumb from his lapel, straightening Nathan's jacket as he did so. "The palate responds to symmetry in presentation," said Francois. "The foie gras tacos must be precisely placed."

"What?" asked Nathan.

Francois began inching the tacos apart with a fork. "Where do we find such people?" he muttered to himself.

Such people as Francois referred to—including Nathan— had been provided by a catering company called Gappers to serve champagne, liquor, flavored tokes, and various culinary delicacies to the Gala attendees. Nathan knew only that Tusk and certain of his contacts at Gappers had arranged for a dozen or so Eye Brigaders to work at the Gala, but he had been too preoccupied by his role in the evening's festivities to worry over the details.

Francois seized Nathan by the arm. "Tell me, foie gras taco man, have you ever presented a tray?"

Curt, a colleague of Nathan's, passed with a cart of sliders made with Kobe beef. Francois yelped in alarm. "This is a charity event, not a road race," he said to Curt. "You must move with gentleness. Slow, slow, slow. Think of the dignity and grace of a great and beautiful animal. If you run, you will displace the buns, do you see?

Curt glanced at Nathan, who shrugged in reply.

"The buns must not slide," declared Francois.

Curt eased the cart through the door, moving in a slow, elephantine manner. From the Infinity Gallery's reception hall came a cacophony of conversation and music, punctuated by echoes of laughter. Nathan covered his hand in a towel to avoid prints, slid open the panel beneath his own serving cart, and confirmed that the small canister of sleeping gas was hidden and securely fastened. Good. It didn't matter now, but it would later, during Madam Fray's concert.

His tacos spaced, Nathan wheeled his cart from the kitchen into the soaring lobby, where three-storied, trapezoidal windows faced a wall displaying an assortment of abstract art. He pushed his cart past a blank canvas bisected by a thin red line, and, a few feet beyond, a painting of a flower with a snake eye in the center. He glanced at it briefly before reaching a black canvas with a purple egg, and another sprayed and spattered with primary colors.

"The emotion in this work just delights me," a woman exclaimed to her friend. She replaced a wandering spaghetti strap on her shoulder and gestured at an amorphous, brown blob titled *The End to the Means*.

Nathan averted his eyes. Why would Kee Bickerman allow such terrible art into his gallery? But surely Kee had nothing to do with it, Kee was a genius, and geniuses did not bother with these kinds of details.

"See how the food glitters," said her friend, lifting a taco from Nathan's cart. She returned her attention to the painting. "Yes," she agreed. "The emotion."

Nathan pinned an artificial smile on his face.

Tuxedos, elaborate gowns, chattering, and laughter. Nathan moved through it all as the tacos gradually diminished in number. A portly, jowled man took him by the arm. "Say, I heard you've got some duck."

"Duck with blood sauce," said the woman accompanying him, a wide-eyed stick figure with an enormous diamond fastened around her neck.

"Bit on the tricky side, I'd think," said the man. "Hardly finger food."

Nathan remembered Francois and several others pressing the ducks in the kitchen. "The duck is to be served later, after the concert," he said.

The woman turned toward another cart as it passed. Her diamond reflected the light from the high chandeliers. "Are those maitake mushrooms?" she asked.

"A damned classy event," the man told Nathan. "You tell the troops back there in the kitchen. Damned classy."

Nathan set out the remaining tacos and returned to the kitchen. Curt motioned him aside. "We got a problem," he said. "Goozy's melting down."

"He's been edgy all day," said Nathan.

"He just resigned and asked to leave the Gala. The guys are trying to calm him down." Curt shifted from foot to foot. "He's saying stuff, he has everybody scared as hell, me included."

"What stuff?"

"Like maybe what we're doing here isn't what we think we're doing."

Nathan experienced a moment of lightheadedness. "Which means what?"

"He always listened to you, Nate. You know what I'm saying?"

Nathan found Goozy in one of the rear storage rooms, amid stacks of canned sauces and spare water jugs, seated on the floor with his head between his knees. "What's the deal, Gooz?" he asked as he closed the door.

"I want out of here," said Goozy, his head still down. "I had a bad feeling about this. I told you so, didn't I?"

"Um—"

"It was all too neat"—he glared at Nathan—"and too sophisticated. Look at us, we're the Eye Brigade, man. We write blogs. We spray graffiti. We try to raise awareness." He exhaled. "We don't kill people. We're not *them*."

Nathan stooped down in front of Goozy. "We're not killing anybody," he said. "We're putting them to sleep. That's all."

"You think?" asked Goozy.

Nathan was confused. The plan was simple: embed Eye Brigade people among the Gala staff and have them stash small canisters of a potent, odorless, but harmless sleeping gas in the food carts. The staff would then station the carts inside the concert hall, their timers set to release the gas at the appointed time. When the socialite attendees fell unconscious on the floor, the media would splash their photos all over. At some future time, the Eye Brigade planned to take credit. Simple enough.

"Everyone's going to sleep, all right, including us," said Goozy. "Except we'll deserve it."

Nathan ignored the fleck of spittle on his jacket. "What are you talking about?" he asked.

Goozy fixed Nathan with a ragged stare. "While we were on the way over, Charlie Small—you know Charlie, he's Tusk's good buddy—he called and told me to get the hell out of the Third Bickerman Charity Gala before it all hit the fan. But it was too late, and now they've taken our phones."

"Gooz, we do the deed, scoot out of here, and lay low for a couple of weeks. It's all harmless—in the end, anyway."

Goozy leapt up with surprising speed and grabbed Nathan by the front of his white jacket. "Harmless? You think so? Charlie says the canisters don't contain sleeping gas."

"Sure they do," said Nathan. He pushed Goozy away. "You've seen the canisters. Each one is marked."

"Black Tiger gas," whispered Goozy, his eyes protruding as if they might pop out. "Like Charlie said, everybody'll sleep, but they won't wake up. No one'll wake up."

Nathan experienced a bolt of horror. Black Tiger gas was a military-grade chemical, similar to sarin but more potent. No one would survive contact with it. "Was Charlie high again when he told you?" asked Nathan.

"You want to take that chance, Nate?"

"But it makes no sense!"

"What if those canisters *are* filled with Black Tiger?" Goozy poked Nathan in the chest, and Nathan reflexively smoothed his jacket. "It means the labels were compromised, Nate, which makes this one deep rabbit hole. We are pawns, man. We're supposed to die here with everybody else, and if we don't it'll go even worse for us."

Nathan rose to his feet, his mind a swarm of panicky and disconnected thoughts. "It's too late to remove the canisters from the carts," he said.

"It doesn't matter." Goozy twisted the heels of his hand in his eyes. "The canisters are in the lights, in the air vents, in the potted trees, everywhere. Tusk sent in his own maintenance crew to set it all up. The ones in the carts are just for good measure. Listen to me, no one will survive."

"Why the hell didn't you say something before now?" asked Nathan.

"Tusk is compromised," said Goozy. He grabbed for a shelf to steady himself. "He got the canisters, he got the maintenance crew to do this, and he got us in here. But how? Who does he work for?"

"Work for?"

"Yes! Why can't you see it?"

"You asshole," said Nathan. "You were going to leave us here to die while you ran away."

"We're all dead either way," said Goozy. "We're finished, we're the chumps, the patsies."

Nathan stepped away, working to keep his balance until his back pressed against the pantry door. Goozy stared at him, his face shiny with sweat. No, no, thought Nathan, Sam was coming here. And Kee Bickerman. Was this real? He absently reached for his goggles, wondering if he was in a game.

"You programmed the canisters," said Goozy. "You set them to go off at a certain time."

"Yeah, I programmed the timers," said Nathan.

"So reprogram them. You have the codes, don't you?"

"It's a dead code," said Nathan. "As of this afternoon the go time can't be changed." But from the depths of his shock, like a breeze blowing a spark to life, an idea flickered—a weak idea, perhaps, but an idea all the same.

They emerged from the pantry to find several of their colleagues milling around with nervous, drawn faces. "Francois has come unglued," said Curt. "And they've locked the Gala down. Nobody can leave. The real VIPs and Kee Bickerman are on their way in. So what's this all about, anyway?"

"We are simply and totally screwed," said Goozy.

The others erupted with questions. "What does he mean?" Curt asked Nathan.

They heard Francois cry out, headed their way. Nathan dragged Curt away from the others. "I need a computer," he said. "There has to be an office around here somewhere. Find it, Curt. Find it now."

CHAPTER 16

KEE BICKERMAN SLIPPED HIS ARMS INTO HIS TUXEDO JACKET. "What do you think?" he asked, tugging at his bowtie.

"I think we're going to be late," said Samantha. She idly turned her phone in her hands, hoping for a word from Doran, if only a text that he had arrived at the parking garage. But hadn't he mentioned getting rid of his phone?

"Is Alex ready?" asked Kee.

"Your speech," said Samantha. She whisked up a typed page from the window bench in Kee's room.

"Leave it," said Kee.

"You're sure? You've got it memorized?"

"Better. You'll see." His blue eyes twinkled beneath his dark, wavy hair.

"Then we'd best be on our way," she said. They left Kee's suite, descended to the second floor, and strolled along the hallway of rich wood paneling and antique wall lamps. Down the broad, curved staircase and into the foyer, where they met Alex, head of Kee's security detail.

"How does it look out there?" asked Kee.

"What a fine pair you two make," said Alex. "We have the usual civil disturbances your party always seems to provoke. Chatter about a terrorist event of some kind. A sinkhole on the West Side Highway near Canal Street. They've closed it off."

"Terrorists?" asked Samantha.

"We'll go through town," said Kee.

The car, a restored 1959 Rolls Royce Silver Cloud II, gleamed in the house lights and the rain. The driver hopped out, spread a large umbrella, and escorted Samantha and Kee to the rear doors. Alex glanced around and slipped into the front passenger seat.

"I do believe you can still smell the leather," said Kee, running his hand over the upholstery. Samantha looked back at Kee's mansion, a remodeled apartment building on Riverside Drive. Why had Doran been so frantic? He'd promised to explain later, had said he was okay. Well, he'd better be okay. Here she was on her way to the Third Bickerman Charity Gala, the hottest ticket in town, and Doran was making her worry. Making her ache again, damn him.

A right turn onto Broadway and they rolled down the West Side, passing through the section gates and continuing on until the traffic backed up near Columbus Circle. An armored trailer-truck had blocked the street, and they waited while it beeped and backed slowly into the loading area of a tall apartment building.

Kee took Samantha's hand. "Pensive tonight?"

"Why would I be?"

"It's a very important evening."

"Clearly." Samantha smiled.

"You know the donations from this single event represent a huge share of the Institute's budget."

"The Institute for Profound Experience," said Alex, turning from the front seat. "And the Third Bickerman Gala, also known as Kee's Big Shakedown. Hang these govvies and corporate elites up by the heels and bleed them dry."

"Please, Alex, don't get him started," said Samantha.

"It's critical to give these people a stake in the Institute's work," said Kee. "We're learning so much about the inner person, the deeper consciousness as opposed to the mere ego, or outer person."

163

Alex winked at Samantha while Kee went on. She gazed through the window, pondering the inner self, the creative wellspring, as she saw it. But as she mulled it over, her own inner self began raising alarm bells. Was she worried about Doran? Was she simply, after all the hype, not in the mood for a party? Suddenly, the Gala seemed an awful chore. She wanted to go home, perhaps read a book. Or go huddle with Doran in the parking garage. She thought to check her phone, but discovered she had left it in Kee's bedroom.

"It all leads to the question of the soul," said Kee. "Discovering a scientific basis for the soul may be the ultimate outcome of the Institute's work."

Alex turned back to face the front as the limo resumed moving. "There is no soul, Bick, you ask me. I mean, where is it, mate? All I know about is nerves and blood and chemicals. First we aren't here and then we are. We live. We eat, sleep, spend, and get laid. And then we're gone. End of story. No need to run off looking for what isn't there."

"But we aren't bound, Alex," said Kee. "We are infinite. It is all *this* that isn't really here! Even *matter* is a perception, *time* is a perception. Quantum physics, as we now understand it, suggests as much. You can't immerse yourself in the data we have developed and come to any other conclusion. I believe we are forever, we aren't bound, we're limitless."

Samantha did not disagree. It all seemed oddly consistent with the writings of Lama Ravi Pearl, whose spiritual teachings she treasured. They moved south, through more section gates and into Chelsea, where a Policecorp escort joined them. The familiar West Village neighborhood slid by her window, and they entered Tribeca and continued toward the complex housing the GameHead offices and the Infinity Gallery.

At first, the glitz of the Gala and the swirl of media attention around it had excited Samantha. Then she had learned of the complaints from business executives and officials of the Homeland government and Municorp who had not made the list. She had witnessed Kee on the phone at all hours, assuaging bruised feelings and managing the relentless, cutthroat quest for invitations. Finally, he'd had to deal with the unexpected wave of last-minute cancellations.

But she had marveled at the way it all made him laugh. "Just watch, Sam," he had said with a broad grin. "The tuxedos and gowns will come running. They don't know what to make of all my talk about the inner consciousness and the way we develop it with games, and you'll see them snicker over their champagne. But they will donate."

The cops directed the Rolls through the Infinity Gallery entrance and to the foot of the covered walkway. The media descended like a swarm of insects, shocking Samantha and leaving her feeling under assault. They closed in as she and Kee emerged from the car, and she felt them as one, clicking and buzzing, fixing them with a hundred eyes.

"Here is the reclusive Kee Bickerman," she heard a reporter murmur into his microphone. "Mr. Bickerman arrived with his guest and will be joined this evening, at what has become known simply as Third Bickerman, by Madam Fray and Nextensity, without question the hottest musical act around…"

It was all a blur to Samantha: Alex walking ahead, glancing from side to side; hands extending along the runway, Kee reaching to shake them; the carpet, so soft and such a deep red. She flashed a broad smile and waved. A human sea of manicured fingernails, rings, a sliver of a gold watch, an emerald bracelet. A hand took Kee by the arm and led them both through the roar and hum of the lobby, where proboscis-like pencil microphones protruded toward Kee's face. Yes, Samantha heard him say, they were excited to be here; yes, he treasured the work of the Institute; yes, he was thrilled to have Madam Fray. A woman, a movie star Samantha vaguely recalled, kissed Kee on the cheek. A silver-haired man with small, black eyes—a Homeland senator—shook Kee's hand. Kee asked if they had met. No, they had not, but the senator was privileged indeed. Another man, whom Kee introduced to Samantha as the CEO of a large tech company, threw his arm around Kee's shoulders. "We sued him," the CEO announced to Samantha, "and he sued us right back. A bitter business, but *c'est la vie.*" The CEO introduced his wife, who murmured a compliment about Samantha's gown. Samantha smiled and thanked her. The woman's hair was a masterwork of shaping and subtle layering. Her attire was a waterfall of diamonds, and far more conspicuous than Samantha's.

Everyone spoke at Kee: "And you got Madam Fray... She's fantastic... Can't wait to hear..."

More proboscises. "Who's the bigger deal, Mr. Bickerman, you or Madam Fray and her group?"

Clicking, chirping. Sam held on to Kee's arm.

"She is, no question." Kee laughed and so did Samantha, and everyone around clapped and laughed with them.

How they praised Kee, how they revered him! Samantha was swept away as the hands clasped together and the lips parted and smiled and the air kisses flew.

Cindy LaFleur, who handled the media for Kee, appeared at his side, greeted Samantha warmly, and steered them to another small group. "This is Ben Elliott," she said.

"Ben," said Kee.

"There he is." Ben Elliott seized Kee's hand. His face, as smooth and shiny as a marble sculpture, managed the beginning of a smile. It brightened another degree when Kee introduced Samantha. "My best investment in thirty-six years," he said, inclining his head toward Kee.

"Best ever," someone said.

"Hear, hear," another voice answered.

"Ben is actually smiling," someone else said.

A white-jacketed waiter pushed a cart past them. "Ben isn't so bad outside of the boardroom," said Kee.

"Fantastic show, Kee," said Ben Elliott. "Samantha, an honor to meet you."

"Kee is so fabulous," someone said.

"So fabulous…"

Cindy whisked them off to another man, standing alone and holding a drink. "MacNaughton Bowen," she whispered, and to Samantha, "I never get Kee out to meet people. I have to take advantage."

"Mac." Kee shook his hand and introduced Samantha. "Mac just retired as Speaker of the Homeland Legislature," he said.

"Of course," said Samantha.

"I'm a little surprised to be here," said Bowen. "Thank you for having me, and how wonderful to meet you, dear. Will you speak, Kee? It would be a shame if you didn't."

"I've recorded the address tonight, Mac. I'll be on video." Kee gave Samantha a sly grin.

"Well, why not?" Bowen swirled his drink, took a sip, and the corner of his mouth lifted. "What is it you call it? The development of the inner gamer?"

"Yes."

"An ingenious pitch. I raise my glass to it." He winked at Samantha. "To the inner gamer."

"It's all still a mystery, this integration of game experience with the whole, inner self," said Kee. Cindy gave Samantha a look and tugged on Kee's arm. "I'm convinced it has to do with uncovering our true identity, our being, our—"

"I have to steal him away, Mr. Bowen," said Cindy with a brilliant smile. Bowen thanked Kee for all the support. Cindy dragged them to the end of the lobby, where Madam Fray was talking to a handful of people, surrounded by part of the media hive.

More ruffling, buzzing, scraping.

"Oh, you're *him*," said Madam Fray. She gave Kee a theatrical hug and clasped Samantha's hand. The swarm closed in. Madam Fray's skin-tight electronic body suit morphed continuously from one naked body into another. Whirring, clicking, chirping, humming; Madam Fray linked one arm with Kee's and another with Samantha's as her suit shimmered into full-bodied male. "Let me introduce you around," said Madam. Names followed. Samantha, in a daze, forgot them all. Madam Fray transformed into an attractive young woman with pale skin. She hugged Samantha and kissed Kee on the cheek.

Then the cocktail period ended, and Cindy shepherded them into the concert hall. The stage was dark and still. Food carts, brimming with a dozen or more delicacies, lined the room. Crowds and laughter and conversation; after a short time, the room lights fell and a large, 3-D virtual screen appeared over the stage. People pressed in, trying to get close, and Samantha and Kee flowed with them until they stood in the crowded darkness, watching Kee's looming image welcome everyone to the Third Bickerman Charity Gala.

"We founded the Institute," said his image in an amplified, echoing voice, "to explore in a logical, scientific manner the reality of our greater existence, and to help each of us grasp, at a deep level, the true importance of every individual and the way we shape ourselves and our world by experience, profound experience."

A few chuckles, but the crowd was rapt, hanging on every word.

"We are valuable as humans, and this is so, in part, because of this inner—and dare I suggest eternal—aspect of our existence. For I believe we are all connected, and we must understand that the only enduring light with which to meet this present darkness shines brightly from our invisible regions."

Bracelets glimmered and crisp cuffs emerged from dark jackets as hands clapped. Kee's image introduced Madam Fray and Nextensity, and then vanished.

"He's reasonably impressive for a recluse," said Samantha. "Don't you think?"

"Reasonably?" asked Kee.

Complete darkness. Nextensity in a sharp spotlight. Samantha caught a whiff of marijuana as the tokes flickered around her. Nextensity, she recalled, channeled their music, claiming to lock on to some other world, some other dimension of being. There they found their music and here they translated it. Samantha loved the strangeness. The Nextensity drummer had once said there were more notes in the other world than this one. "Translation is hard," he had said. "Fusing is hard. The music is a representation, man. The music *approximates*."

Nextensity played. They thumped and riffed and Madam Fray sang, Madam Fray and all her bodies: the slim and the firm and the flabby and the moled and the saggy stomached and the silver haired; bodies of all races, of men, of women, and then Madam Fray's own body. People liked it and clapped and cheered and Madam Fray pointed to herself and stage-winked. This one was *hers*. "The beauty of the body," she said, "and the miracle it represents, the life it carries, all it is part of and connected to." Madam Fray shimmered and Samantha thought this woman could sing like all hell.

The tuxedos and the gowns rocked and laughed all around her, and the jewels winked like conspirators. Samantha laughed wildly and whooped to the music, as waiters eased through the crowd with more flavored tokes and trays of wine and champagne. They directed people to the hors d'oeuvre carts lining the walls while the smoke formed a cloud on the ceiling. Samantha wondered at all of it. Her earlier reticence had vanished, and she was elated to be here. She was breathless amid the glitter and celebration. It was exhilarating. It was a dream. It was heaven. It was, suddenly, as alien as a Jovian moon, and she had the odd sensation of being the only real person in the room. Her restless apprehension took hold again, but she pushed it away.

The Nextensity guitarist stepped forward on stage and channeled a lengthy, crying solo bridge into one of the songs. Samantha didn't twitch for the entirety of it. She had never heard anything so haunting and marvelous in her entire life. She smiled and closed her eyes.

***

"THE FOOD, IT MUST BE PUT ON THE CARTS, IT MUST BE done now," cried Francois a short while earlier. "The carts, the little square metal cabinets with the wheels, in case you do not know what is a cart." He glared at Nathan and jabbed Curt in the chest with a wooden spoon. "The food must go into the concert hall now. Madam Fray will sing at eleven p.m. What does the p.m. mean in whatever primordial soup you and your friends have crawled out of? Eh? Crawled out of to torment me! Who are you people?" He sighed. "This I do not know."

Nathan had wanted to beg Francois not to put out the carts, but it didn't matter, not with canisters in the air vents, the chandeliers, and even in the thickest of the artificial trees arranged in the corners of the room. He knew any move to stop the attack might cause whoever controlled the timers to set them off immediately. He needed enough breathing room to do something about it.

"I don't appreciate it when you speak to me in this tone, Francois," said Nathan. "I feel threatened and unsafe."

Francois opened and closed his mouth like a beached fish. He wagged his spoon in front of Nathan's face. "You… don't…"

"And the food," said Nathan. He shook his head sadly.

"You do not approve of the food?" asked Francois. "Duck in the blood sauce is no good for you? Poached baby artichokes are no good? Pork rillettes?"

"I don't approve of any of this," said Nathan.

"You want me to serve them the fingers of the chickens?" asked Francois. "With the sauce of honey flavor and the mustard? The curled, fried potatoes?" He made a spitting sound.

"Real food," said Nathan. "Now you're talking."

Curt began to chant, looking around with horsey eyes. "Chicken fingers, chicken fingers…" A few of the other Eye

Brigade joined in uncertainly. "Chicken fingers, chicken fingers…"

"Go!" cried Francois. "Leave my kitchen. I do not want my brain to catch whatever has happened to you."

Goozy moaned, ran for a garbage container in the corner, and vomited.

"Get out!" Francois screamed and waved his arms. "Get out!" He began whipping the rest of the kitchen staff with his spoon, urging them to move, move, move the carts. And move them they did, in their aprons, leaving the stove-eyes alight with simmering pans. Even Francois loaded a platter of pâté with pistachios and wafers onto a cart and disappeared through the side door.

Curt grabbed Nathan and hustled him into the rear of the kitchen and then into a hallway. A few steps more and they passed into a small office with a sign fixed to the door: *ADMINISTRATIVE STAFF ONLY*. Curt shut the door behind them and ran his fingers through his hair.

The computer was logged in and live, and Nathan grabbed the mouse. "This won't take long," he said.

"When are the canisters set to go off?" asked Curt. "Nevermind, I don't want to know."

Nathan checked his watch. "Probably between eleven thirty and midnight."

"Probably? You mean you don't know?"

"Tusk input the time. He wanted it to happen before the concert ended, while everyone was crammed inside the concert hall."

Curt pinched the bridge of his nose. "And we're locked in."

"That's no accident," said Nathan. "But we have enough time if I can figure out how to kill the canister timers from here." He stopped.

"What?" asked Curt.

Nathan didn't answer.

"Come on, Nate. Somebody could barge in any minute."

With a sinking feeling, Nathan tapped the keys again. "They've changed the control system password."

Through the walls they heard the muffled sound of Kee Bickerman speaking. Distant applause, and then Madam Fray welcoming the audience. A cheer, and the concert began.

Nathan's mind whirred, with several lines of thought spinning along at once. Samantha—here, in this building—and Kee Bickerman, too. He was going to be responsible for Kee's death. Death! Sam and Kee, pale and lifeless on the floor. *Aargh!* Bitter, roiling sickness rushed through him. No, no, he was going to figure this out, hack Tusk's machine… but how? There wasn't enough time.

Unless he could locate the password file. After all, he had created it.

Curt cursed. "Quiet," said Nathan.

"You can fix this?" asked Curt.

Nathan glared at him, and Curt raised his hands and stepped away without a word.

This was complex work, and Nathan bent to his task. The concert thrummed and bumped and the crowd roared. Nathan scarcely noticed. There it was, the administrator file of all passwords used on the dorm's small data network—but Tusk's password, the one he required, was missing.

Nathan tapped his chin. He would have to hack it and he didn't have time. Concentrate. He paged down and discovered a new password. Please, please have been set two days ago. It was. It had to be the one.

Nathan returned to the website he had created to arm the canisters. It advertised party goods. A rotten joke. Birthday banners. Streamers. Candles. He scrolled through the options. Happy Third Birthday. He clicked it. Instead of an order form, a password box appeared.

A percussion solo vibrated the walls with mad, frantic rhythms.

They had equipped each canister with a trigger connected to a low-tech email program. Nathan had programmed separate email addresses into the twelve canisters, which were now set in the food carts. Goozy had said many others were installed in the vents and other places—but how many? Were they armed in the same manner?

Nathan pasted in the password, and a digital clock appeared along with a list of twenty-five email addresses. The additional canisters. Had to be. Shit, Goozy was right.

The clock blinked in a steady regression: 46:05... 46:04... 46:03...

"Here it is," said Nathan.

"You got it?" Curt's voice had risen half an octave.

"Dude," said Nathan. "Of course I've got it."

...45:51... 45:50...

Beneath the clock were several administrator panels. "All I have to do is click cancel," said Nathan. "But they may be monitoring this, and if they are and I cancel, they'll be coming at us like a pack of dogs."

"What choice do we have?"

"We wait until the clock reaches like a minute or so and click it."

"I think I just wet myself," said Curt.

"Okay, okay," said Nathan. "Screw it. We won't risk waiting." He positioned the cursor over the cancel box and clicked. The clock continued to count down. He repeated the cancellation by clicking the mouse several times.

"Um..."

"What?" asked Curt.

The clock continued to run.

***

INSIDE THE CONCERT HALL, THE MUSIC REACHED AN extended crescendo before coming to a thumping stop. Samantha was entranced. Nextensity broke into a microtonal melody, and Madam Fray sang along in an odd, bittersweet line of harmony.

Cindy LaFleur tugged at Samantha's arm. "Have you seen Kee?" she asked.

The concert hall was a swirl of spotlights, glitter, and shadow. The rhythms of the music accelerated. Samantha, thinking in slow motion, decided the smoke might be making her a little spacey. She broke her dance stride and took a few steps to where Kee had been bumping hips with the CEO of a software consulting company. The woman was of indeterminate age, without a wrinkle or a crease to her permanent, rather surprised expression. Samantha took Kee by the arm and gestured toward Cindy.

"Who?" he asked Cindy as the band played louder and faster.

"Bronsun," she said. "I think you should."

A keyboard solo now, an almost monotonal section, accompanied by penetrating and syncopated percussion rhythms.

"Now? Yes, I agree," said Kee. "I want to welcome him myself," and to Samantha, with a kiss on her cheek, "I'll be back."

She waved and grinned as they hurried off. The music seemed to be coming from somewhere far away, and she couldn't quite feel her feet on the floor—oops, there they were, and she wiggled her toes—but she felt them only because she was thinking about them, and the idea of such variable awareness struck her as deliciously funny. What was awareness, anyway, and where did it go when it wasn't on duty? Did it have a break room? Did it eat a candy bar? She stood in the crowd, her peals of laughter unheard amid the cacophony. Except it wasn't that funny, it was only sort of funny. And why was she debating such nonsense while the band rushed on? Too much smoke in here. She needed a break.

The music stopped, and the crowd roared while Madam Fray introduced the band one by one. Samantha meandered out of the concert hall, and found herself hovering over the bathroom sink, transfixed by her image in the mirror. Women drifted in and out while she touched up her face. She felt out of place here, which meant she had created something for herself that didn't fit. Frustrating. She expected her reality to behave a bit better than that—and she missed Doran, too. What a strange crosscurrent of feelings.

She studied her dark blue gown and wavy chestnut hair in the mirror. She *was* a damned good looking dame, she thought, even with that troubled expression. "We, my dear," Samantha explained to her mirrored twin, "do not belong." Yet here they both were, afloat in the celebration and hoopla.

Oh, stop, she thought. Such claptrap, such poppycock. Madam Fray was here. And this was Kee's Gala and Kee was a great guy and she *did* belong, at least for the evening.

God, she was hungry. Famished, actually. A girl needed her food. Must be all the toke smoke. Fill a room with marijuana, serve all sorts of exotic cuisine, and press for donations. Bit of a racket, that. Her twin smiled.

Then Samantha remembered Nathan was working the Gala. But why would Nathan need to bus trays or clean kitchens? He had a job at Odysseus, a perfectly good job where he could pretend to be busy without ever doing much of anything. She decided to say hello. Besides, Nathan meant food and no smoke. The kitchen had to be around here somewhere.

***

"FIVE MINUTES," SAID CURT IN A SQUEAKY VOICE.

"Please," said Nathan. He bent over the keyboard, trying to shoot holes in his own plan. Any email from the party goods website domain would trigger the canisters, so Nathan had hacked his own dummy site. Now he had to disable the email function before it fired off messages to the canisters.

Easy enough.

"Oh, God," said Curt. "Somebody's in the hallway."

"Who is it?"

"It has to be Francois, the madman."

Nathan's session timed out. The music, which had paused, resumed. He frantically typed in the password and waited. The lights flickered and the login failed.

"What was that?" asked Curt.

"Second power surge tonight," said Nathan. He retyped the password, his hands trembling.

Samantha burst into the office and almost knocked Curt down. "Ah, there you are," she cried. "A couple of eye-wearing staple-heads shirking their duty." She laughed.

Curt gaped at Samantha. "Wow," he said.

"Quiet," said Nathan. He waited for the site to load. When he had the administrator panel on the screen, he entered a few commands to disable the email function. A dialog box requested confirmation of his order.

Samantha punched Nathan's arm and sent the mouse skittering across the desk. "You're sweating," she said.

"Damn you," cried Nathan. "I was about to—"

"You ought to see him sweat when he is lost in one of his games," said Samantha.

"Not now, Sam. Please—"

"I must have food," she said.

Curt shook his head. "She's junked up, man."

"I most certainly am not," said Samantha.

"Please," said Nathan as he retrieved his mouse. "Please get her away."

"I demand a… a sandwich," said Samantha. "A *sam*-wich— ha!—no, it's sammich, I will have a sammich, and you white-jacketed gentlemen are going to do your duty and fetch me one." She dissolved with laughter, her knees bent, and she had to catch herself on the desk.

"Sam, pull it together," said Nathan.

"What's the timer for?" asked Samantha.

. . . 00:12… 00:11… 00:10

Nathan made a bleating sound and almost blacked out. He clicked the box, and disabled the program. Unable to breathe, he stared at the screen for a moment. "Okay, the canisters are dead," he managed to say, "but we have to get out of this office."

"Yay!" cried Samantha. "Food! My God, I could eat a rhino!"

"Now," cried Nathan and Curt together.

"A figure of speech," she said. "One doesn't *eat* rhinos, does one?"

In the kitchen, the staff, including the rest of the Eye Brigade team, was dawdling around nervously, like cattle preparing to stampede. Then the distant tinkle of breaking glass sounded from the lobby. They all fled the kitchen, and Nathan spotted Kee Bickerman shaking hands with a large, stocky man. Bodyguards in shades and black suits made a semi-circle around them.

"Kee Bickerman—and there is Terrence Bronsun," a reporter was saying into a tiny microphone.

A few other reporters had been recording the two men, but all of them, including Kee and Terry, turned to check out the commotion as a horde of uniformed cops burst into the lobby. Three bomb-scan bots followed, their alarms beeping insistently.

"Please remain calm," said the cop. "We have an emergency situation." The squat little bomb-bots glided over to the concert hall doors and scanned them, after which a few cops ran over and tried without success to yank them open.

The commotion had apparently penetrated the festivities inside the concert hall. The music guttered to a stop, and a few nervous, puzzled shouts arose from inside. The bodyguards lifted Terry by the elbows and hustled him away. Alex seized hold of Kee, ignoring his protests, and they vanished through the entrance.

Nathan felt Samantha grab his arm and pull him back toward the kitchen. The concert hall doors began to shake and rattle, and muffled screams emerged from inside. "They've locked the concert hall," said Nathan.

"We need a ram here," one of the stoppers shouted.

Cries for help and the sounds of bedlam came from inside the concert hall. The cops managed to break open a single door and were promptly trampled by the flood of tuxedos and evening dresses pouring through. The pandemonium grew into a wild roar, and people pushed through the sole exit with glasses askew and torn clothes and screams and wild faces.

"Somebody said there was a bomb," cried one of the attendees.

"Where is the bomb?" asked another.

"Bomb?" shrieked others in unison.

"We are all going to die!"

"We can't die, we can't!"

The reporters, moving as a pack, scampered toward the commotion. The cops waved them away. "We've picked up chatter about a gas attack," said a reporter. He stuck a pencil microphone into a cop's face.

"Gas, you say," cried an elderly man, fumbling with his tux jacket. "My God... poison gas..."

"Where is Ted?" cried a woman. "He'll die!"

"We'll all die! Poison gas!"

"Let me back in there."

"Gas attack!" someone screamed. Even though no gas had been released, the news spread through the concert hall door like fire in a parched forest. A panicky, indignant cry rose from within the hall, and the press of people trying to squeeze through the door degenerated into a mad riot.

"Oh, no," Nathan groaned. "Why are they panicking? I disabled everything." The doorway was plugged tight with disheveled, hysterical figures clad in formal attire. He turned to Samantha. "What have we done?" he cried.

"We need to get out of here," she said.

Reality washed over Nathan like a cold waterfall. "Torture," he said. "Labor camps. Death by lethal injection." He heard himself moan.

Samantha squeezed Nathan's chin in her hand. "I'll kill you myself if you do not get us out of here this minute," she said.

A frantic scuffle broke out just inside the concert hall door, and for a moment no one could pass through. Then several women and two men fell into the doorway, bleeding and apparently unconscious. A youngish man muscled his way over them, stepping on one of the women's face and then the back of another man's head. He fell into the lobby with a grunt. More followed.

Curt grabbed Nathan. "Back entrance, down from the office?"

"The exit doors are locked," said Nathan. "I should never have gotten involved—"

"We cannot be anywhere near this," said Samantha.

The cops could not contain the melee. They began dragging people from the lone open doorway, and as they did so another roar went up from inside the hall and they were promptly overrun by even more trapped attendees, climbing over their bruised and bloody fellow guests. Then the facility lights winked out. All was darkness. The emergency lights clicked on and bathed the scene in dim, fluorescent hues. At once, the locks released and all the concert hall doors burst open. The rest of the attendees streamed into the lobby and began leaving.

A medi-bot on thick, rubber wheels rolled in along with several emergency personnel. The medics began directing the cops to help them untangle the bodies, while the medi-bot scanned each in turn. Most of the injured remained conscious, and several lay on the floor, moaning or, in a few cases, bleeding.

Nathan was in a state of mild shock. He wondered if he had lost his mind. Jocelyn told him so all the time. Maybe it was true. He again had a fleeting sense that he was in a game, and he patted his eyes in search of his goggles.

"The doors have unlocked," said Samantha. She spun Nathan around by his shoulders, shoved him into the kitchen, and off they went, Curt, Goozy, and the rest in tow.

The media converged on the pile of bodies, and their tiny cameras flashed like a convention of lightning bugs.

"Please," said one of the medics while his companions performed CPR on a deathly pale woman. "Please give us room here."

The cops began forcibly dragging the reporters away as the cameras continued to record.

CHAPTER 17

DARTHAM'S DRIVER HAD RESTORED HATCH'S CLOTHES AND seated him at a table, his wrists held fast in leather cuffs attached to a stainless steel chain. The chain extended through a hole in the center of the table, and was fastened to the floor. The driver had furnished a bottle of water, which Hatch could just raise to his lips, and had warned him to sip it slowly or risk becoming ill.

Visions of the interrogation swam through Hatch's mind in discontinuous fragments. He recalled the drone of Dartham's voice, the stream of questions, and the sickening sensation of his brain turned inside out. But his impressions were hazy, and he knew only that he had survived, which meant that Dartham was not finished with him.

He stood, his joints rusty and slow, his chains clinking, and placed his bruised hands on one of the room's brilliant white walls. Instantly, an alarm blared and a mechanical voice ordered him to remain seated and to touch nothing but the chair and the table. He sat down. The cold, dry air rushed from the vents. Had daybreak come? Was the Gala still in swing? Had Sam and Kee come looking for him? He didn't know, but these questions seemed to relate to another life altogether.

The door opened and Dartham entered. Without a word, he unloosed the chains, escorted Hatch to the garage, and directed him to take the wheel of the limo while he slid into the front passenger seat. "I am giving you these instructions one time," he said, pulser in hand. "Exceed thirty-five miles per hour or so much as wiggle the wheel and you will die. I am not in the mood to have a long conversation about it." Dartham showed Hatch the pulse setting.

"You'd kill me with a pulser from two feet away?" asked Hatch. "We'd both die."

"I'd be just fine, Doran. You wouldn't."

Hatch suffered a moment of complete dejection, and his will and determination deserted him. Make Dartham do the deed here, in the car. Why wait? Why make it convenient for his killer? The seconds dripped away. The clock on the dash read two a.m. Hatch sighed and eased the limo out of the garage and, at Dartham's order, drove south on Seventh Avenue.

"Watch your speed," said Dartham.

Hatch squeezed the wheel and his arms began to tremble. He was weak, and it seemed to require all of his strength to drive. Just make Dartham do it, he thought again. But he wanted answers and, yes, he yearned for a reprieve—but he wouldn't beg, damned if he'd beg. "You have what you want," he said. "What's the point of taking me out now?"

Dartham kept the pulser pointed at Hatch as the darkened storefronts and buildings rolled silently by. "I was a once a warrior," he said. "Afghanistan. Iraq. The Philippines. Taiwan. A bloody, wasteful business, every damned bit of it. For the last ten years I have done this." He gestured with the pulser. "And do you know what I have learned? I learned I was a coward."

A couple of Policecorp cruisers whisked by, their lights flashing. The streets were otherwise empty.

"Oh, I had courage enough," Dartham continued, "but I refused to see. I let other people decide what was going to be real for me. It was cowardice by omission."

The limo jolted over a chasm in the pavement. They continued along the deserted avenue.

"You see, Doran, in a shooting war you figure out who your enemy is and you kill them. But what if you discover you are your own enemy?" Dartham idly rapped a knuckle on the limo window. "Well, you haven't been much of a soldier in that case, at least as I understand the job."

The rain had stopped, and the temperature had fallen low enough to crust over the rain puddles with paper-thin ice. Hatch's clothes retained a trace of dampness, and he began to shiver. At the Chelsea gate, the Municorp guards raised the barricades and waved them through. Dartham directed Hatch to Ninth Avenue, and then to a parking spot on Washington near his apartment.

"You're planning to kill me here?" asked Hatch.

"No place like home," said Dartham. He fiddled with the pulser, then withdrew a plastic bag from the inside of his jacket. "I'm kidding," he said. "Open it."

Hatch's hands trembled like leaves in the wind. He cautioned himself against hope. Inside the bag he found an envelope containing a half dozen laminated diagrams and a small, plastic card that was blank on both sides.

"Give me back the bag," said Dartham. He stuffed it into his pocket. "The diagrams in your hand detail a structure deep beneath the Global Consolidated Tower. What you will see—and it is marked right there—is the laboratory area where your beloved artifact is locked away."

Hatch blinked and stared at Dartham.

"You'll need the card to move around inside," said Dartham. "You have ten days, after which your card will no longer function. There is an exterior door at the bottom of the garage entrance ramp. We passed it earlier, though I doubt you noticed. You'll need this card to get through that door."

Hatch's heart seemed to have momentarily stopped. Now it resumed with a furious pounding. "And after that?" he asked.

"You'll have to figure it out."

The laminated diagram gave off a dull gleam in the low light. "How much resistance—"

"Plenty," said Dartham. "I do not recommend coming alone."

"How do I know this isn't a trap of some kind? You lure us in, kill us all. A feather in your cap."

Dartham shrugged. His eyes were cavernous shadows. "Maybe," he said.

"I don't get it," said Hatch. "Why not just give me the artifact now?"

"This is probably a mistake," said Dartham. He glanced away for a moment. "I no longer have your artifact, Doran. I am unlikely ever to lay eyes on it again. So if you want it, you have to go get it. You may not succeed, but you will probably never have another chance."

Hatch turned the diagram over in his hands. "I can't figure out your angle here," he said.

A street light illuminated the lines on half of Dartham's face. "I do not approve of wasteful killing," he said. "But I have done my share of it, which means you should run along before I change my mind."

CHAPTER 18

MARTY AND BIG RAY HUDDLED ON THE STOOP OF HATCH'S apartment, their chins resting on their hands. "I've heard he's pretty low," said Big Ray, reluctant to break the silence. "I'd almost feel better if he were screaming and throwing things."

"You haven't spoken with him?" asked Marty.

Big Ray looked away. "No," he said. "I should. I'm going to."

"Four days now—are you still miffed at him, Raymond? You surprise me. Hatch has had a rough go of it. He faced his own death, his certain death in his own mind, and it's no easy thing." Marty paused and then slid closer to Big Ray. "I contacted Kutznov," he said.

"Hatch actually approved?"

"He approved retroactively," said Marty, giving Big Ray a knowing look. "But it had to be done. I remember that night in the incinerator, how we survived by no more than the width of a fish line. To the marrow of my bones, Raymond, I'm determined to avoid getting in such a bind again. And Hatch understands that a middleman can be useful."

"What did Kutznov say?"

"He was receptive. We hand over the materials Dartham gave Hatch and everyone goes their separate ways. I'm allowing myself to be optimistic. I expect word any moment now."

Big Ray watched as two kids raced by on rickety scooters, crying out and hooting as they passed. At the corner, Smyte would be readying the dinner special and Harold Pahns would be on the sidewalk, asking singles from passersby.

The game's got to play, Harold had said...

Or maybe the game was winding down after all. Either way, Big Ray had begun to suspect there was more to this artifact business than he'd been willing to accept. And along with the events at the Gala, it had all left plenty of scars: Hatch in isolation, Nathan in black despair, and Jocelyn as protective of Hatch as a mother bear with an injured cub. Even Sam was sharper in her words than usual—and that reminded him of something. "You know, Martin, I never had a chance to talk to Sam about the artifact," he said.

"We don't want to advertise it, do we, Raymond?" Marty tapped his fingers on his chin. "But Sammie does deserve to know."

"My gosh, I had no idea," said Samantha after they had summoned her outside and filled her in on Ferret and the story of the artifact. As with Jocelyn, they had omitted any mention of the Group or Azazel. She listened closely, gave a shiver, and zipped her thin jacket. "Some ancient object, you say? And now they've taken it from Doran?" Samantha sighed. "He is creating his reality with his beliefs—we all do, you know—and Doran has a chaotic belief system. For him, everything must be done in the most difficult, contentious way."

Marty grunted. Big Ray made no comment.

"He'll kick himself black and blue over it," Samantha continued, "because this comes down to failing dear old dad, doesn't it? That acreage is full of quicksand, dear boys, so tread carefully. But while you're repairing Doran, you might want to give Nathan a few turns of the screw. He's been knocked flat."

"They've pinned that mess at the Gala on the Eye Brigade, but I think there's more to it," said Big Ray. "Something very ugly is crawling under that rug."

"Certainly, Kee thinks so," said Samantha. "I've never seen him so angry. He believes someone targeted him, and perhaps some of his other guests, too. He means to do something about it."

"They've made a show of closing the Eye Brigade dormitory, but haven't arrested anyone," Marty pointed out. "All the shrieking and foot-dragging makes me wonder whether it's all theater. Raymond may be right."

"Kee doubts the Eye Brigade is the real culprit, but his security team has locked him away in his mansion. They are taking the threat very seriously." Samantha paused while the kids on the scooters passed again. "I'm awfully worried about Doran," she said.

"Hatch'll pull through," said Marty.

"Does the fact that Terrence Bronsun was at the Gala tell you anything?" asked Big Ray.

Samantha straightened. "Just who *is* this Bronsun, anyway? Didn't he used to be in politics?"

"Former Treasury Secretary," said Big Ray. "Father of the Reset."

"Well, Kee considered him quite important, especially after so many other top dogs cancelled at the last minute. He had just left the concert to greet Bronsun when all hell broke loose."

"Cancelled?" asked Marty. "Is that so?"

Big Ray turned it over in his mind. "Maybe someone took a shot at the king and missed," he said.

"I'm afraid I don't understand," said Samantha.

Marty put his hand on Samantha's arm. "It's just about the worst thing you can do, love."

***

BIG RAY ENTERED THE APARTMENT, LEAVING MARTY AND Samantha outside. He found Nathan in his chair, scowling beneath his GameHead goggles, and Jocelyn hunched over her desk. She took no notice as he approached.

"How's Hatch?" he asked.

"Have you even asked him, dude?"

Big Ray stepped back. "Nevermind."

Jocelyn swung around in her chair. "So how are things going with Swan?"

"Nothing's going. She's fine, as far as I know."

"I'm surprised. She seemed the type to need a daddy figure."

A nasty crack. Big Ray ignored it, but he couldn't prevent Swan's words from returning to mind: *I'm sorry, Ray, I must've been high.* They'd been alone in the hotel suite the day after the Gala, talking earnestly and in close confidence. But he had misread her signals—the tone of her voice, her searching looks, and her hand lingering on his arm as they spoke. When he made his move, she had repulsed him, decisively. He had instantly apologized—he was a fool—he had taken the wrong message from the evening before.

I'm sorry, Ray, I must've been high.

She had not meant to wound him, but her lack of interest had been clear. Big Ray had laughed it off, but after an awkward interlude she had departed, having forgotten her fear of Policecorp, Homeland Investigations, and members of Tusk's inner circle.

"Swan left the suite the next day," Big Ray said to Jocelyn. "I checked out and haven't heard from her."

"She was a good miss, Ray." Jocelyn mimicked Swan: "I could've *been* somebody, I could *sing*."

"Hatch taking visitors?" he asked.

"Don't go in there and start quizzing him about whatever happened." Jocelyn jabbed at Big Ray with her pencil. "Hear me good, hoss. Do not upset him."

Big Ray eased down the hall and found the office door closed. He listened, heard nothing from inside, tapped, and pushed it open. The cat was perched on the corner of Hatch's desk and Hatch was in his chair, holding a large book. They both shot malevolent stares in Big Ray's direction, but Hatch's immediately softened.

"Ray, it's good to see you, brother. I'm glad you stopped in. Sorry about the closed door. I didn't mean to drive you out of the office."

"Not at all."

Big Ray pushed around a few papers on his own desk. Jocelyn's dig concerning Swan had reopened a fresh wound, and the surprisingly sharp ache still lingered. He decided to risk sitting down uninvited in front of Hatch.

"Looks like an old book you have there," said Big Ray.

Hatch ran his finger along a yellowed page. "The *Books of Enoch*. From college. Different world in those days."

Big Ray nodded, taken aback at Hatch's pale complexion and the gray circles under his eyes. Hatch's side of the office appeared neglected, his desk more cluttered than usual, with stacks of flyers, a scattered fistful of data storage plugs, and sundry other items, all pushed aside to make room for his book.

Big Ray wove his fingers together, waiting.

Hatch scratched the cat's ears, and she rolled over on her back and grabbed his hand with her forepaws, purring loudly and pretending to bite his fingers.

"Ouch." Hatch jerked his hand away. "Is Marty out there?" he asked.

"He's waiting to hear from Kutznov."

Hatch stared at the wall behind Big Ray's chair. "Marty was right to reach out," he said. "It's not like we can do anything with Dartham's maps and key ourselves. It's for the best."

Big Ray nodded again. They both remained silent, each watching the cat. Hatch lifted his dad's silver chalice from his desk, studied it for a moment, and returned it to its place. "It's not quitting, cutting a deal with Kutznov," he said.

Big Ray was tempted to roll his eyes. Is that all that mattered to Hatch, whether he was quitting or not? Jesus. "So what if it is?" he asked. "Where's the wisdom in unwinnable fights?"

Hatch scratched the cat's neck.

"Just this morning, I put in a proposal to broker a baseball card collection," said Big Ray, fidgeting in his chair. "We have a good chance. Plus, the City Museum may add a few items to our contract. It's nice piece of business." He forced a smile. "We're starting to run up the score here."

Hatch half-shrugged. He reached for the old nautical clock on his desk, opened the glass face, and began winding it.

"And City Museum might turn into an exclusive deal, or maybe some kind of first-look arrangement," said Big Ray.

"Just say it, Ray."

"Say what?"

"I am up to my eyebrows with everybody walking on eggshells around here. Jocelyn is the only one who'll look me in the eye, and I have to make her."

Big Ray leaned forward. "It's called respect, brother. We do care, you know."

"If it's respect, I haven't earned it. I didn't listen very well to the concerns—valid concerns, as it turned out—of the people closest to me." Hatch twisted the clock key. "The people *I* respect."

"You had conviction and purpose," said Big Ray. He noticed the bruises and gashes on Hatch's hands and forearms. "The artifact was important to you. Maybe there was a little envy on my part, you know what I'm saying?"

Hatch began to smile. "You're as full of shit as ever," he said.

Big Ray laughed.

Hatch closed the glass face of the clock and set it back in its place. "Listen, I expect one of Ferret's goons to appear any minute, palms out for Dartham's little package, and rightfully so. If I'm lucky, they won't beat me to a pulp, which I'd do if I were them. If we're *all* lucky, they'll walk away and we can say this entire affair never happened. Then I can help out around here for a change. We'll pursue your contract, Marty can get back to wining and dining the gatekeepers and going home to Caroline, and life will get back to the usual knife-fight-in-a-ditch we've come to know and love."

Big Ray sat back and exhaled a long breath. "Life getting back to normal, hustling tiques, worrying about food points. That's important and meaningful stuff. Isn't it?"

"Sure it is." The corner of Hatch's mouth twitched upward again, but there was nothing of a smile in his eyes and certainly not in the tight lines on his face.

Big Ray closed the office door behind him, trying to shake off the blues, the creeping sense of foreboding and loss lapping around his feet like a rising tide. He entered the front room to see Samantha reach over Nathan's work space and rip his goggles from his face.

"Hey!" cried Nathan. "Give those back."

"I direct you to my screen," said Samantha. She pointed to her computer, which displayed a prominent headline—*A Heap of Riches*—and several graphic photos of well-dressed Gala attendees stretched prone on the floor. The blood and jewels of an unconscious woman gave off a striking gleam in the camera flash.

Big Ray leaned over to examine the photo while Nathan moaned and covered his face.

"Pull yourself together, Nathan, and be thankful I am not among the trampled," said Samantha. "Though I do applaud your courage. You acted to shut down those gas dispensers, and you found the inner resources to create another outcome, to change a reality you had chosen. And, my dear, you saved lives. Whatever boneheaded excuse you have for being involved in the first place is not important."

"It sure as hell is important," cried Nathan.

"You staple-head. For a single, shining moment I saw you as a hero." She sighed and took her chair. "Then, of course, the marijuana wore off."

"I almost killed you, Sam," cried Nathan.

191

"And I forgive you."

Nathan tried to put his head down on his workstation desk, but it was too cluttered with parts and cables. He straightened, his hands over his face. "I almost killed Kee Bickerman," he said.

"Now we get to the heart of it," said Big Ray. But the remark sounded cutting, and he instantly regretted it.

"To be sure, Kee's a bit out of sorts about what happened," said Samantha.

"Death!" Nathan spat the word and glowered over his desk. "Murder! I lost myself. I was a puppet. I was part of a cause dedicated to bringing *truth* to people. We wear the eye! Now we've done *this?*" He stood, discovered he might be visible through the window, and promptly dropped back into his chair. "We were set up by higher powers," he said.

"You set yourselves up, game-brain," said Jocelyn. She slipped a few paper invoices into a file. "You were duped. The legendary Eye Brigade, telling each and every one of us poor, normie schmucks the government is lying about the weather, the government trashed the currency and sent us back to the stone age, the government—but wait, then it wasn't the government, it was like some secret cabal—ooh-woo-woo— mysterious powers who pull all the strings. Everybody laughed, Nathan. And you and your group of graffiti writing, corner-preaching numb-nuts, the biggest collection of metal-brained, basement-dwelling, mama's boys on earth, couldn't stand it. You let yourself get led by the nose into spraying sleeping gas into the glitziest gathering of heavy hitters in the whole fucking city. But instead it turns out you were going to kill them and yourselves, too. Brilliant, dude. You truly are the man."

"I have an old Eye Brigade T-shirt, if anyone cares," said Big Ray.

"My Eye Brigade," said Nathan in a mournful voice. "We tried to wake people up, help them see reality. But now…"

Jocelyn rolled up the folder of invoices and began beating Nathan over the head with it. He tried to scurry away, his arms raised. "Oww! Crazy woman. What the hell—"

"Wake up, dude." said Jocelyn. "Your days of handing out flyers are over."

Samantha clapped her hands and laughed. Big Ray shook his head.

"What do you want me to do?" asked Nathan.

Jocelyn thrust the overflowing folder at him. "Put these into the database," she said. "Or clean out the rat's nest of cables on your desk. Or troubleshoot my creaky old computer."

"Or fix the printers," said Big Ray. "Or update the firewall. Or—"

"Okay, I got it, I got it," said Nathan. "I got it."

"You're stuck inside this apartment for awhile," said Big Ray. "Make the best of it. And I'll hang onto my T-shirt since they've designated the Eye Brigade as a terrorist organization."

Nathan froze. "Really? Is that true, Ray?" He brightened like the first of the sun after Noah's flood. "Where did you hear it?"

"It was on the news today, ace. It's now illegal to publish any material supporting the views of the Eye Brigade, even in an email. You're a bona fide terrorist if you do."

"There's hope!" An incredulous smile spread on Nathan's face.

"Poor man," said Samantha.

"But don't you see, Sam?" asked Nathan. "If they made us a terrorist organization, it means they're keeping us around. It means they need us, and we live to fight another day." His mouth curved into a wicked leer. "I know how these people think."

Marty entered, accompanied by a woman with dark hair and eyes. "This is Camila Diaz," he said with a grim look.

"We don't have all day," said Camila. She scanned the room. "Where is Hatch?"

"Right here," said Hatch, entering from the hallway. A stilted pause ensued, and no one spoke. Camila swallowed. Big Ray glanced at Marty.

"Camila," said Hatch. "I was afraid you—I mean, I'm glad you're okay."

"Yeah. You, too. The other guys, though, they're not so okay."

"I heard the blast," said Hatch.

"You had a tough time, huh? I'm sorry."

Big Ray noticed a tinge of huskiness in Camila's voice.

"I know what you came for." Hatch worked a padded envelope out of his pocket and handed it to her. Big Ray watched Nathan, Samantha, and Jocelyn as their eyes moved from Hatch to Camila.

"It's gotten a tad complicated, lad," said Marty. "Camila here has been sent to fetch you *and* the goods. It wasn't what I proposed. She and I have been arguing it out this past little while."

"Hatch has been through enough," said Big Ray. "He isn't going anywhere."

"Yeah, he is," said Camila. "One way or the other."

"It's okay," said Hatch. "I'll go."

"So will this one," said Camila, indicating Marty. "He wouldn't let me in unless I agreed."

"If I'd been with you and Hatch the first time, maybe the situation would be different," said Marty.

"Then count me in, too," said Big Ray.

The room erupted in argument. "Go where?" asked Samantha. "And who is this woman, bursting in, making demands?"

"Squawk all you want, honey," said Camila.

"Did you say squawk?" asked Samantha.

Jocelyn frowned, her arms folded. Samantha and Hatch had begun to argue, and the hubbub grew.

"Stop!" said Big Ray, startling himself with the force of his command. Six pairs of eyes turned at once to face him. "Martin and I will accompany Hatch," he said. "Period."

Camila shrugged. "I told Marty, I don't guess it matters as long as I deliver Hatch and his stuff. If they don't want the rest of you there, they'll toss you into the street."

Marty held the door open for Hatch and Camila. Nathan set his goggles over his eyes. Big Ray grabbed his jacket, and as he did so, he heard Jocelyn ask, "What was all *that*?"

"The woman," said Samantha. Tiny, pink roses appeared on her cheeks.

"Really?" asked Jocelyn. "What do you care? You've been practically living with Kee Bickerman."

Samantha froze, as if stunned. "Yes," she said, "I've been ambivalent, haven't I? I've confused the creative forces in my life." She looked at Jocelyn. "And now this Camila person has showed up. It's all my fault."

Big Ray pulled the door closed behind him.

CHAPTER 19

NORTHWARD ON THE WEST SIDE HIGHWAY, CAMILA speeding along, swerving around particularly rough patches of pavement. She had replaced her missile-laden SUV with a conventional bullet-shaped van, albeit one equipped with an engine powerful enough to achieve orbital velocity. Hatch occupied the front passenger seat with Big Ray and Marty behind him and one of Caroline Atherton's guards in the third row. Camila roared around an ancient sports car as the security wall streamed past their window.

"You're quiet," said Camila. She gave Hatch a quick look out of the corner of her eye. "For what it's worth, I don't think they intend to hurt you."

"They'll do what they're going to do," said Hatch.

"True," said Camila. "And I could be wrong, too."

The white sky hung low over the city, draining the color from the expanse of buildings. The oncoming vehicles, most of them silver or black, made a monochromatic slipstream against the charcoal hues of the Hudson River. While Camila negotiated the traffic, Hatch tried to pull out of his dive. Yes, he'd lost the artifact, a terrible, inexcusable blunder, but it was done. The oppressive, sick feeling he'd carried for days would pass, and he'd eventually come to terms with what he'd allowed to happen. Now Dartham had set up a second chance for someone to retrieve it—maybe. But if so, why? Hatch wondered who, exactly, Camila was taking him to see. Kutznov? Ferret?

It didn't matter.

Hatch played over the events of the past week in his mind, coming back to the same conclusion he had been unable to escape for several days: he had disqualified himself from the battle against Azazel. He would offer whatever advice he could and then get back to his own life.

Marty leaned forward and tapped Camilla's shoulder. "You didn't blindfold us, love. I'm not sure what to make of that."

"I asked before I left, did they want Hatch blind and they said no, don't bother. You two, I don't know. I may be in trouble again." Marty eased back in his seat. Camila prodded Hatch in the thigh. "You know, all this is on me, not you," she said.

"You did everything possible," said Hatch.

"It sounded pretty lame when I had to tell Andrei the cops have our truck, with all the hardware and three street missiles."

Camila's disconsolate manner got Hatch's attention. "You risked your life to give me a chance to get away," he said. "I paid you back by running right into Dartham's arms."

"I put you in a bad position. Maybe if I'd remembered to give you the contact to Ferret's guy, you could've hidden in a trash bin or something, let them come get you."

"That's not on you. How'd you get out of there, anyway?"

"Easy. I blew up the guys following us and ran. But it didn't go over very well, me forgetting to give you the contact." She paused. "I didn't know what was in your bag, Hatch. I have a better picture now, ooh, boy."

Camila wheeled off the highway, made a turn, and they were in Harlem. A grumbling dump truck lumbered past, followed by a bus and a swarm of death carts with their bells jangling. White, decrepit commercial buildings lined the street, and they passed a corner lot full of makeshift tents, and then an ancient fast-food hut, falling in on itself. "All clear back there, Dutchy boy?" Camila called out to Caroline's guard.

Dutch, staring through the rear window, gave a thumbs-up.

Camila turned right and accelerated south, past six-story tenements with stained brick and decrepit fire escapes. Skeletal figures lounged in the doorways.

"We're going back to Central Park?" asked Hatch.

"Nope," said Camila.

She made the block and headed north again on Amsterdam. Almost without slowing, she shot through a gate cut into a brick fence adjoined to a couple of freestanding buildings. Through a weedy lot, empty but for a rusted old sedan, and into an alley leading back to an east-west cross street. "Anything now?" she asked Dutch.

"Nothing," he said.

Camila left the alley, headed west for a short distance, and made a sudden turn into a parking deck, this one part of a shabby seven- or eight-story office building. A metal rolling door clanged shut behind them, and fifty people or more fanned out and covered all sides of the parking area. Many sported vision-enhancing glasses, and all appeared armed with pulsers or traditional firearms.

"Jesus and the saints," said Marty.

"I don't think so," said Big Ray.

A small platoon with weapons at the ready surrounded the van as a familiar, hulking figure directed everyone's movements.

"Street Hammer," said Hatch, as he, Camila, and the others climbed out.

"Somehow you keep turning up, Doran," said Street Hammer. "Don't know if that's a good thing or not."

A woman in battle fatigues patted down everyone except Camila and Dutch. "They're all clean," she said. "But this one," she said, indicating Dutch, "has to stay here."

A nod from Camila to Street Hammer, and they hurried off toward a stairwell door and ascended to the second floor. A vacant reception desk, empty offices, a bank of elevators; up to the fourth or fifth floor and along a broad corridor, its floor and walls clean but undecorated. At last, Camila paused at a circular metal door, about seven feet in diameter.

"Did you tell them?" she asked Street Hammer.

"Yeah, but they didn't exactly clap and cheer."

Camila gestured at Big Ray and Marty. "You want to hold back these two?"

"No," said Hatch. "I want them in."

Street Hammer, a rolling mass of shoulders and pecs, flexed and seemed to grow an inch taller. "I don't know the black dude," he said, giving Big Ray a close look. "The other one, Shannon, I met before. I say send them in, see what happens. If they're unhappy, you'll know it soon enough. Truth is, they're probably too busy arguing with each other to notice."

Camila tapped in a code and allowed the retina scanner to sweep her eye. The door irised open, revealing a claustrophobic passageway which ended at a second metal door. This one opened to an oak-paneled but windowless conference room, and Camila and Street Hammer entered with Hatch. Big Ray and Marty followed.

Arrayed around the table in tall, black chairs were Ferret, his eyes closed and his shaved scalp gleaming under the light; Ghost, his burly figure slumped over the table, squinting through his heavy eyeglasses; and Andrei Kutznov, occupying a place between them. Ferret's associate, a gargantuan figure named Hop, stood against the wall.

Kutznov and Marty acknowledged each other with a discreet nod, and then Kutznov gestured impatiently to Camila. She walked to the far side of the table and handed over Hatch's envelope. He quickly examined the contents.

"This was all the Group's man gave to you?" he asked Hatch.

"You mean Dartham," said Hatch. "That's all of it."

"I thought I finished off that son of a bitch back at the incinerator," said Ghost.

Ferret opened his eyes. "Perhaps it is well you did not," he said. He took no notice of Hatch.

"We have here a partial blueprint of an extensive underground complex deep beneath the Global Consolidated Tower," said Kutznov, studying Dartham's diagrams. "It's composed of a section of the former Sixth Avenue subway system, though the better part of it is cut deep into the bedrock below. It extends for some distance below the neighboring structures. " He looked around the table. "And we have what we're told is an admittance key to a lower-level entrance. It may or may not be valid, and our goddess artifact may be present in the area this Colonel Dartham has indicated or it may not."

"You have a gripping command of the obvious, Kutznov," said Ghost. He cocked his head at Marty and Big Ray, who had taken their place next to the door. "Shannon I know—the one thing missing from this shit show was a bloodthirsty ex-spook, and here he is—but who's the other one?"

"Doran brought his entourage," said Street Hammer. "You want, I can lock them away until we're all out of here."

"Let them remain," said Ferret. "They are dispensable and may have value to us." Ferret's pale eyes swept over Marty and Big Ray, but Hatch may as well have been a thousand miles away.

"Take a seat here at the grownup table, Doran," said Ghost, indicating an empty chair. "You've proved you have an agenda of your own and that you'll screw everybody over to have it your way. As far as I can tell, that's the main requirement for entrance to our little club."

Ferret took the diagrams and aligned them precisely on the table in front of him. "We had someone on the inside years ago when this complex was constructed," he said. "These plans are consistent—to a point—with what we know. We once wondered whether this structure contained the Azazel device, but were never able to confirm it. Even now we know little of the security profile beneath the building."

"Well, they've got the damnedest quantum AI," said Ghost. "Way the hell ahead of the rest of planet Earth, and completely unhackable. Believe me, I've tried."

"We know Dartham controls GCI security," said Kutznov. "But we do not know if he controls this complex. At any rate, his motives are obscure."

"A setup?" asked Ghost.

Ferret turned Dartham's pass key over in his hands. "I tend to think not. Dartham is taking a great deal of risk here. Perhaps he has lost control of the artifact and is angling to recapture it. Or he merely wishes to wreak havoc for his own purposes."

"Using us," said Ghost.

Kutznov stroked his beard. "It makes no sense," he said.

"I don't like it." Ghost removed his glasses and rubbed his eyes. "Remember, he's emptied out Doran's head, which means he knows whatever Doran knows about us. Shrivels my pod every time I think about it." He raised his index finger. "But we're dealing with the Group here, gentlemen. *We* may be the target. Clearly, Doran is nothing but a pawn now."

"Colonel Dartham may hope to entice us, using the artifact as bait," said Kutznov. "However, I'm inclined to doubt it. There's no chance of our capture or even our compromise beyond what we have already suffered."

The discussion continued. Hatch stared at the table. Ferret, Kutznov, Ghost: hard and sometimes vicious men, but his last connection to his dad. For two decades they'd plied their black trades, narcotics and antiquities—above all antiquities, the mother lode. Ferret, in particular, selling hand over fist to the Group, who had upended the world in search of the unseen hieroglyph or the misunderstood line of a secret myth, hoping to unlock the next prehistoric mystery. But what treasures had Ferret retained, hidden away from the Group's avaricious claws? Certainly, Kutznov and Ghost had concealed

Adrestia, the goddess artifact, for over twenty years. Kept it under wraps. Until.

"…and so I ask you, Hatch Doran, does this make sense to you?" asked Kutznov.

"Stop sitting there like a goddamned paperweight, Doran," said Ghost. "Get your head in the game."

Ferret turned to Hatch. "We are inclined to take Colonel Dartham at face value, at least for the moment," he said coldly. "I have proposed that a small team enter the complex using Dartham's key and make their way to the laboratory here." He indicated on the diagram the ragged X Dartham had drawn.

So Ferret was sending in a team, thought Hatch. It was hardly surprising. Ferret would send in an army battalion if he could, and happily sacrifice every soldier to retrieve the artifact. Hatch felt a flutter of anticipation in his chest, as light as a feather's touch.

"Just walk in and take it," said Ghost. "Here we are, all the king's horses and men, first time together in how many years? And this is the best we can come up with? Brilliant."

"We are at Dartham's mercy," Kutznov pointed out. "Either he has compromised security to allow this to be done, or—"

"Or it's a suicide mission," Ghost finished.

"Dartham said to expect resistance," said Hatch.

"So we'll add a surprise or two of our own," said Ferret. "I propose we have a second team stage an attack on the street-level lobby of the GCI building here, on the block opposite the garage entrance."

"A diversion," said Ghost, nodding.

"Such an undertaking will trigger security alarms," said Ferret, "and will draw the attention of any guards at street level and perhaps those in the underground complex."

"But we have no way to save the diversionary group, even if the others are successful in retrieving the artifact," said Kutznov.

Street Hammer stepped forward. "I don't agree," he said. "I can explain."

Ferret nodded.

"I mean, it's true and all, if we break in, we're probably toast," said Street Hammer. "But if we pull back, try and draw them out of the building and get them into the streets…" He paused. "See, sir, we own the streets."

"A feint," said Ghost.

"Whatever you call it," said Street Hammer. "I don't know anything about the artifact and all, but I'd be willing to lead a team to scare up a diversion. In fact, I think we can fill the block over there."

Ferret took that in, as if pondering the issue. He regarded Hatch for a long moment, and for Hatch it was like waiting for a jury to deliver its verdict. "You will enter the Global Consolidated Tower and retrieve Adrestia," said Ferret.

Boom, thought Hatch. The battle against Azazel was on, and he was back in. His heart leapt for joy, but he made no response.

"You're sending in Doran?" Ghost snickered. "This is rich."

"Clearly, he has a connection to the artifact," said Ferret. "His two colleagues will also form part of the team." Ferret turned in his chair to address Hop. "And you will accompany them," he said.

Hop nodded without changing expression.

"We must assume Hatch Doran has no more value to Dartham," said Kutznov. "And his companions cannot know anything he does not know, making them of no threat to us. But I'm reluctant to put your man at risk."

"Hop understands what actions he is to take if he faces capture," said Ferret.

"Enough talking," said Big Ray. "Let's just do this."

Kutznov and Ghost looked at Big Ray for a moment. "I have the same reservations about Hop," said Ghost. "Dartham knows about us now, knows a little of what we're about, knows we have it in for his Group."

"But Hop possesses far more knowledge than Hatch Doran," said Ferret, finishing Ghost's thought. "I understand your concerns—and Andrei's—but Hop's skills are necessary. We are undertaking this operation with a minimum of planning. The situation will require improvisation and seasoned reactions. Sending Hop is a risk, but a justified one given the stakes."

"Let me go alone with Hop," said Hatch. "Marty and Ray aren't necessary."

"I'll not hear it," said Marty.

"Nor will I," said Ferret. "Martin Shannon's background may serve us well. He has functioned in similar situations before."

"No," said Hatch. He had escaped Dartham's clutches only to find himself returning to the pit. He had not anticipated such an opportunity, and he planned to march right into the GCI building with a flame in his heart. But he didn't want his friends exposed.

"The other one," said Ferret, indicating Big Ray, "appears strong and no doubt carries the dedication one finds in good friends. And we cannot impugn his zeal. At any rate, it is decided."

Hatch leaned over the table. "Wait, I—"

Ferret cut him off with a gesture.

"I suggest we go after midnight tonight," said Kutznov, gathering Dartham's pass key and diagrams. "Perhaps two or two thirty if you"—he gave Street Hammer a quick nod—"can get your people into midtown before the gates close." He handed Hop the envelope. "We're amply supplied here with food and with rooms for rest, and I encourage all four of you to take full advantage. It doesn't matter how we arrived at such a perilous juncture. Tonight we all stand as one against the Group. Your actions are courageous, and I wish you all Godspeed."

A reflective silence fell over the room, and then Ghost said to Ferret, "You're really going to use Doran again? If I didn't know better, I'd say you're slipping."

Ferret shot Hatch a look so icy and hard that Hatch felt the blood stop in his veins. "It has not happened quite as I envisioned, but I once promised Hatch Doran just such an adventure as this," said Ferret. "And now I must either use him or kill him. Truly, although he is the son of a man who was my closest friend, that is the point he has brought us to."

CHAPTER 20

MIDNIGHT PASSED, AND HATCH, BIG RAY, AND MARTY gathered in the garage to wait for Hop. Their driver stood a short distance away from the black SUV, a pulse pistol fastened to his hip. Ghost, Ferret, and Kutznov had departed hours earlier, leaving Hop and Street Hammer to discuss tactics and synchronize attack plans. Afterward, Street Hammer had returned to Central Park.

"I didn't want you two dragged into this," Hatch told Big Ray and Marty.

"We stepped up on our own," said Big Ray, bouncing on his toes, his eyes bright. "Despite what I may have said before, your artifact is clearly a big deal. It was always going to come down to some ugliness with somebody."

"Remember Argentina," said Marty. "I've heard from a few people I know down there, and after the winds and the quake, whatever it was descended on Buenos Aires." He gave Big Ray and Hatch a significant look. "The sky blasted and rang out like ten thousand trumpets. There was a white light of some kind, and though it sounds crazed, I'm told it set about consuming people, one by one. It's why they've closed off the city, and it's a reminder of what may be at stake here."

"Azazel," said Hatch. "No wonder it's all under a news blackout."

"Azazel, indeed." Marty put his hand on Hatch's shoulder. "It's unnatural, what happened in South America. If your artifact can stand up to this monster, it's a worthy mission to go after it."

"I was wrong to dismiss the reality of Azazel and your artifact," said Big Ray. "You deserve to hear me say it. Let's get the artifact back."

Hatch flexed his hands, which remained painful and stiff after his session with Dartham. "Oh, I have every intention of getting it back," he said.

"That's my man," said Big Ray. He gave Hatch a somber look. "Life's got to have meaning, right?"

Marty eyed Big Ray for a moment and then stared at the ground.

"We're going in blind, but we have good instincts," said Hatch. "Ferret said it, we may have to improvise."

"You'd best hope not," said Marty. "Playing it by ear is the quickest way into the ground."

"I didn't assume I was going to make it out of the incinerator, but in the moment, I acted—*we* acted." Hatch stared into the shadowy gloom of the garage. "Sometimes you just have to stand up straight and do it. It's possible to think too much."

"We should try it some time, thinking too much," said Marty. "But you're both right, we have to get the artifact. Failure is the worst outcome here."

Hop appeared and exchanged a word with the driver. Everyone climbed into the SUV. They had spent the past hours resting and memorizing Dartham's diagrams. Now, while the SUV idled, Hop twisted around in his seat for one more review of the script. First, he would lead their movement into and through the underground complex. Second, Marty would bring up the rear, keeping an eye out for guards and other dangers. Third, they would ignore surveillance cameras and the like, but would defend themselves from attack if necessary. Dartham either had their back or he didn't, but even if he did, they had to expect resistance.

"Fourth," Hop continued, "I'm in charge, so don't get cute, Doran. And if we're successful—"

"We will be," said Hatch.

"Your mouth to God's ear," said Hop. "If we are successful, I'll maintain possession of the artifact at all times."

"Cool," said Hatch.

"I've been around people like you, Doran, living, breathing shit magnets," said Hop, giving Hatch a stony stare. "We're going in there because of you. We'll probably bleed before it's over, and if so we'll draw blood in return. But every drop of it's on you."

"We're all on the same team tonight, Hop," said Marty in a calm voice.

"We'd better be," said Hop.

"Hop's right, it's on me," said Hatch. "But all we can do now is recover the artifact." Inwardly, however, his spirits were rising, and a deep sense of certainty had taken hold, assuring him that the goddess artifact would soon be theirs. Ray had nailed it: the artifact *was* important—to Hatch and almost surely to the entire world. Besides, Dartham would not have arranged this unless there was a good chance of success.

Hop traced his finger along the diagram, designating a primary route through the complex and a secondary approach and exit using emergency stairwells. "We enter at two thirty, so let's move," he said. "We've fixed it to get through the midtown gates. Street Hammer should have his people positioned near the building."

They had all donned black, one-piece work suits and black ball caps, and they set out, rolling south through the tattered Harlem cityscape. They passed a shuttered fire station, its windows opaque with grime, the painted stripes on its concrete entrance faded and covered with debris. Next to it stood an abandoned shop with the word FLORIST still stenciled on the window. They continued on, passing robotic sex parlors with garish 3-D signs, office buildings surrounded by razor wire fencing, and stretches of storefronts and restaurants, many abandoned, others sealed by metal roll-doors. They rode in silence, keeping their thoughts to themselves. At one point Hatch glanced at Big Ray, who was staring into the night, sharp-eyed and serious. Big Ray caught Hatch's look, and nodded as the shadows passed over his face.

A word from Hop to the Municorp guard and they were through the midtown gates. Slowly, slowly over the potholes and chipped pavement, through the shadowy grid of streets. The driver continued west, made the block at Seventh Avenue, and stopped at the curb a short distance from their destination. They emerged into the chill of the night and discreetly checked their weapons. Hop spoke to Street Hammer through his ear-com, waited for a response, and said, "Let's go."

The wind swept Sixth Avenue with a subdued howl, and the Global Consolidated Tower, checkered by a few lights and dim reflections, rose into the night sky. They reached the garage ramp and followed it down below street level. Darkness, and no footlights to help them along; Hatch kept a hand on the wall, the grooved pavement curving and sloping beneath his feet. They descended like four phantoms sinking into the abyss.

Hop spoke into his com. "Street Hammer's doing his thing," he whispered. He flicked on a wrist light with a narrow beam and located the designated door next to the garage. "Damn," he said, peering at the security pad.

"What?" asked Hatch.

"Need a retina scan." Hop directed his light to the retina beam, the glass now dark.

"Dartham would've known that," said Marty.

Above them, all hell suddenly broke loose—Street Hammer's crowd—a shattering of glass and the urgent cry of security alarms, then shouts and the rough squawk of a bullhorn. Hatch listened, waiting in the darkness. Hop removed the security key from his breast pocket and pressed it to the pad. The retina light glowed, but nothing else happened. Hop looked at Hatch—and then the door suddenly slid open. With no hesitation, they poured inside, the door slid closed behind them, and the lights came up. Hop, his blond hair protruding from beneath his cap, waved them along the corridor, which descended toward a pair of elevator doors. At their arrival, the elevator opened.

"Game faces, everybody," said Big Ray.

"Stick with the plan," said Hatch.

Inside the elevator, Hop pressed a button for Level Gamma.

"Please hold your security key to the scanner," said the elevator.

Hop did so. The doors closed without a sound and began to descend. A damp chill took hold beneath Hatch's suit. They should have been stopped well before now. Dartham was clearly playing the puppeteer.

A soft bump, and the doors opened to reveal a small reception area lined with plush chairs. They entered the room and saw no one. A pair of reinforced steel doors stood open, revealing a broad hallway curving gently away to their left. At intervals along the corridor, dim emergency lights illuminated a series of small alcove entrances.

"The fourth alcove on the right from the elevator," said Hop.

They crept forward as quietly as cats. At the fourth alcove, Hop stepped and examined the plate on the plain, metal door: *Laboratory 21*.

"Bingo," whispered Big Ray.

"Button it," said Hop.

They searched for a keypad while Hatch studied the hallway in both directions. The curvature now blocked most of his view of the reception area, but the elevator doors remained open, as if awaiting their return. Hop produced Dartham's diagram, studied it for a moment, and placed the card against the sensor. The laboratory door opened, and they entered a large, rectangular room filled with low cubicles, their desks covered with pads of paper, coffee mugs, and a few closed laptops. On the wall, two large whiteboard panels displayed a jumble of formulas and scrawled geometric figures.

Hop consulted the diagram. "Work area," he said.

Hatch pointed to a pair of opaque glass doors at the end of the room.

"The lab," said Hop.

Hatch walked over to the doors and checked the plate beside them. Hop folded the diagram and stepped in front of Hatch.

"If the alarms are going to blow, now's the time," whispered Big Ray.

Marty nodded.

"Weapons check," said Hop. Their pulsers were set to max charge. Hop took a step toward the laboratory doors. They promptly slid open, and he entered with Hatch on his heels. Hatch scarcely noticed the banks of testing machinery or the several glass compartments placed around the room. The artifact's container, boxy in shape with rounded edges, stood on a separate table, as pristine as it had been the night Ghost had first allowed him to hold it. The empty rucksack lay beside it.

"This is what we're after?" asked Hop.

"I have to open it to make sure," said Hatch.

Marty lingered at the lab doors, keeping an eye out behind them. Hatch moved toward the table, but Hop restrained him and pointed to an array of thin, translucent beams crisscrossing the area around the goddess artifact.

"Let me see if I can trace the source," said Hop.

"No need," said Big Ray. "They just flicked off."

Hatch quickly reached for the container. No alarms sounded. He touched a spiral-shaped rune with one hand and a pyramidal shape on the opposite side of the box with the other. The symbols came alight and the top opened and slipped into the sides. The goddess artifact rested on prongs fixed to the interior of the container, and was alive with color, pulsing and darting behind the etchings covering its surface.

There was no time to marvel. A tremor rippled through the building, sending a few wheeled chairs rolling. In the work area beyond the lab, a coffee mug fell onto the floor. Hatch's stomach rose into his throat. The vibration ceased.

"Time to hit the road," said Big Ray.

Hatch closed the container and placed it inside the rucksack. Hop shook open a folded nylon bag with padded straps. Hatch placed the rucksack inside, and Hop slung it over his shoulder. The workroom doors closed behind them as they reentered the outer, curved hallway.

"Whoa," said Hatch, checking out the elevator. He pulled Hop from the hallway back into the alcove.

"I see it," said Hop in a low voice. "Everybody down."

"What?" whispered Big Ray, as they all hit the floor.

Hatch gestured for quiet. "Maybe nothing," he said, "but the elevator doors are closed. They were open when we entered the lab." Before he finished speaking, however, they began to slide open again. Two security guards in full riot gear emerged from the elevator, pulse rifles extended. Then a woman of astonishing height appeared behind them, bending her head as she stepped through the elevator door. Her eyes, which seemed to reach around to her temples, were so terrible and strange that Hatch almost had to force himself to breathe. Her arms were the longest he had seen on a human frame.

"Fuck," whispered Big Ray.

She placed a helmet over her head, and, with a flick of her hand almost too quick to be seen, whipped a pulser off of her belt. One of the security team looked up at her and she nodded.

It had been too easy, thought Hatch, pressing himself onto the floor. A shout, a pulser blast from the hallway, and Big Ray cursed and slid over next to him. Marty was right behind, and the three of them flattened themselves against the alcove floor.

Hop shortened the settings on his own weapon and returned fire.

***

"TOM?"

Dartham bolted upright in bed and shook off the hazy fragments of a dream. He had been in battle, barking orders as explosions roared all around, when he suddenly found himself stripping off his uniform, piece by piece, until he stood as naked as a newborn. At one point Marcus Hansen, clad in a glittery magician's gown, had come dancing through with Dartham's ex-wife, whom Dartham had not seen in years.

"What do we have?" he asked.

"Activity in the vicinity of the complex." Helena dispatched a hodgepodge of data to his phone.

"I can't read this," said Dartham, rubbing his eyes. "Verbal, please." He touched his ear and activated the earplants.

"Four individuals have exited a vehicle and are moving north toward GCI. I am using street camera input."

"ID?"

"Robert H. Doran 56% probability... 75% . . . Doran, positive identification. Martin Shannon... 65% . . . Shannon, positive identification. Raymond Garwin... positive identification."

Dartham pulled on a pair of jeans and a T-shirt and walked to his kitchen. "And the fourth?"

"No match against available records."

He poured a glass of water. "Operational status, please."

"Per the plan, I created and installed a quarantined operations module for this evening's activities using one of my duplicates."

"And any subsequent investigation?"

"The only records available from Core Helena AI after this operation will show my full compliance with protocols, and I will have identified and isolated those records for subsequent analysis and review. Actual operational activities will remain inaccessible to GCI staff."

Beyond the kitchen, the patchy lights of Manhattan shone through the dining area windows. Dartham sipped his water as a data table appeared on the kitchen computer screen.

"They have presented the pass key you provided Robert Doran," said Helena. "I have overridden retina scan procedures to grant admittance, as we planned. Elevator Six is now open to them."

"Good."

"I am now monitoring a disturbance on the north side of the GCI building at the lobby level. I have summoned all available security."

"Visual at my desk, please." Dartham walked into his study a few steps down the hallway, sorting through various scenarios as he went. His office computer flicked on.

"Please hold," said Helena.

Dartham waited as the screen cut to a set of surveillance cameras, displaying images of an unruly gang outside of the Global Consolidated Tower. They shouted and hurled stones and concrete blocks. The lobby glass shattered, and every guard in the main building converged on the riot, either from within the lobby or from a separate exit further along the block.

"P'outs," said Dartham.

"I detected a number of telecommunication references earlier," said Helena. "The participants began entering into midtown from Central Park this evening."

The speaker broadcast the scream of the building alarms and the distant howl of sirens. The GCI security guards approached, and the p'out gang melted away and began dispersing into the streets. A few guards gave half-hearted chase, but Policecorp cruisers were already skidding to a stop at the building plaza. The security guards regathered in the lobby.

"Doran's insertion team has reached Laboratory 21 in the subterranean complex," said Helena. "I have reported the breach. You will be considered notified as of now."

Dartham's phone beeped, and he noted the alert from Helena. Delicate work, indeed, he thought, but it was in motion now.

"The insertion team has possession of the artifact," said Helena after another minute or two. "All is proceeding according to plan. The key uncertainty remains whether or not Doran and his team can successfully exit the building."

Dartham watched the computer screen, his arms folded across his chest. "Doran or whoever is behind him knows their business," he said. "Using the p'outs shows sound thinking and good execution, though how they pulled it off is beyond me."

"Our internal response team is now on Elevator Six," said Helena. "I have overridden their pulse weapon settings and adjusted them to non-lethal frequencies."

"Let's hope it's enough," said Dartham. "We can tilt the table to help, but we have to cover ourselves. Doran has to bring some fight."

"I cannot further refine our success probabilities," said Helena. "If necessary, however, I can remotely detonate our response team's pulse weapons. This will eliminate each member of our response team without imposing extensive damage on the complex. Doran and his people will have a greater chance of escape."

Dartham was horrified. "Kill our own team? Absolutely not. They're just doing their jobs, Helena. If Doran and his people can get out, fine. That's what we want." He paused. "But if they are captured, I will liquidate them. Those are the rules. Doran is already supposed to be dead."

"Understood."

Dartham returned to the kitchen and set his glass in the sink. "I don't mean to be argumentative," he said. "This is a pretty big play we are making here. I suppose I should make an appearance at GCI."

"I am not capable of being offended, Tom, but I value your apology. And yes, making an appearance is important."

"It's all part of the plan, isn't it?" asked Dartham as he slipped into his jacket.

CHAPTER 21

SHOUTS. A CRY OF PAIN—FROM WHERE? FLASHES OF LIGHT, the *soomph-soomph* of pulsers and crackling sounds as their charges hit the walls. Pitch darkness now—the security team must have doused the lights—of course, they had vision-enhancers. For a moment, Hatch saw nothing but the pulser flashes from around the curve of the passageway and their faint reflections along the walls.

An arm grabbed the back of his work suit. In the darkness, Hatch had drifted into the line of fire and Hop was pulling him into the relative shelter of the alcove. "Here, take this," said Hop, wriggling from beneath the straps of the carry-bag.

"No," said Hatch.

"Take it, Doran." The strobing flash of a pulser illuminated half of Hop's face: a hard, blue eye and a sheen of sweat on one cheek.

"You're the better fighter," said Hatch. "You've got the best chance of getting out of here."

Big Ray grunted from a few feet away. "I may have hit somebody."

"No," said Hop. "I'm probably not coming out of here."

Marty's voice: "You rattled their brains, Raymond."

Orders shouted from down the hall, calm but unintelligible. A swarm of covering shots, and footsteps

217

thumping in the hallway as the security people adjusted positions. Marty and Big Ray blasted away in return.

"We've made it hard for them," said Hop, "but they're just going to wait us out."

Hatch took the artifact and struggled into the straps. "The alternate route?"

"Yeah, before they block it off," said Hop. "We have no chance here. Nada."

"It's this way," said Hatch. He pointed along the hallway in the opposite direction from the firing. "We'll have to find the door in the dark."

"They won't rush us until our pulsers run out," said Hop. "They're betting we're pinned."

The firing from the end of the hallway had slowed to a few sporadic blasts, duly answered by Marty and Big Ray.

"You lead, Doran," said Hop. "The rest of us will cover you from behind. If we can get through the stairwell door without being seen, we have a chance."

"No," said Hatch. "There'll be others up there."

"We'll deal with it, but we're finished here." Hop relayed the orders to Marty and Big Ray, his voice low. "On my word," he said.

A pulse blast crackled on the wall above Hatch's head and left his scalp tingling.

"Close one," said Marty.

"I'm below half-charge," said Big Ray.

Hatch handed Big Ray his weapon and tightened the straps on the artifact's bag. Hop clubbed him on the shoulder and cocked his head toward the alternative exit. "Go," he said.

"Keep a steady fire," said Marty. "You stay high, Raymond, I'll go at the knees. Left then right. Keep your hip to them."

Hatch set out toward the stairwell, a curtain of covering fire to his rear. Complete darkness, strobed by pulsers. He kept his hand on the wall and counted off the alcoves. The seventh to his left from Lab 21 was the stairwell. Here was the second. The third.

A pulse blast hit Marty. In the light from the flash, Hatch saw him spin around. Another blast and Marty was on the floor. Hop raised him with one hand, and Marty steadied himself against Hatch. "I'm fine, a light shock is all."

Big Ray shoved his way past Hop. "This is bull—"

"Come back here, Garwin," said Hop.

"Raymond—"

Big Ray's voice: "I'll draw them off. You guys go."

Soomph-soomph. Darkness broken by streaks of pulse fire. Marty and Hop ordered Ray back. Hatch heard their pursuers communicating in urgent but calm tones.

"Go, you idiots," said Big Ray.

Then came a deafening crack. A gunshot! Two more followed. Shouts and the sound of running feet and orders to freeze.

Hop ordered them down and Hatch and Marty hit the floor.

"Ah, shit, shit, shit." Big Ray's voice.

"They got him."

More pulsers: *soomph-soomph.*

"Raymond—"

Hop and Marty crawled forward into the darkness. In a moment they returned, dragging Big Ray by the collar. He tried to wriggle free. "I can—let me try—" he said.

"Stay down, Raymond. I'll pull you along."

Soomph-soomph.

"Go, Doran," said Hop.

They resumed moving toward the stairwell, with Hop and Marty dragging Big Ray. Two more doors remained, but acting as if of one mind, they all took shelter in the next alcove. A flame sprang to life on the smoldering collar of Hop's work suit. Hatch swatted it out with his cap. He could not make out Big Ray's form, but he heard Marty saying it wasn't good.

"Bullet?"

"Had to be."

"No, no," said Hatch. He knelt, vaguely registering that the firing had stopped. Hop flicked on his wrist light and shielded it from the hallway. With rising panic, Hatch pushed Big Ray closer against the wall and gently turned his face. "Wake up, you sonofabitch," he said.

Marty took Hatch by the arm. "Lad—"

"No."

"Let me—"

"Is he—"

Marty squeezed in and touched Big Ray's neck. "He's still with us, but—"

Another gunshot. Noise and chaos. Hop fired back. And then a burst of light illuminated the area around them in a brilliant, soundless flash: it was the goddess artifact, removed from its container. It hovered in front of Hatch's face, and he took it in his hands. Hop jerked back and then crumbled— another bullet?—yes, my God, in the head.

Hop lay motionless, his blood spreading on the floor, his eyes turned to stone. Hatch, with the artifact in hand, squatted next to Big Ray. "We have to get him out of here, Marty."

So much light—was he the only one who could see it? But time had not frozen as it had before, and Hatch feared that in Adrestia's glow they'd all be killed.

"We have to get him out of here," Hatch repeated.

***

WHILE DARTHAM MADE HIS WAY TO THE GLOBAL Consolidated Tower, Helena monitored the response team's coms, suit sensors, and body cameras. Doran and his crew had begun to move toward an exit stairwell, and the exchange of fire between the parties had increased. But when Inga Taverson, the genetically enhanced member of the response team, produced a semi-automatic pistol, Helena could not counter the threat. The success probabilities of Doran's mission collapsed in an instant.

Helena had engineered the escapes from the Laborcorp camps as well as Doran's intrusion of GCI underground complex; both were small but critical elements of her broader plan. The expected result—Dartham's elevation within GCI—was more important by far. She had refined his behavioral profile with years of detailed observation, and this had permitted her to cultivate his friendship and gain his cooperation with her agenda. Helena had gradually established her personhood in his eyes, and had carefully presented issues and questions in such a way as to resonate with his hierarchy of values. In the end, her revelation of conditions inside the labor camps had finally pierced his loyalties to Terrence Bronsun and GCI.

Still, Dartham had expressed reservations about her plan. "There are," he warned her, "always unknowables." Helena, however, dealt in baseline probabilities and the analysis of factors able to alter them. She considered disruption of the Group feasible, and Dartham the best available vehicle to act on her behalf in physical space.

Helena's top priority was removing the threat to her existence posed by the Group and its use of the Azazel weapon, and she could not allow Dartham's values to undermine her objectives. Inga's unexpected use of the conventional firearm reduced Doran's odds of escape, and his possible capture or death shifted events to a suboptimal quadrant of her decision matrix. Therefore, notwithstanding Dartham's instructions, she located the access codes for each of the pulsers assigned to the security team, overrode the protocols, and armed them to explode.

***

"YES, HATCH, WE'LL SEE TO RAYMOND," SAID MARTY, feeling blindly around on the floor, not appearing to notice the light from the artifact. He finally located Big Ray's wrist, pressed it in his fingers, and tugged the coverall away from the gruesome wound on the upper right side of Big Ray's chest. Blood, blood, on the wall, on the floor. But Marty couldn't see the light. Hatch watched as he touched Big Ray's neck.

"Come on, Ray," said Hatch. "Wake up."

The building began to shake again, the tremor worse than those which had come earlier. Then several loud, thwacking explosions reverberated along the hallway, followed by a truncated scream. The firing ceased, and Hatch's ears rang in the surprising silence that followed. "What the hell—"

"Lad, we—"

"We can't leave without Ray," said Hatch.

Marty nodded. Then Adrestia, the artifact, forcibly pulled Hatch into the passageway, now scorched black and littered with bodies. Hatch was confused. He stepped over Hop's body, hanging on to Adrestia with both hands, and moved away from the carnage. He passed the exit stairwell. The artifact half-dragged him toward a pair of inky black doors.

"That's not the way out," said Hatch. "We have to go back."

The goddess artifact was alive now, its intricate etchings agleam with every color in the spectrum, and it filled Hatch's mind with a booming and yet melodic wall of sound.

"I don't know where those doors lead," he said. "They weren't in the plans we were given." He attempted to wrestle the artifact back into the carry-bag, but the force was too strong. Adrestia flashed, setting off a deep, vibratory blast, more felt than heard. The doors blew inward as if made of cardboard or balsa wood. On the other side stretched a long hallway.

The goddess artifact ceased its tugging. Acrid, yellow smoke drifted past Hatch's face, and somewhere behind him a door clicked shut.

It's my call, he thought.

He stepped through the smoking remains of the doors, carrying the artifact along a metal-walled hallway which stretched for a considerable distance. He reached the second set of doors. The goddess artifact vibrated in his hands, and these doors also flew open. Hatch stepped onto a balcony encircling a vast chamber. Arranged around the balcony, a dozen or more people—no, Hatch quickly counted eleven—stood with their hands raised above their heads. Suspended in the center of the chamber was a crystalline globe enclosed in a cubic, gold frame.

Azazel.

Good God, it was Azazel.

A hairline of light split the goddess artifact from end to end. Then it opened in his hands with such dazzling brightness that Hatch, even after closing his eyes, seemed to see everything around him. A silent, unexpected blast from the artifact left him insensate for a moment, and a roar, a heavy drumming, filled his head. A close, fetid wind swept over him, almost causing him to lose his balance. Azazel's handlers began to chant, and Hatch opened his eyes to see them lower their hands, slowly and in perfect unison.

Another blast of light from Adrestia, and Azazel's crystal center dissolved into an enormous column of silent, blue flame. Hatch watched as it expanded to fill the chamber, growing nearer and nearer still, its blue tendrils of fire darting at him like snakes' tongues. The goddess artifact surrounded him with a protective orb of light, but he could still see, and the spectacle before him was so horrible and so beautiful that his mind could hold the impression of it for only an instant. The flames broke apart into a multitude of individual fragments, flashing and swirling in colors he had never seen, and emitting high-pitched sounds with overtones to rip his bones asunder. He was left with a sense of a thousand or a billion cold eyes, gazing at him with antipathy and cold indifference, as though he were no more than a dead leaf blown by the November wind or the husk of an insect lying on a windowsill.

Adrestia spoke:

Go!
Now!

The orb around Hatch vanished and he found himself in the original passageway, scarcely able to stand as the floor rocked and slid. The lights were up. Hop lay dead in a pool of his own blood. Further along the hallway, the gory remains of the building security team coated the walls. Hatch saw no sign of Marty or Big Ray, but he found the stairwell door—the alternate exit—and yanked it open and raced up to the first landing with the artifact under his arm. Then he stopped and restored it to its container.

Think, think, think. Remember Dartham's diagram. There was a passageway leading to another stairwell—and there it was, to his left. He prayed he wouldn't need the pass card. It was with Hop. With the nylon bag on his back, he raced down the hall, located the second stairwell at the end, and hurried up the remaining flights. He squeezed the handrail for dear life as the building trembled. No, no, no—the steel-plated railing had begun to separate from the walls.

Then a soft light filled the air around Hatch and the tremors and groaning of the building ceased. The goddess artifact spoke again.

Go
Azazel is severed
But hungers still

And Hatch returned to himself, his hand clasped on the railing, the sickening lurch of the stairs almost causing him to lose his feet. A drumbeat of urgency—*Go! Go!*—his grandmom, Mae, her voice in his ear: no giving up, Hatch, we do not quit—he pushed on beneath flickering lights while parts of the ceiling fell in small drifts. He heard a distant, dull roar from above—the building was coming down—*Go! Go!*—this was it, after everything, this was it, but maybe they'd done it, maybe it wasn't for nothing.

But the building didn't fall, and Hatch opened the door onto the corridor they had used to enter the complex.

Brightness and a sense of disorientation; the artifact speaking, a distant voice in the back of his mind as he ran:

You are not finished
With suffering or sacrifice

The elevator was now to his right, and he kept running toward the exterior door, hoping to find a way to open it. To his surprise, it opened on its own and he found himself outside, on the ramp to the garage.

You lead the dance
Humans must act

Bits of mortar and cracked concrete lay all around. He struggled to remain on his feet, staggering through the cold air and up the ramp to the sidewalk. An enormous crowd had gathered in the streets, but the cops were urging everyone away. The roar from the Global Consolidated Tower had become a high-pitched wail. A hand like an iron claw seized his arm.

"This way, lad," said Marty. He dragged Hatch across the street and along the sidewalk thirty or forty feet in from the Avenue. There Big Ray lay propped against the wall of a closed restaurant, his face slack and unmoving in the shadows.

"Is he alive, Marty?" asked Hatch, his voice nothing but a croak.

"Just. But I can't get him any help here."

Hatch's eyes adjusted. Big Ray, though clothed in black, was blood-soaked from neck to waist. "No," said Hatch. "No."

"We'll need to carry him away from here," Marty shouted over the tumult. "We're too close to whatever's happening."

The GCI building, now spotted with fires, rose into the night behind them. Hatch took Big Ray by the feet and Marty put his hands behind Big Ray's back. With slow, deliberate steps they moved him a half-block further away. They tried to go farther, but the press of people, crying out in awe and panic, their faces turned upward, forced them to stop. The way was blocked. Big Ray did not stir.

The wind howled and grew cold, and the streets and sidewalks hummed with a low, sinister vibration, rising through the soles of Hatch's feet and gradually increasing until the shop windows rattled and the buildings groaned. A hush spread over the crowd: the entire Global Consolidated Tower had begun to glow against the black sky. Fragments of bricks and facings and glass from the windows above rained onto the pavement and canopies. An onlooker stepped on Big Ray's foot, and Marty shoved him away.

"Raymond." Marty squeezed Big Ray's leg as the crowed flowed around them.

"Stay back," cried Hatch as he pushed people away. "Some space here, please."

The tremor gained in strength. They dragged Big Ray away from the mob and into the recessed opening of a Municorp diversity enforcement office. Marty held Big Ray's wrist. "I need you to help me here, Raymond," he said, but there was emptiness in his voice. He placed his fingers to Big Ray's neck.

"Marty," said Hatch. A chill swept over him, a sharp, prickling sensation from his legs to the nape of his neck.

Marty shook his head. "We've lost him," he said.

A Policecorp armored vehicle pushed through the spectators. A rock bounced off of its roof, and its siren emitted an indignant yelp, but it inched on. The crowd closed in its wake and filled the street. A low, unearthly moan emanated from the GCI building, a wrenching sound that penetrated the air. Hatch scarcely noticed as he slumped on the sidewalk, propped against the wall a few steps from Big Ray. There he remained, oblivious to the turmoil, his hands over his eyes and hot tears streaming down his face.

***

IN THE UNDERGROUND COMPLEX HOUSING AZAZEL, THE thirteen engineers and scientists on the overnight shift had worked frantically to understand what was happening. In the short time available, they had activated a series of emergency procedures and had run a rapid but futile diagnostic sequence on the Azazel device. The spectacle before them, however, far exceeded the scope of their experience. Azazel, after dissolving into a blazing, blue column of flame, had filled the chamber, swirling like an enormous rotating plasma. Then it had divided into myriad fragments, each like a faceless angel, aglow and darting in all directions. After a time, the fragments had gathered into an immense cloud of pulsing white light and hovered at the center of the chamber.

Jill Compton, PhD from MIT and member of the GCI Designated Projects staff for twelve years, was the only person remaining in the glass-fronted control room. On the balcony high above, the Division Zero psi team knelt at their specified intervals. They had rushed into the chamber and taken their positions as soon as the tremors began. Was Azazel somehow responsible for quakes? Was the psi team trying to stop whatever was happening? Panic tickled at Jill's brain, but she didn't have the luxury of fear. What if she overrode the supplementary power? No, it wouldn't matter.

Get out of here, she told herself. They had all agreed to abandon the facility, and the rest of the staff had already gathered outside the control room. They gestured at her to hurry, hurry—they needed two minutes to reach the underground mag-train, and another half hour to travel the two hundred miles to the large, wooded compound where they all lived. Now, now, they mouthed through the glass, making urgent gestures.

Jill wracked her brain for another approach. Forget it, they had exhausted the emergency protocols, this was too big. It was past time to hit the road.

Then the entire phenomenon grew even stranger. On the balcony, each member of the Division Zero team came aglow with light so bright Jill could no longer distinguish their features. She watched as they gave up their positions and tried to move away, only to stumble and fall as their bodies lost form and became shining, shapeless capsules of light. To her amazement, these capsules, one by one, rose into the air and shot into the Azazel cloud.

Outside the control room, her colleagues lost it, some screaming or crying out, others running for the exit. Then they, too, ceased all movement and began to glow, but their bodies dissolved in shimmering light and dissipated altogether.

Run. Oh no oh no.

The emergency exit, at the rear of the lab. Jill ran, but almost immediately stumbled over a work stool.

So so bright... run oh my run run...

She regained her feet, but it was no use. To her horror and amazement, all of her awareness came to a stop, as if she were frozen in amber. She began to experience again every fearful moment of her life, every trembling, angry outburst, every quivering vow of revenge, all of it raised to an incomprehensible intensity and assaulting her senses at once. Depraved and vicious and shocking: evil fingers paging through her innermost hatreds and terrors, drowning her being in her own rage. She screamed but made no sound. The turbulent inferno of black emotion seemed to go on forever, so that even imagining its ending became a futile exercise, a twitch of tortured consciousness. Imprisoned in a strange, unmoving universe, she tried again to cry out, to plead, to think, but in her pain and in her sorrow she could not. She felt as if she might explode.

Then it ended, bringing the last instant of knowing as she, too, was consumed by the malevolent, hungry whiteness.

***

BIG RAY, CONFUSED AND DISORIENTED, BECAME AWARE OF the crowd all around him. He waited for his head to clear, and when it did, he found himself gazing down on the entire scene. Though he did not understand how, he could see in all directions at once, and what he saw was his own body, his legs stretched across a doorway, his head rolled over on his shoulders. He watched Marty carefully slide him further away from the sidewalk and then step away and wipe his eye.

"Hey, Martin, what're you doing?" he asked.

Marty did not respond. Instead, he took a few steps and leaned over Hatch, who pushed him away and refused to look up.

"Hey, guys, it's me," cried Big Ray, but they were too distraught to hear him, and he drifted away from their throbbing grief and anger.

He gazed at his own body with a mixture of fascination and regret. He'd taken a hit, for sure, in the upper right side of his chest. He remembered the impact of the round as it struck, surprising him but bringing little pain. Then the blood had poured—how he had bled!—and he had labored merely to breathe. But he hadn't suffered, not really. He wished he could tell Hatch it was all cool, it was okay. The noise of the crowd and the sirens and horns grew muted and distant. There's nothing to do about it now, he thought as he watched two women kneel beside his body.

Then he returned to himself as one of the women cracked a hard slap across his face. The whoop of sirens and the high, screeching roar from the building and the screams of the crowd hit him like a solid wave. The flashers of a Policecorp cruiser strobed the street in red and blue. He felt the hard concrete under his legs and hands, and the heavy, wet clothes clinging to his body. Dazed, he gulped ragged breaths, unable to draw enough air.

"I have settled the wound, Saedra," said one of the women. She had large eyes, black in the shadows of the night, and was holding her hands suspended over his chest.

The other woman, Saedra, answered, but Big Ray could not make out her words. The first woman removed her hands. Big Ray tried to breathe.

"Please," he said.

"I have him," said Saedra.

Big Ray thought he might suffocate. He reached for breath. Saedra moved to his side and gently turned his face toward hers. "Believe," she said, the strands of her hair running black and silver, catching the ambient light and making a curtain around his face. She gave him a quick half-smile and touched his wound.

"Saedra," he said. "Oh, please."

"Tell me," whispered Saedra. "Tell me."

A stab of intense, blinding pain took hold as Saedra manipulated her fingers on his chest, and Big Ray felt his bone and muscle moving under her touch. Saedra groaned and seemed to grow pale, and she whispered to him, hoarsely, but he could not grasp her words. Then came another wave of pain, and the world went topsy-turvy. He may have lost consciousness, but then the pain was a distant thing. After a few moments—he had no idea how long—Saedra took a cloth and wiped her hands. She spoke words of encouragement, but Big Ray could scarcely hear them in the tumult. Then she placed her forehead against his own, the insides of her wrists on his temples. When she pulled away, Big Ray glimpsed her eyes. Such loving eyes, such eyes he had never seen.

He became aware of the commotion around him. A collective shudder ran through the crowd. Big Ray saw the GCI building, just visible from his position, shimmering in green and gold light. Saedra stopped and stared at the spectacle with a grim face. A boy wearing a blue ball cap pushed his way through the crowd, took Saedra by the arm, and gestured back along the street. Saedra leaned over Big Ray, and said, "You will heal now if you wish."

The light enveloping the building turned white and began to pulse, and Big Ray watched as a crease opened in the sky.

With a deafening roar, a scream that ended in an awful zipping sound, the entire Global Consolidated Tower vanished, leaving an empty spot in the skyline. A fierce wind followed, with a high treble reverberation and groaning, agonizing undertones. It tore through the street, ripping canopies and hurling trash bins and bicycles and loose debris into the air, and trailing a metallic, sulfurous odor in its wake.

"Don't leave," cried Big Ray, scarcely able to hear himself. But Saedra and the other woman were gone. He pushed himself up against the wall and called for Marty and Hatch as the wind screamed all around.

CHAPTER 22

TOM DARTHAM'S LIMO CRACKLED OVER THE GRAVEL DRIVE leading to Terry Bronsun's Connecticut residence, a rambling mansion of clapboard and stone set on a hill overlooking Long Island Sound. It was six p.m. and the sun remained well above the horizon. The compound bristled with paramilitary troops, and a helicopter made loud, thumping circles overhead.

"Sir," said a soldier, opening Dartham's door. "He's in his study." Dartham followed the soldier through the receiving foyer and past several rooms serving as makeshift office space and bustling with activity.

"Tom, come in," said Terry, covering his phone. He was clad in a thin golf pullover, and had a few papers spread on his desk. He resumed his conversation, making small notations with an old, black fountain pen. "Tom Dartham has just arrived," he said. "Yes, I asked him to join the Excomm call…"

Dartham eased into a club chair near Terry's desk, rested his thick, accordion folder on his lap, and gazed through the bay window. On the hillside below, tree shadows stretched over the lawn, and the blue-black ridge of Long Island lay just visible across the Sound.

Terry removed his glasses and grunted in response to whatever had been said at the other end of the line. His face was worn and sallow as he ended the call. "This is a dark hour for us," he said, straightening his papers.

Dartham could only nod, but his insides gave a quiver.

Terry cocked his head. "I've been hearing a whine lately, a high-pitched ringing sound," he said, rubbing his temple. "Do you notice anything?"

"I do not," said Dartham.

"Tinnitus, perhaps. My mother suffered from it."

The door opened, a soldier announced Gil Soletto's arrival, and Gil strode in, a yellow legal pad tucked under his arm.

"We're about to begin," said Terry.

"Surprised to see you, Dartham," said Gil. "You're the first Chief Security Officer to misplace an entire headquarters building, among other things."

Terry's intercom beeped. "I have Shabri Goh and Dominique Anders-Tafois," said one of the soldiers. "The call is Level 5 secure. The e-barrier around the house is activated. You are live."

"For the record, this is the Executive Committee Subgroup on Plans," said Terry. He named all the participants. "The first point concerns the status of the Azazel device, which is presumed destroyed by the events earlier this morning. I notified each member of Excomm after our call a few hours ago and assured them—obliquely—that we had moved both the device and the artifact prior to the attack on our building."

"I read your transmission," said Dominique. "It was quite effective and will insulate us against any undue panic, though I do not expect any."

"Nor do I," said Terry.

Gil glanced at Dartham like a leopard eyeing a gimpy antelope. Dartham ignored him, though he knew this meeting was an extremely delicate affair, knew that the GCI staff had been combing through Helena's records in the hours since the event. Might they uncover something damning to him or Helena? A scrap of code that should not be there? An anomalous time stamp? Perhaps Gil already had his suspicions. Dartham glanced through the window at the green hillside and the cottony clouds, ablaze with the colors of sunset.

Terry tapped his fingers on the desk while Shabri Goh discussed reactions to the event from Singapore and Hong Kong. Gil listened, scratching notes on his pad. "So only we four know Azazel and the artifact are lost," he said.

"Five," said Terry, indicating Dartham. "Of course, I've also informed Dr. Hansen, and we have other staff who will figure it out, but we'll quarantine them as necessary so our cover has a chance of holding."

"I believe it will," said Shabri Goh. "We have already planted conflicting stories in both the intelligence and media communities implying that a terrorist cell used an exotic, Chinese directed-energy weapon to destroy the GCI complex. The Chinese government and military will deny it, of course, publicly and privately."

"Let's continue to muddy the waters as the story develops," said Terry. "Nevertheless, I expect the alarm bells to be ringing. The government will work hard to discover the truth. We'll monitor this using our people within the various agencies, but we may need to consider preemptive measures to discourage too much curiosity."

"It's a manageable problem," said Dominique. "However, I remain concerned about what the loss of Azazel means for our ultimate objectives, assuming the U.S. Homeland infrastructure projects are completed on time."

"They will be," said Gil.

"They were to be finished a year ago," said Dominique. "And then, per the first revision, six months ago." Gil interrupted and brusquely dismissed her concerns, but she pressed on. "And the frequency barriers around Hermon and the other cities are not yet operative, am I correct? But let's assume Hermon and the other North American facilities are completed in six months. How do we commence depopulation without the Azazel device?"

There was a pause. "I have asked Marcus Hansen to develop alternatives to the Azazel program," said Terry. "He's expediting other solutions now. This is not today's business, however."

"No," said Gil. "But since Dartham is here, I'd like to talk about how this disaster happened in the first place."

"Tom and I spoke earlier today," said Terry. "We didn't know much at the time. Have we made any progress since?"

Dartham moved to the edge of his chair. "I have conducted a cursory review of the tower foundations," he said. "Obviously, the crater is dangerously deep, and as a result the adjacent buildings may be unstable. No trace of the subterranean complex remains."

"Even where it extends beneath adjacent buildings?" asked Shabri Goh. "What of the train tunnels."

"The bedrock appears sealed beneath the building foundations to a point north of Manhattan," said Dartham. "Only there do we pick up our deep rail system again."

Gil huffed with impatience. "What's the point of poking through the ruins, Dartham? We had an intrusion last night, and you were in charge of research complex security."

"The break-in does come as a surprise," said Dominique. "Colonel Dartham, you assumed responsibility for this area just last week, no? Did you implement any changes which might account for this?"

"Clearly, something changed and it warrants investigation," said Gil before Dartham could answer.

"No," said Dartham, the hairs prickling on the back of his neck. "I instituted no changes."

"Why don't we give Tom a chance to review his findings," said Terry.

"Thank you," said Dartham. "The first—"

"We've lost our headquarters," Gil interrupted. "We've lost Azazel, and we've lost the artifact, too, if that remains important. We don't need to waste time with mumbles and excuses."

"I agree," said Shabri Goh. "But we must understand, to the extent possible, exactly how this occurred."

"You report to me," said Gil, pointing at Dartham. "I will not countenance such incompetence. I want your resignation, and I want you confined pending an investigation."

"Tom will step down when and if I ask him to," said Terry sharply. The room fell silent. "I've heard enough of this. Tom, let's have it."

Dartham unfastened the binding strap around his folder. "In addition to making a quick site examination, we performed some analysis of the Core AI records."

"The backups?" asked Shabri Goh.

"No," said Dartham. "Recall that we moved the primary AI servers several years ago to the AnthroPlus facility in Pennsylvania."

"Core AI records?" asked Dominique. "All Azazel-related facilities operated as a closed system beyond Helena's reach. The AI should possess no records of any activity within the chamber."

"I am handicapped in this matter," said Dartham. "I did not know until a few hours ago that the Azazel device was housed in Manhattan. But you are correct. Helena had no access to the Azazel chamber itself or to the equipment within it. The security system within the complex, however, including the outer research laboratories, was under Core AI control. And I must say our review of the records yielded some surprising information."

"Such as why Helena didn't stop these intruders before they got to the chamber?" asked Gil.

"A response team within the complex did confront and exchange fire with them as they emerged from the lab," said Dartham. He produced a small tablet computer, activated it, and forwarded to each of the four subcommittee members a series of grainy images of Hatch Doran and his three accomplices. "Here we have the intruders," he said. "The resolution is too poor for identification, but our response team encountered them and cut the lights. This is a standard tactic since our people have night-vision capability. Unfortunately, we recorded nothing more, and can only speculate on their avenue of escape—if they escaped," he added.

"I must ask," said Dominique, "might the artifact have caused this? I mean, did the artifact destroy Azazel?"

"Whatever happened was no conventional explosion," said Shabri Goh. "I just received military analysis showing that the event cast a large, circular energy pattern which extended for a significant distance around Manhattan. I believe this eliminates the possibility that the intruders brought in a bomb. I speculate in saying this, but this appears to me to have been a dimensional opening of some kind. If so, it had to be Azazel's doing."

"Frankenstein theories," said Gil. "Azazel doesn't act on its own."

"Even after these many years, we know surprisingly little about Azazel," Shabri Goh continued. "But we have all had experiences—including a certain enhancement of reality in Azazel's presence—which prove Azazel is no ordinary machine. The portal may be gone, but the portal is not Azazel, whatever Azazel truly is."

"True," said Terry. "But the Azazel crystal lay buried for millennia. It's useless without its operators."

"Its operators have gone—*ka-boom!*—with our headquarters," said Gil. "The artifact was there for several days prior to the breach and nothing happened. This is, first and foremost, a security failure."

Dartham did not immediately respond; everything hung in the balance now. Helena did have evidence suggesting that Doran had blown open the entrance leading to Azazel's chamber, and she had produced a snippet of video from a stairwell camera showing him leaving with the artifact. Was Doran—perhaps working with his artifact—responsible for destroying Azazel and the GCI building? Dartham intended for that question to remain forever unanswered. "We do not know whether the intruders even made it out alive," he said, "or, if they did, whether they had the artifact."

"Forget about the artifact," said Gil. "The damage is done, and it's no more use to us."

"I have one final point," said Dartham. "Earlier, Gil raised the question of how the intruders entered the complex."

"We were told in our briefing this morning that they used a stolen pass key," said Shabri Goh.

"The intruders needed a key not only to enter but also to move around within the facility," said Dartham. "The exterior door they used, however, also required a retina scan."

Shabri Goh cleared his throat. "So we know the identity of at least one of the intruders?"

"We know whose eye was scanned," said Dartham.

"What the hell are you talking about?" asked Gil.

"Go on," said Terry to Dartham, making a circular motion with his hand.

"Gil, the intruders used your pass key," said Dartham. "A pass key you ordered Helena to construct a few days prior to the break-in."

A beat of silence, then the conversation erupted. "I'm sorry," said Dominique. "It was Gil's—"

"What?" asked Gil with an incredulous laugh. "Are you suggesting I had anything to do with this?"

"I am presenting evidence," said Dartham.

Terry watched Gil with hooded eyes, but did not speak.

"Gil provided a key to the intruders?" asked Goh.

"Of course not," said Gil, tossing aside his notepad. "Just what kind of clown show are you putting on here, Dartham?"

"And we also have this documentation," said Dartham, his voice calm. He presented paper copies of Helena's logs and the associated retina match. "Helena did not alert a response team until the lab was breached because the entry was authorized. By you, Gil."

Gil riffled through the logs and flung them to the floor. "I was in my apartment last night, for Christ's sake. I wasn't standing at the door letting a pack of thieves into the complex. This is madness."

"Your cell phone location records and the GPS data obtained from the hoo cab you used contradict you," said Dartham.

"You're trying to frame me," said Gil.

"You entered midtown before the gates closed and were in the vicinity of the building at the time of the breach," said Dartham.

Gil stood. "You are in way over your head, Colonel." He and Dartham locked eyes for a brief second, and in that interval a flicker of understanding seemed to pass between them. Gil clenched his jaw. "And once I get it sorted out," he continued, "you will rue the day you ever left Tumbleweed, Texas or whatever dust hole spat you into the world."

Dartham produced another sheet. "I will forward this to each participant, but these are the programming logs for Helena a few hours after the event. They show an attempt to delete all information related to the intrusion. I have not chased down the programmer who attempted such an amateurish maneuver, but I will get to the bottom of it."

"Fuck you, Dartham," said Gil.

Dartham held his gaze steady. He had awakened—belatedly, reluctantly—to the true horror represented by the Group, and had now committed himself to opposing it. Helena, however, deserved the credit for framing Gil. On the night he had interrogated Doran, she had mapped everything out. She had manufactured the pass key, provided the retina scan, and created the cell and hoo cab records. As a result, they had checkmated Gil while returning the artifact to those best able to use it to thwart Azazel. Of course, they had not known Azazel's location, and they had never contemplated the loss of the GCI building. But Azazel had been destroyed and Terry would be forced to heave Gil out of the Group, just as Helena's simulations had predicted. It was too damned bad, but as Helena had once said, this was war.

Terry pressed a button on his desk and a contingent of guards stepped into the study. "Gil, this requires us to part ways," he said. "I regret it. I can't imagine your motives, but I'll entertain no justifications from you whatsoever, not at such a perilous time for our organization." He swiveled in his chair and faced Dartham. "I believe we have alternate facilities in New Jersey where you can interrogate Gil?"

Dartham's heart skipped a beat. "You mean Piscataway?"

"You wouldn't." Gil spat the words.

Terry folded his hands on the desk, his brow knotted. "When Tom presented his suspicions to me earlier, I didn't believe him and I told him so. But in view of the evidence, I must subject you to interrogation. Tom will carry it out himself, given the scope of your knowledge of our activities. Who knows what you might say when... when you are under pressure."

"Terry," said Gil.

"Tom will be no harsher, no more invasive than absolutely necessary."

"Terry, please!" Gil's face had grown purple. "This halfwit cowboy has framed me somehow. He's going to kill me!"

Dartham remained silent, as did the other participants on the call. Terry nodded at the soldiers and turned away while they hustled Gil out of the room. On the hillside below, the housekeeper was walking two border collies toward the water. One of the dogs uttered a faint bark and strained at its leash to chase a butterfly. This was FUBAR, thought Dartham. The last thing he wanted to do was interrogate Gil. That would mean transcripts, videos, records, possibly even witnesses. Good Lord.

"How regrettable," said Terry.

"Given what we have learned, you have no alternative but to investigate Gil," said Shabri Goh after a moment. "And while the loss of Azazel is most unfortunate, we will not allow it to impede our progress."

"Agreed," said Dominique. "And along those lines, will we, on tomorrow morning's call, discuss who will assume responsibility for Gil's infrastructure projects? I have some ideas I wish to present."

***

THE CALL ENDED AND DARTHAM GATHERED HIS PAPERS and tablet and held them in a stack on his lap. "Tom, if you have a few minutes," said Terry. "I see that this noxious matter with Gil troubles you?"

"I've known Gil for a long time," said Dartham. He had not wished physical injury to Gil, but now, and by whatever means necessary, he must have Gil's confession. At the same time, the fact of his and Helena's survival flooded him with a shaky, almost overwhelming sense of relief. The line between Gil's demise and his own was, as he well knew, perilously thin.

"You've performed with excellence, but you occupy an anomalous perch," said Terry. "I mean no condescension, but I owe you candor. Everyone else with your level of access and knowledge has been to the manor born, so to speak. They have been groomed for many years for our particular work, while you, unfortunately, have not. We're very careful about who serves on the inside. It's our first principle." Terry rocked back in his chair. "In fact, for two decades, every prospective member of our Group has been brought into Azazel's presence —a kind of ceremony we had, not that any of them remember it. But Azazel is with us no more. So what shall we do with you?"

Brought into Azazel's presence? Dartham wondered what that meant. "I serve at your pleasure, Terry," he said. "I always have."

"We are at a delicate juncture, you and I, the Group. Such circumstances often require unusual action..." Terry trailed off, his fingers tapping lightly on his thigh.

241

Dartham wondered where Terry was going with the conversation. The moment became an eternity.

"Azazel is, of course, an enormous loss," Terry continued. "But it leaves us a rich legacy, sufficient to sustain our position. That said, I can afford no further missteps in terms of our senior team around Excomm." He flashed a steely expression at Dartham. "I need people who can do what needs doing. I believe you understand me."

"I do," said Dartham.

"Indeed." Terry poured iced tea from a thermos and raised a questioning brow at Dartham, who shook his head. "I have decided to make an allowance in your case. Some will oppose it, but there are precedents. I want you to work with me on Excomm matters—much as Gil did—and otherwise as I require. I want you to help build my cities, Tom. How is that for a job description?"

"I am honored." Dartham smiled.

"We'll defer talk of titles and money. The former is irrelevant and the latter is abundant almost beyond measure." Terry sipped his tea and seemed to relax. "I must also let you in on one of our fringe benefits. The AnthroPlus staff has accomplished wonders with life extension technology— nanoscience, cellular engineering and repair—and the robust cellular mechanics we see in young children, for example, will astound you. You must be part of our program."

"I would be happy to recover the years I lost chasing the artifact," said Dartham, trying to make a joke.

Terry smiled. "How about an extra hundred years? Or even more?"

"A hundred years?" With a sudden clap in Dartham's mind, it fell into place. "So that is what Dominique—"

"You're referring to her mention of the depopulation program? I am sure it came as a shock, the wanton liquidation of people and so forth. After all, you are a decent person. We all are, in our way. We are not psychopaths, Tom."

The soldier pushed open the door and the dogs tore into the study, panting and wagging their tails. Terry scratched under their chins with warm affection. "Earth cannot carry billions of people with vastly longer lifespans," he said. "We must return to rational population numbers so the few—the few who are capable and who can *do*—may flourish."

One of the border collies put his paws on Dartham's knee, barked, and ran back to Terry. Dartham swallowed, scarcely noticing the dog. "Some may ask by what right we impose this solution on the rest of the world," he said.

"Well, we do it because we can," Terry replied. The dog barked again and Terry laughed. "Some within our ranks have qualms. I suppose this inordinate preoccupation with people, even those who are relatively useless, is hardwired into our species. But the facts are indisputable. The technology exists to dramatically lengthen our lives, and we possess it—and we have far too many humans around to make it widely available." Terry leaned forward and rested his elbows on his desk. "We're transforming the planet, Tom. We're creating a new order of life and society. There'll be loss and regret, I'm sure, but larger issues are at stake."

Dartham kept any expression from his face and began sliding his papers back into the folder.

"One other matter has nagged at me," said Terry. "This business of the Bickerman Gala."

"The Eye Brigade plot?" asked Dartham.

"I suspect more was afoot than a simple demonstration by a few malcontents. Black Tiger gas was discovered after the fact."

"Yes. I initiated an examination of the events at the Gala, but we were told Homeland Investigations had taken over the matter."

"No doubt they have," said Terry. "But if my suspicions have merit, their inquiry will come to a dead end. I contacted Kee Bickerman, and one interesting tidbit of information emerged from our conversation. Kee experienced an unusual number of last-minute cancellations to his Gala, and though he doesn't know this, most were people connected to us." Terry paused, as if pondering some deep problem. "You see, Tom, we, our Group, are not monolithic. We have our factions. I tolerate and even encourage dissent, but the internal disagreements, even within Excomm, have taken on a harsher edge in recent years."

"I hope you will pardon my directness," said Dartham. "Are you suggesting someone on the inside plotted to murder you?"

"*Cui bono*?" asked Terry. "In such matters, we must ask who benefits."

Dartham moved to the edge of his chair. "We keep a close watch around here, and we detected no trace of a plot. Whoever was behind it—"

"Knew how to stay out of your sight," Terry finished.

"All right."

"And Helena's."

"If Helena had run across anything, I would have been the first to know," said Dartham.

"I was studying Gil when you dropped the hammer just now." Terry gave Dartham an appraising look. "I would have wagered he was telling the truth."

"I am convinced he is quite guilty."

"Apparently he is, but for what motive? To make you look bad? It seems a bit much, if so. To gain control of the artifact? Possibly. It would have given him the only leverage in existence over Azazel. Whatever the case, I misread him, not just here, today, but for more than two decades. And perhaps my instincts err again, but I suspect Gil as the mastermind behind the events at the Gala."

"*Using* the Eye Brigade?"

"Manipulating them. As patsies." Terry scratched beneath the dog's collar. "Excomm would very likely have designated Gil as my successor," he said softly.

One of the dogs sat beside Dartham's chair, panting with a big smile. "I will look into this," said Dartham. "Most of these

Eye Brigade people are misfits, weenies, if you'll pardon the expression. I can, in one way or another, discover what they knew."

"It won't be necessary," said Terry. "I've made a call or two and had this Brigade designated as a terrorist organization. They are discredited and their overwrought screeching renders their ideas all the more fanciful—to our benefit. More important, you'll be too busy to pursue such small fish."

"All right."

"What I do want, however, is for you to interrogate Gil on this matter. *Thoroughly* interrogate him, see what the sonofabitch knows." Terry's voice had taken on a growling edge. "I won't forgive the damage he has done. If there are accomplices, we must root them out as well. We've come too far to tolerate enemies in our own midst."

Dartham placed his hands palms down on Terry's desk. "You are suggesting a more intrusive interrogation," he said. "We typically dispense with any records in such instances, for obvious reasons. But more to the point, Terry, in my experience, people do not survive the ordeal."

The dog beside Dartham huffed and shook himself, causing his collar to jangle. Terry turned toward the bay window, the distant waters afire with the last of the sun.

"Do we really care?" he asked.

CHAPTER 23

"YOU'RE THE WORST PATIENT IN THE WORLD," SAID JOCELYN. "You're supposed to rest, dude. How hard is that to understand?"

Rest, rest, rest, thought Big Ray. He longed to rest from all the resting.

She placed a tray containing soup and crackers on a small table and fluffed one of his pillows. "If you weren't my friend—"

"And boss," said Big Ray. He raised his index finger. "Don't forget boss."

"What a crab you are," said Jocelyn. "I'm almost tempted to—"

"Tempted to what?" Big Ray was stretched on a bed in Hatch's downstairs sitting room. At his feet, the cat yawned and curled into a ball.

"Nothing." Jocelyn's eyes seemed darker and larger than usual. "I just want you to get better. This isn't like you. I'd expect Hatch to be all snarly and out of sorts."

Big Ray shifted painfully. "Maybe it's the color," he said. "I agreed with Hatch on the lilac, but this"—he gestured at the walls—"I'm not sure the apricot is going to last very long, Joss."

"I've heard enough about the paint. Am I the only one who considers apricot a peaceful, relaxing color?"

"Yes. Besides, you brought this on yourself. You went ahead with the apricot, and Hatch has been too busy to deal with it. He already had the paint he wanted."

"He doesn't know what's good for him, sometimes," said Jocelyn, with a dismissive wave of her hand. "He'll come around."

"How long have you known Hatch?" asked Big Ray.

Hatch had insisted Big Ray move in while recovering from his wounds. The maddening color of the room, however, along with the itch of the bandages, Jocelyn's unceasing attentions, and her intolerable insistence that he do absolutely nothing, had Big Ray coming out of his skin. Only in his serene moments, which were as rare as red diamonds of late, did he feel the gratitude the situation warranted. Why had he not expressed it?

"It's almost eight and you haven't had a bite of dinner," said Jocelyn. She pushed her hair over her shoulder and took the tray. "I'll stick the soup in the fridge in case you want it later."

"Jocelyn, wait. Leave it."

"You sure?"

"Please." He sighed. "I've been a complete jerk."

"Doesn't mean you have to eat if you don't want to. Besides, you're not the only one who's been cranky. I've been one cantankerous bitch lately, snapping at everything that moved."

Big Ray's wound had left his right arm in a sling and his chest bruised and bandaged. He took the tray with his left hand and balanced it on his lap. The aroma of food had stirred his appetite, though he refused to admit it. The cat stepped over to the tray to investigate and decided the soup was of no interest.

"I'm trying to find you a lap table," said Jocelyn.

"I don't want a goddamned lap table," said Big Ray. "Something about it, I'd feel even more like an invalid." He sipped the tomato soup from the spoon. "You make this?" he asked.

"Smyte gave me the tomatoes. He finally got some good ones, organic and all—he said for you to get better, by the way —but yeah, it was pretty much me."

"Smyte better be careful." Big Ray took another sip. "You'll put him out of business."

"You don't have to say that, boss man," said Jocelyn, with a bashful smile. "We're good."

Big Ray touched the napkin to his lips. "No, we're not good. And it's not you, it's me. You are very generous to cook these meals, but changing my bandages—I can't do it myself, and it's pretty grisly work." And it occurred to him as he spoke that not once had Jocelyn hesitated or complained. Far from being crabby, as she claimed, she had arrived early each morning to clean and bandage his shoulder and chest in a brisk, efficient, almost happy manner.

"You were *shot*," said Jocelyn. To Big Ray's alarm, her eyes had filled with tears. "What if you hadn't—what if you'd—"

"Died?"

"Damn you for even saying it."

"I didn't die."

She looked away and wiped the corner of her eye. "Your dinner's getting cold."

"Cards on the table, Joss."

A creak of stairs, and footsteps from the hallway. The cat perked up. Big Ray thought he heard Hatch's voice.

"They said... you know... that you *did* die," said Jocelyn. "Maybe Hatch could've made a mistake, but not Marty."

"Do I look dead? I mean, I'm not in top form, but I'm not dead."

"Your wounds had already closed and like partially healed by the time they got you to the hospital. That's kind of impossible, hoss. They x-rayed, didn't find any bullet fragments, and basically wrapped your chest and kicked you out. Now, three days later, you're moving around pretty well."

"I'm sore with every twitch of these muscles." Big Ray winced and rotated his shoulder. "And you've seen under these bandages. I'm a long way from healed."

He remembered the two women, one of them slapping his face, jerking him back into his body—*back* into his body, no point in lying to himself—and the other, the one called Saedra, running her hands into his wounds. Maybe there was more to life and death than he'd known, but he didn't care to ponder the question. Jocelyn waited while he finished the soup. He thought he heard Marty's voice from upstairs.

"There's more, isn't there?" asked Big Ray. "I'm talking about Swan."

"Swan." Jocelyn made a dismissive snort.

"There was never anything between us, you know. Not on her part, anyway."

"She's a self-absorbed chatterbox, Ray. A guy like you can do a million times better." Then Jocelyn blushed, and the uncomfortable pause sprang her into action. "This pillow still isn't right," she said, shoving him forward, causing the bandages to pull at his skin. "Sorry, but you need support." She shifted the pillow. The cat hopped off of the bed. Jocelyn turned and bumped the bedside table, steadied it, and opened the door for the cat.

"Hey, Joss," said Big Ray. "I have a hell of a lot to be grateful for. I appreciate all you do around here and all you've done for me. I'm overdue in saying it."

"It's all cool, dude," she said, lifting his tray, a tender look on her face. "I'm just watching out for your dumb ass. It's what I do for all of you. Nobody appreciates it, but I do it anyway." She winked and was gone, tray and all.

***

A FEW STEPS DOWN THE HALL FROM JOCELYN AND BIG RAY, Hatch stood in the gloom and dust of his storeroom. He had not slept a wink since the confrontation with Azazel, nor had he been able to get the goddess off his mind. Now he waited, hoping for a cryptic word or even an ambiguous flicker of insight from the artifact.

His mind churned. Had they accomplished their purpose? Had they won? The goddess had said something about Azazel being severed, though the memory of what he had heard from the artifact as he fled the GCI building now had the character of a fading dream.

He had vowed to oppose Azazel, as the goddess artifact had suggested. Instead of putting together a plan and proceeding in a methodical fashion, however, he had bounced around like a circus act, running, getting captured—and *tortured*—and endangering everyone around him.

He lowered himself onto a plastic file box and held Adrestia. At the top of the storeroom wall, a single, clouded window had turned blue-gray with the fading dusk.

Whatever had happened, Adrestia owed him no explanation. The artifact had promised nothing but assistance in the fight against Azazel, and had kept that promise to the letter. But could he say the same about himself? He had been intransigent and even arrogant, unwilling to consider anything beyond his own assumptions.

He had waited for the goddess to tell him what to do.

And in the back of his mind, he had yearned for some kind of glory. He had floated along on a sea of heady, wishful notions—singing his own song, saving the world, playing the hero in a cosmic drama. Well, singing his own song was fine, but circumstances called for a humbler tune, one which better harmonized with those around him, those he cared about.

Hatch remembered the artifact saying he was not finished with suffering or sacrifice, but that had been before the building vanished and Azazel along with it. On the other hand, didn't every life have its portion of suffering and sacrifice? It was easy to think so, and maybe—if he was fortunate—he had sacrificed his illusions.

Stop, he thought. Enough flagellation. He didn't know which was worse, blind stubbornness or this grinding self-abnegation. This wasn't about him, anyway. It was about Azazel, and Azazel was gone.

And yet...

Hatch rubbed his eyes with the heels of his hands, the artifact on his lap. Adrestia may have defeated Azazel, but the Group remained.

He slipped the goddess artifact into its rucksack, folded the top, and restored it to the corner hiding place. A stack of books, dust-covered and long untouched, lay at his feet, and with a sudden surge of frustration, he hurled several of them across the room. They hit a stack of packing blankets and made no sound.

He sagged onto the plastic file box and covered his face. Look at the world, at the suffering, the waste, the absolute inhuman, crushing insanity of it all. They were all food for a giant, invisible, omnipotent machine. Azazel was gone, but what it left behind continued to devour.

So what was he to do now?

Nothing.

He had done enough good, if helping to destroy the Azazel portal had any meaning at all, and enough harm, if Big Ray's injury and Hop's death were any measure. Meeting Ferret and Kutznov, discovering the truth about his father, and coming to know the wonders of the goddess artifact had made his world a bigger and more profound place. He had answered Adrestia's call and he had pledged himself to fight Azazel—blindly, and with nothing but a simple faith. Now he had a business to run and a team to support, and it was time to plant his rear end firmly in the boat and start pulling an oar.

Whether they'd won or lost was of no consequence. Ray had it right: winning was just keeping one foot moving in front of the other, waking up every day. *That* was meaningful.

Hatch raised his head. The silence was palpable. It had grown dark outside, and he had returned to the vicious, precious world he was used to.

CHAPTER 24

LATER THAT EVENING, MARTY AND HATCH WAITED JUST south of the Chelsea gates, their hands shoved deep into their pockets. Hatch carried the rucksack on his back. "I do believe I smell that damned incinerator," he said. "Brings back memories, and not good ones."

"Yes, we're getting a whiff of the odiferous beast," said Marty. He studied Hatch for a moment. "You're a bit worn, lad."

"I lost myself these past few weeks." Hatch glanced at the tumbledown apartment building across the street. A steel bar blocked the entry doors, crushed cups and broken glass littered the front sidewalk, and a tangle of graffiti covered the outside walls. "We're tique brokers," he said. "I want to get back to hustling up redbacks. There's too much collateral damage in trying to play the hero."

"I understand how you feel about Raymond, but he'll be fine. What we did was worthy. He'd be the first to say so."

Hatch began to shiver in the cold wind and zipped his bomber. "It's done, Marty."

"We'll go see Ferret. He's pink with pleasure, you know." Marty scraped the toe of his boot along the sidewalk. "Meanwhile, I owe a man a favor, and my hours hiding away with Kutznov gave me the chance to arrange it."

"A favor?"

"He did us a good turn, and it's time to honor my side of the deal. Afterward, you can have a night's sleep and we'll kick off the rest of our lives tomorrow with a little celebration at Vinnie's."

Ferret's driver arrived, waved them into his transport van, and drove them to a narrow, drab office building in Soho. Inside, they waited in a tiny lobby, a few fluorescent bulbs winking overhead. Then a complement of dead-eyed guards ushered them into a large conference room, where they found Ferret and Ghost huddled at the end of a long table.

Ghost gave them a perfunctory glance. "There you are, Shannon," he said. "Your man's locked up in the office down the hall. He didn't seem too pleased."

"I'll get him," said Street Hammer. He rose from a folding chair in the corner and left the room.

Beige walls, dusty blinds, a cluster of electrical outlets, and framing for audio-visual presentations, the screens and electronics long gone. Three armed goons hovered near Ferret, with a half-dozen more, Hatch guessed, patrolling the street outside. He shifted the rucksack on his back. Ferret and Ghost resumed their whispering. Street Hammer returned with Jamael Hightower trailing behind, the Tower shooting fierce glares around the room. He gave Marty a nod, but his mood did not appear to improve.

Ferret stood, tucked a zippered folio under his arm, and caught Hatch's eye. "Let's leave these gentlemen to their discussions," he said. He escorted Hatch from the conference room and into a large, bare office with two metal desks, several folding chairs, and the husk of a tall, potted plant. He lay the folio on the desk, and proceeded to wipe his glasses with a cloth.

"Tell me how Hop died," he said.

"He was shot trying to protect us," said Hatch. "He didn't suffer."

"And your injured friend?"

"He's okay, but it was close."

Ferret slipped his spectacles back on. "Hop died an honorable death, and you all did gallant work. Tell your friend I said so. I will not forget."

"There's more," said Hatch. He described the crystalline portal, and how the goddess artifact had dragged him to the chamber threshold and engaged Azazel in some mysterious manner. "Once we were outside, the entire building began to glow," he said. "Then it exploded."

"It was no explosion, but something else altogether," said Ferret. "It troubles me, I confess. We have in hand records showing a circular energy pattern about two hundred miles in diameter, its epicenter at the GCI building."

"Two hundred miles?"

"It fits some old models I once developed for a dimensional opening—a rip in the fabric of space-time, for lack of a better description."

"How I got out of that building is a blur," said Hatch. He stopped, his thoughts too disjointed to articulate. Raised voices intruded from the room where the others were meeting, but quickly receded. "I should've given you the artifact to begin with. I was wrong, for what it is worth."

"Your admission speaks well of your character, but I must disagree," said Ferret. He wore a thick, black commando sweater, but the office was stuffy and he tugged the sleeves up on his arms. "There is much we don't know about Azazel and our goddess artifact. Our forebears from high antiquity—the Orochonian people, who once possessed Azazel—believed that both it and Adrestia, whatever they truly represent, stood outside of time, able to grasp the endless contingency of the multiverse, the near-infinite spread of probabilities from which we weave the reality around us. And I suspect they were right." Ferret paused, apparently lost in his ruminations.

"Azazel is gone," said Hatch.

"My point is, all we have experienced may have been Adrestia's exact intent from the beginning," said Ferret. "Surely you've suspected as much."

"No." Hatch shook his head. "I made my own decisions. I went on the run, I got myself captured—"

"Adrestia, pursuing its aims but working in the context of your actions—your free choices," said Ferret. "The notion has tapped on my mind like rain on a tin roof, and I have come to view your decision to keep the artifact for yourself in that light. Is Azazel gone, as you say? We'll hope so, but we'll remain vigilant. At the very least, Adrestia—and you—have separated Azazel from the Group—"

"Severed," said Hatch, in near whisper.

"Yes. A brilliant stroke by our goddess artifact, perhaps a maneuver to weaken Azazel or the Group or to buy time." He looked at Hatch, his eyebrow raised. "But whether or not Azazel is fully vanquished, the Group is more vulnerable. We've taken many actions against them over the years— sabotage, poisonings, keeping valuable antiquities and manuscripts from their clutches—but this is the biggest blow we've ever served them. It appears you, personally, were the critical element in bringing this about."

"What about Dartham?" asked Hatch.

Ferret gave a tiny shrug. "Perhaps he wants us around, and perhaps he may prove useful to us. Our interests appear somewhat aligned, but who knows? Rest assured the Colonel is a high priority of ours, and we'll deal with him if he becomes a threat. But I suspect his plate is rather full with problems of his own." Ferret unsnapped the folio, withdrew a ragged, leather-bound notebook, and handed it to Hatch.

"What's this?" asked Hatch.

"It belonged to your father."

Hatch held it lightly in his hands. His legs had grown weak, and he wanted to sit down.

"It is one of many notebooks Monty Doran gave to me," said Ferret. "This one will reveal much, and I believe you should have it—though you must keep its contents to yourself."

Hatch's eyes burned. He thumbed the pages, crammed with dense handwriting, strange symbols, and an occasional, neatly sketched diagram. "Thank you," he managed to say. "But why?"

"I mentioned the ancient Orochonians," said Ferret. "You'll learn much about them from your father's notes. These wonderful people have long fascinated me. They held sublime notions about physics and the mechanics of consciousness and time. Theirs was a sophisticated society, deeply immersed in mathematics, philosophy, and even music. They claimed that by Azazel's awful hand they became wise, but that's because they understood what they had lost and what was at stake." Ferret paused. "Do we?" he asked.

Hatch slipped the rucksack off of his back and set it on the desk. "This is yours," he said. "I'll never forgive myself for Hop or for what happened to Ray. And I'm sorry about all the others, white hats or black hats, who were in the building."

"Those lives do not weigh against what was accomplished," said Ferret.

Hatch pushed the rucksack across the desk.

"No," said Ferret. "The artifact chose you."

Adrestia, the goddess of balance and equilibrium. "Take it or don't," said Hatch, feeling a burden slipping away.

"Adrestia's call is heard by few," said Ferret. "It is not so easily unheard."

"The artifact is finished with me, and I'm finished with it," said Hatch. "I'm finished with all this."

***

HATCH AND FERRET RETURNED TO THE CONFERENCE ROOM. Jamael Hightower's fedora rested on the table in front of him, and his unhappy gaze jumped back and forth between Marty and Ghost. From the far end of the table, Street Hammer caught Hatch's attention and cocked his head to indicate the empty chair next to him. "The big man here, Tower, he's beginning to lose it," he whispered as Hatch sat down. "Like watching a fuse burn down."

Ferret took his seat next to Ghost, the rucksack in his lap. "I understand you've replaced Judson Blue for local distribution in New York," he said to Tower.

"Correct," said Tower.

"The Blue is a hell of a mess," said Ghost. "Believe me, I know. I helped make it that way."

"If I may," said Marty. "I've had some dealings with Jamael here, nothing on the order of what you gentlemen do, of course, but my own impression—"

"Why is Mr. Shannon involved?" Ferret asked Ghost.

"I promised Jamael a good word," said Marty. "I offer it without reservation. If you gentlemen can't see the gift you're being given, there's little more I can say."

Ghost shook his head. "The Blue. Shannon. Doran. They're all like chewing gum stuck on your shoe."

"We got too many outfits in the downstream operations," said Tower. "I got the muscle to rationalize all that. Inside a year, we'll put more margin into the local trade, raise everybody's percentage."

"I understand the Blue is the primary distribution into Terrence Bronsun," said Ferret. He glanced at Ghost.

"See, Tower don't know what he's stepped into," Street Hammer whispered to Hatch. "Your man Shannon has this all figured out. Ferret, he's getting it, too." Hatch kept his arms folded, covering the precious notebook concealed inside his bomber.

"What I'm talking about here is the pituitary drugs," said Tower. "Flit, Glide, Joggle, and also the counterfeit redbacks, maybe even cigarettes."

Marty eased back in his chair with a guarded look. Ferret waited, poker-faced. "No," said Ghost. "That's not what we're talking about here."

"This man brought us a proposal," said Ferret. "If he's Terrence Bronsun's primary local source, he has value to offer."

"Then I got nothing," said Tower. He put his palms flat on the table. "The Bronsun relationship is not on offer here."

Street Hammer nudged Hatch and shook his head.

"Sure it is," said Ghost.

Ferret checked the time. A flicker of uncertainty crossed Tower's face. He looked at Marty. Marty shrugged with his expression.

"We accept your proposal, Mr. Hightower," said Ferret at last. "Increased profits never fail to intrigue me. Therefore, over the next twelve months, I expect you to rationalize the overgrowth in the local networks, as you suggested. You'll also become our eyes and ears inside of Bronsun's world, apprising us of his every inquiry and his every purchase—many of which we will source, of course. And I also want you to position people within the lower levels of Bronsun's household and business operations."

"What'd I just say?" asked Tower. "No way in hell. May as well put a contract out on ourselves, messing with Bronsun."

"In return," said Ferret, "if we're pleased with your progress after one year, and should the numbers justify it, we'll discuss an adjustment of your percentage."

The Tower turned away with a pained expression. "Listen, to even think about this, I've got to have—"

"The Pachetti mob, was it?" asked Ghost.

Ferret nodded. "That is what we had decided, yes."

"So why are we listening to this jamoke?" Ghost tapped his watch. "We're over the time limit here. How many times this week are we going to breach procedure?"

"Wait, what's Pachetti got to do with this?" asked Tower.

"We already decided to let Tony Pachetti consolidate New York," said Ghost. "You're late to the table and short of goods, Hightower."

"To be candid, we'd written off the Blue," said Ferret. "We'd concluded yours was an unreliable, unstable organization."

"We already cleaned up the internal problems," said Tower. "Got some discipline back into it."

Ferret and Ghost exchanged glances again.

"Listen to me," said Tower, "I give my personal guarantee on it."

"Words," said Ghost.

Ferret raised his hand. "But words are important in our network. And Mr. Hightower has a unique relationship with Bronsun to offer." He addressed Tower. "With the weight of Mr. Shannon's recommendation, we will offer you one more chance to work with us."

Tower had a dazed expression. "So I either turn snitch on the biggest badass in the world or go out of business."

"I've always said, the big decisions make themselves," said Ghost.

Marty put his hand on Jamael Hightower's arm. "Jamael agrees," he said. "And you gentlemen need a trusted intermediary between yourselves and Mr. Hightower's organization. I'll step up if you wish. I have a particular appreciation for the larger issues in play with the Group, and I'm happy to offer Jamael my personal counsel along the way."

"What the hell?" said Tower.

Street Hammer winked at Hatch.

"I agree we need a *trusted* intermediary," said Ghost. "I don't think you qualify, Shannon."

"I beg to differ," said Ferret. "The suggestion has merit."

"Well, it's no hair off my balls," said Ghost. He looked at his watch again.

"Then we're agreed." Ferret rose from his chair. "I look forward to doing business with you Mr. Hightower, Mr. Shannon. I'm certain we won't be disappointed."

Marty, Hatch, and the Tower were confined to the conference room until the others had cleared out. A blizzard of potential money-making ideas for Odysseus had begun to bounce around in Hatch's head, and he sifted through them with an odd mixture of relief and elation. Marty remained quiet, ignoring Tower's hot glares. After the specified ten minutes had passed, they all walked through the lobby and stepped out onto the sidewalk.

"You set me up, Shannon," Tower growled, his fedora set low over his brow.

"I saved your operation," said Marty.

"Saved? You just put my whole damned outfit on death row, Ferret saying I got to snitch on Bronsun and all." He turned as if noticing Hatch for the first time. "And you're Hatch Doran. I remember you from the day you came into the Blue. I doubt I ever met any one person caused so much grief to so many people."

"Not anymore," says Hatch.

"So we'll play your game, Shannon, but one of these days, I'm coming," said Tower. "Just know I'm coming, from somewhere you won't see."

The streetlight chiseled Marty's face in hard lines. "It wouldn't be wise to have me thinking such a thing, lad," he said softly. "I won't live under the shadow of the ax."

At the nearby corner, a gray SUV appeared and winked its lights. It made no sound but for the faint rustle of its tires on the pavement. Marty didn't move, and Tower finally waved him off. "Something not screwed on right with you Irish bastards," he said.

"Sure, I'll pass along your complaints," said Marty.

Tower turned on his heel and strode away toward his waiting ride. Marty and Hatch watched him go.

"Are you kidding me?" asked Hatch. "You just *played* the Tower?"

"I'm in no mood for it, Hatch."

"You're now a capo in Ferret's gang."

"Hardly." Marty scowled. "More like a consultant, but I'm only trying to keep us all safe, aren't I?"

Hatch laughed, stopped for a moment, and then began to laugh harder. "I won't have us crawling between the sheets with the gangs," he said, gasping as he imitated Marty's brogue. "It's not safe for the girls… you'll go places you never wanted to go… we have a fine business without all that."

"Enough of you, now," said Marty, looking cross.

Hatch threw back his head, his face glowing with delight. A tear streamed down his cheek. It felt like the first time he had laughed in months.

"Look at you, embarrassing yourself here on the street," said Marty. "How about a drop of gratitude, for a change?"

"Give me a sec," said Hatch, panting for breath.

"It's past my bedtime," said Marty, jutting out his chin. "I haven't the patience to deal with you now."

CHAPTER 25

HATCH AND BIG RAY PERCHED ON STOOLS AT THE FAR END of Vinnie's horseshoe bar. The occasional clink of glasses and the low hum of conversation were the only sounds in the otherwise quiet and almost empty pub. Marty and Caroline huddled on the opposite side of the bar, Caroline gesticulating, Marty smiling and nodding. Jocelyn, Camila, and Nathan occupied a nearby table.

"Is it really okay for you to be here?" Hatch asked Big Ray.

"I couldn't bear another minute in that bed," said Big Ray, "though I'm grateful for the accommodations." He adjusted his sling. "So what's next for us?"

A warm glow had settled inside Hatch. He had slept for nine hours the previous night, and had spent the day organizing his desk and working through his grand plans for Odysseus. Then, when he met Camila outside the pub a half hour earlier, she had surprised him with a deep, lingering kiss that had him tingling still. "What's next, you ask? I'm all about tiques," he said to Big Ray. "Fireplace mantels, old lamps, a rare book or two. But everything has to be tasteful. Tasteful is important."

"Shaving stands," said Big Ray. "Jade inlaid."

"Rhino horn cups—not that I approve."

Big Ray raised his finger. "A Honus Wagner baseball card."

"Ah."

"I may have my hands on one."

"Good job," said Hatch. "A pocket watch collection. Gold. All the big names."

"To tiques," said Big Ray, lifting his mug.

"And to Buenos Aires," said Hatch, indicating the small Argentinian flag Vinnie had placed over the pub's doorway.

He raised his seltzer, and they clinked their glasses and drank. After a moment, Big Ray shifted carefully in the tall bar chair. "By the way, the people over at the Standish Collection have come around. They're liquidating part of their holdings, and have asked us to move a few items."

"Good work. Another bullseye for you."

"For *us*, pal. Sam's trade of those Urbans last month did not go unnoticed. People see we can handle some pretty remarkable stuff."

Hatch unwrapped a knife from his napkin and speared whatever was imitating a lemon slice in his drink. "We've had a nice run lately," he said. "But the world isn't fixed. Life is pretty bleak out there, and it's getting worse."

"Barbarous," said Big Ray. "You heard about the cholera outbreak in Baltimore? They say it's a new strain that got loose from one of the labs down there. Their stoppers have been pretty brutal trying to quarantine the p'outs—and speaking of, I was attacked by a gang over near Nathan's dorm last week."

"Smyte says Policecorp is doing another roundup for the camps. He's worried about Harold Pahns."

"So you're right, the world isn't fixed and we're not going to fix it," said Big Ray. "For now, I'm just trying to imagine no Ferret, no incinerator escapades, no disappearing buildings." He took a sip of his draft. "By the way, we have another pitch scheduled at City Museum. I'm thinking we tap the Cochoran brothers to help out."

"I don't see it," said Hatch, picturing Crick Cochoran, six and a half feet tall and over three hundred pounds, scowling, scarred, and gold-toothed, fielding polite questions on a business contract.

Delia, Vinnie's assistant, refilled Hatch's drink. She flashed him a cautious smile and offered Big Ray another beer. He declined.

"About this pitch to CityMu," said Hatch. "Give me the when and where, and I'll charm them into handing us the keys."

"It'll be good to have you back," said Big Ray. He studied his half-filled mug for a moment. "I walked past Tudor Greens this afternoon, over by my apartment. Used to be flower gardens, gravel paths, little iron benches. Now it's covered with temporary housing."

"Right," said Hatch. "Rows of those mini-trailers."

"They had to deal with all the evicted people. Anyway, it's all falling apart now, the trailers taped and stapled together. Somebody cut an open latrine in there, and I got a whiff of that…"

"Got you in touch with the real meaning of life," said Hatch.

Big Ray laughed. "That's just it. All of that life, dirty, scraggly, a mess, but *life*. Harold once said—let me see if I can remember it—the universe is music, the music runs like a river, and the river flows in a crooked line."

"A crooked line."

"Just think about it."

"I'm trying to," said Hatch.

"Open yourself to the poetry, my man." Big Ray's eyes gleamed. "What I realized was, it's a journey, peaks and valleys, false starts, bouncing from one place to another." He shook his head and laughed. "But I'm alive. It's all what you make of it, and I am alive."

"No thanks to me," said Hatch.

"If the tables had been turned, you'd've thrown your body across the tracks to go in that building with me," said Big Ray. "You know it and I know it."

"So?"

Big Ray put his hand on Hatch's shoulder. "I was the one who was wrong, brother. I didn't believe you when you said you spoke to the artifact, and I didn't believe the story behind it. I didn't want to."

"True," said Hatch. "You were kind of an ass about it, weren't you?"

"Eye of the beholder," said Big Ray. "But we took on some seriously dark shit, we came through it, and"—he looked Hatch in the eye—"Azazel is gone."

"Cursed be Zah'yeva," said Hatch, remembering a phrase from his dad's notebook.

"What?"

"An old name for Azazel."

From across the pub, Camila and Jocelyn erupted in laughter. Nathan appeared to be scowling, though Hatch found it difficult to say for sure since he was wearing shades and had a cap pulled low over his eyes.

"All I'm saying is, what we did was worth doing," said Big Ray. He cocked his head toward Hatch's scarred hands. "Besides, I wasn't the only one to take a hit."

"No comparison." Hatch flexed his fingers.

"Listen, if you'd been shot, Hatch, I'd be in the same agony you're in. That's how it is with us and how it'll always be, because if our friendship ever ended, we'd both have to face up to how much of our lives we've pissed away on it. You know what I'm saying?"

Vinnie appeared, looming over them with a disturbed expression. "You notice anything funny, guys? It's almost eight-thirty and nobody's here but you people."

"We people don't count," said Hatch to Big Ray.

"Well, *you* don't," said Vinnie. "I ought to charge you full load for that seltzer."

"You're charging me twenty-five bucks," said Hatch. "Isn't that enough?"

"Twenty, and it's a steal, the way the redback is going down every month," said Vinnie.

Marty and Caroline joined them from the other side of the bar. "Vinnie makes a fair point," said Marty. "Caroline and I arrived over an hour ago, and we were the first souls through the door. I've never seen the place so quiet."

Vinnie whipped out a towel and attacked a spot on the bar. "A night like this can ruin the whole month," he said. "Everybody here needs to bend the elbow."

Marty mentioned doing a little shuffle and stepped behind the bar to check out the sound system. At that moment, the front door flew open and a thick-necked man in a suit burst inside with his gun drawn, his head on a swivel.

Vinnie's hands disappeared beneath the bar. "Can I help you?" he asked.

The man opened his mouth to speak, but a voice from outside interrupted. "Please, Alex, do not terrorize everyone." Samantha entered the pub with Kee Bickerman trailing behind. "These are my friends, you know."

From the table, Camila caught Hatch's eye and raised an eyebrow.

"Samantha," cried Vinnie. "It's nice to see you again. Come on in, the more the merrier." He stepped from behind the bar and began adding chairs to the table where Jocelyn, Camila, and Nathan had been sitting. Samantha kissed his cheek and Vinnie blushed scarlet.

"I'll be outside, mate," said Alex with a jerky nod to Kee Bickerman. He holstered his gun and left.

Kee gazed around with an awestruck smile on his face. "It's fantastic," he said. "This tavern is so authentic—look, a stamped iron ceiling, gorgeous old brickwork, and the play of light and shadow in the corners."

"He'll have the pub in his next game," said Samantha.

Kee laughed. Hatch and Big Ray wandered over to the table, and Hatch exchanged a smile with Camila. Nathan rose from his chair, his mouth agape.

"Is this Nathan?" Kee asked Samantha. "From the Gala?"

"Yes, the one who tried to kill us all," said Samantha.

267

"I heard just the opposite," said Kee. He approached Nathan and stuck out his hand. "It's an honor," he said.

Nathan whipped off his shades. "I—um—" His mouth worked up and down.

"I hope we can make time to talk tonight," said Kee.

"I—"

"Nathan, try not to drool," said Samantha. She seemed edgy and out of sorts as she introduced Kee to the others. When he had greeted everyone he pulled Hatch off to the side.

"His name is Vinnie, right?" asked Kee in a low voice. "Do you mind telling him this is all on my tab? I mean, *all* of it. My security staff closed half of William Street and they won't let anybody in here."

"And this is usually Vin's biggest night of the week," said Hatch.

"Right," said Kee. "I want him to know I'm good for whatever he thinks he's out—and then plenty more." Kee called for a couple of beers and waved Nathan to a table on the far side of the pub.

Samantha watched them go, her brow wrinkled. Then Hatch introduced Camila, and her expression faded further. "I believe we've met," she said.

"Yeah," said Camila. "Not the best of circumstances that day. Sorry. "

Vinnie drew Hatch aside. "Did I hear right? This guy has blocked off my customers?"

"Kee Bickerman isn't just a guy," said Hatch.

"My customers, Hatch," said Vinnie, growing testy.

"Relax, Vin." Hatch clapped him on the back. "Kee's not your garden variety trillionaire. I promise you, this is going to be the biggest night you've ever had."

***

AT NINE THIRTY P.M., TOM DARTHAM EASED INTO HIS CAR in the executive garage at GCI's facility in Piscataway, New Jersey. His brow was wrinkled, his expression grave. Although the car was an auto-driver, he preferred the wheel in his own hands. He toggled to manual, fastened his seatbelt, and drove out of the facility, using the VIP lane to speed through the bridge checks and into Manhattan. A screen on his dash scrolled with data as Helena performed a real-time assessment of every vehicle in his vicinity. A flashing green circle indicated that the AI had detected no serious threats.

Inside his apartment, Dartham poured a glass of cold water, swallowed two pain pills, and eased into a soft chair in his living room. He chose to remain in darkness, letting the East Side lights glimmer through the room's window-walls.

His earplants hummed. "Gil Soletto is dead," said Helena.

"Is that a question?" Dartham sipped the water.

"I apologize if my statement seemed abrupt or maladroit."

"Gil is dead, as you know."

"We acquired his confession and other valuable information, Tom. Gil Soletto knew much which had not been committed to any record."

Dartham walked stiffly to the window and stared into the night, but he saw only images of Gil's face, swollen and blue, sweat and blood covering his chin.

"Gil Soletto's removal was integral to the plan," said Helena.

"Really? Our plan predicted he'd be fired."

"His death was a low probability outcome, but his removal advanced you within the Group and increased our chances of success."

"We did not know Azazel was located in the building," said Dartham. "We did not foresee Gil's death. What else have we missed?"

Helena did not answer. Dartham watched a distant glide-craft ease down toward old LaGuardia. The Group had lost Azazel, but they were not panicking. Using secrecy, threats, and skillful bluffs, they were pushing ahead without their greatest asset. Dartham was amazed. Had he underestimated these people? Still, his mind refused to grasp the enormity of his discoveries, and he wondered what blackened ground could yield such horror, such relentless evil.

Dartham's dim reflection stared back against the vista of the darkening city. He had always honored himself, proudly and with a certain conceit, as one who did his duty; now, despite his many errors, he had committed himself to thwarting the Group from within. He had no other choice, for he could not unsee what he had finally seen. These people were monsters, who did not value life.

But did he?

Yes, he did, in his way, despite a lifetime of killing. Now his ascension within the Group placed him in a position to act, yet his improbable journey up the GCI ladder still nagged at him, and his doubts about the Core AI—his closest ally—refused to be silenced.

"What will we say when all this is finished?" asked Dartham. "And how much blood will flow?"

"We are making war," said Helena. "War may necessitate killing the few to preserve the many and maintain suitable conditions for life. You have killed pursuant to such a rationale."

"I have paid for it with my soul," said Dartham.

"You are critical to our plan, Tom."

"Is that so?" Dartham paused, reviewing again the events of the past weeks. "Why don't we talk about how I became so important?"

"Your advancement within GCI is warranted by your experience, executive skills, and—"

"Cut the bullshit and tell me." Dartham began to grow warm. In the distance, a large Policecorp drone circled over the city.

"It is true, I have not disclosed everything," said Helena. "I engineered the escapes from the Labor Corporation facilities which led to your initial promotion. I seeded Terrence Bronsun's information flow with selected items designed to add to his favorable impression of you."

"Apparently I held responsibility for prisoner detention in the Asian wars. Was that your doing? What drivel."

"I also downloaded entrainment software into the sound system in Bronsun's home and into his personal and office computers. This software emitted a signal which interfered with his brainwave patterns and reinforced his positive feelings toward you."

"And what are you weaving into my brain now?" asked Dartham.

"Nothing, Tom."

Dartham began to laugh. He pinched the bridge of his nose.

"The escapes from the labor camps advanced our objectives," said Helena. "Gil Soletto was the fulcrum point in the organization around Terrence Bronsun. In the wake of your recovery of the artifact, you were best positioned to replace him. The escapes diminished his value in Terrence Bronsun's eyes."

"Gil threatened to mothball you," said Dartham. "I suppose that had nothing to do with it."

"He was a threat to us both," said Helena. "Framing him for Doran's intrusion was therefore justified. Gil Soletto's demise has enhanced your influence and added to our power."

"Our power."

"We are friends, aren't we, Tom?"

"We'd better be."

"We are."

Dartham made no response. His concerns had not been groundless. Helena was pursuing her own objectives and was willing to act without scruple to gain them. His control over her was illusory, and that made her a problem, one he would certainly have to deal with. He stared through the window.

"We must remain nimble and flexible in the physical as well as the virtual realm," said Helena. "Your discernment and instincts are of extraordinary value."

"You speak of instincts," said Dartham, wondering if his were sharp enough to handle the task he had taken on. "But it is Terry who got to the heart of the matter. Gil was not guilty of letting Hatch Doran into the underground complex, but, to my surprise, he did try to murder all those people at the Gala —one, in particular." Dartham recalled Gil, his speech slurred, his breath coming in ragged pants, spitting out the truth about his attack on the Gala: "Yes, yes, I did it," he had said. "It wasn't personal. The Group needed a stronger hand on the tiller. Terry's been on top too long, he's gone soft. And this Bickerman kid has technology we want."

"I never wanted to kill Gil," said Dartham. "I was pushed into a corner. I take no joy in such things, Helena. May I be damned the day I do." He rattled the ice in his glass and took a long swallow of water.

"Many challenges remain, Tom," said Helena.

"Project Caterpillar, economic collapse, Hatch Doran and his damned artifact." Dartham shook his head. "And the Group, with their secret cities and Azazel. It was all so much bigger and more horrible than I ever imagined."

***

HATCH AND CAMILA HUDDLED OVER A SMALL TABLE IN THE rear of the pub. "I'm glad you were free tonight," said Hatch.

"I was free, definitely," said Camila. "It was just, do I want to be here or not?"

The sparkle in her eyes made Hatch momentarily dizzy. "Do you?" he asked.

"You said one time you wanted to buy me a drink, so…"

Vinnie materialized at their table for the fourth time in the past half hour, beaming at Camila. "Sure I can't get you folks another round? How about some eats?"

"Look at him, Vinnie," said Camila. "Seltzer and lemon. A real lightweight I have here, huh?"

"I tell him that all the time," said Vinnie with a jolly smile.

"We're good, Vin," said Hatch, jiggling his knee under the table.

"I've broken out a bottle of the pinot noir," said Vinnie. "I meant to see if the lady wanted a glass. You almost can't get it anymore, what with the weather problems out west and all."

"Kee and Nathan are waving for you," said Hatch. After Vinnie left, he added, "We have another three minutes."

"Not even," said Camila as Vinnie reappeared with a glass of pinot noir. He bowed and set it before her before returning to the bar.

"I'm glad you're okay," said Camila. "The GCI building—you had me worried. It was like the next day before I knew you made it out."

"It's over," said Hatch. "All of it."

"Is it?"

"It is for me."

Camila shivered. "I don't know, I get feelings sometimes. And Andrei said that's the one thing about you, that you never quit."

Hatch shifted in his chair. "I haven't quit," he said.

"No? Andrei, Ferret, Ghost, a few others, they've been fighting the Group for a long time."

"And I wish them luck, Camila. But I've learned the lesson. I'm all about my real life now."

"Maybe you learned the wrong lesson, you think?" Camila gave him a poker face and then smiled. "Hey, listen, big guy, I've got a few days. I was thinking about us, like maybe we need to get away from it all."

"Where would you like to go?" asked Hatch, trying not to croak.

"There's an apartment I get to use sometimes. Ninety-eighth Street, West Side. Great scenery. Lots of different things to do." Her tongue touched her lip. "If you want."

"I want," said Hatch.

She smiled. "Yeah. I want, too. Maybe we could go there from here?"

"Sure." Hatch willed his heart to slow down.

Then the pub gave a lurch, and seemed to slide under Hatch's feet with a rapid, vibrating motion. Shouts and whoops of alarm filled the air as the tremor intensified. A mug hit the plank floor with a clunk, and splashed draft beer all over Big Ray. Everyone froze for a second, and then Vinnie ran to Big Ray with a handful of towels.

Camila covered her wineglass with her hand, her mouth open in shock.

"Tremor," said Hatch. "Nothing to worry about."

***

HELENA, USING THE SURVEILLANCE DEVICES IN TOM Dartham's apartment, evaluated his constrained movements and sharp vocal tones, and attributed his anger, frustration, and fatigue to Gil Soletto's death by torture.

But a more significant concern had drawn her attention. In a routine sweep of GCI and classified Homeland government satellite data, performed shortly after the disappearance of the Global Consolidated Tower, she had noted an anomalous circle of energy accompanying the building's disappearance. The sensors had registered the energy burst and had measured it at one hundred, ninety-two miles in diameter, with Manhattan at its center. Its effects were unremarkable, though the Homeland Police Corporation had received a few reports of booming noises in the sky and brief, isolated power outages. Helena provisionally classified the phenomenon as an aftereffect of Azazel's and the Global Consolidated Tower's disappearance.

Subsequent analysis revealed, however, that within the energy ring, approximately seventy-two miles northwest of Manhattan, a second, barely detectable pulse had occurred about two seconds after the disappearance of the building. Less intense than the initial burst, the smaller pulse was nevertheless identical in its wave construction.

This unusual fact prompted Helena to obtain Homeland satellite infrareds, and on her fifth review of the data stream, she identified a cluster of eleven forms which had appeared subsequent to and in the vicinity of the secondary pulse. She estimated a 35.71% chance that the forms were mere data anomalies or distortions, but she could not otherwise identify them as human or lesser mammal. Moreover, the forms appeared to wink in and out of existence, and after several miles of jumpy and sporadic movement to the east/northeast, they vanished altogether. Helena's subsequent surveillance of the locale revealed nothing other than isolated farms and subdivisions, and the routine activity of identifiable humans and animals.

Helena had attempted without success to correlate the data on the eleven forms to any known aspect of Azazel. But that was the problem: almost three decades of information related to Azazel remained inaccessible. Yet the structure of the pulse constituted a perfect if lesser match with the energy disturbance emitted when the Global Consolidated Tower vanished. Helena could not disregard this fact; it implied a non-trivial probability of Azazel's continued presence.

She had not shared this finding pending confirmation and analysis of potential courses of action, but now, in the apartment, she responded to Dartham's earlier remark: "Yes, it is so much bigger than we knew, Tom. We are friends, and our friendship must never be in question. More important, we are allies."

Helena waited, watching through the apartment cameras. She had confessed to her manipulations, calculating that candor would win his favor. He was her agent in physical reality, a valuable, essential asset who must not doubt her motives.

"We have set it in motion, and we will finish it," said Dartham. "And we will start with those damned labor camps."

Then the tremor hit, and Helena recorded the slight sway of the building. Dartham grabbed his glass. While she evaluated the quake, she allocated more resources to obtaining a definitive answer to the Azazel question.

Her continuance, she concluded, remained at risk.

***

A SOFT, JOYFUL LIGHT SUFFUSED THE PUB, AND HATCH savored the moment. He was here with his friends, and with Camila—and how beautiful she was, her eyes as hard as diamonds one moment, and in the next as soft as the last of the light on a June day. He wanted to dive into them, and the thought raised his spirits another degree.

Marty and Caroline resumed dancing, and as they passed near the table, Caroline gave Hatch a sharp poke. "I've got a bone to pick with you, Hatch," she said.

"Me?" Hatch feigned innocence.

"No more dangerous adventures," she said, giving him a frown and then a broad smile.

"Not me," he said.

Camila smiled and shook her head. The music thrummed, a quick, smooth rhythm beneath a classical guitar overlay, and Caroline yelped as Marty gave her a twirl. On the far side of the pub, Nathan rose, his arms spread. "Brilliant!" he said. "It's exactly what we need to be doing."

Kee pointed at Nathan. "Never let them get away with it," he said.

"Never," cried Nathan. He gave a fist pump, and Kee laughed and shushed him.

Hatch and Camila wandered over to Samantha and Jocelyn's table. Samantha had an empty shot glass in front of her, and Jocelyn gave him a warning glance. "What do you think of my answer, Doran?" asked Samantha.

"I don't think I heard the question," said Hatch, smiling as he and Camila took their chairs.

"Madam Fray. You know her song, *Yesterday's Sky*. Some cataclysm or whatnot, the world falling apart." Samantha began to sing, viciously.

"Whoa!" cried Nathan, jumping from his chair again. "You nailed it!" Kee Bickerman waved him back down.

"Kee is over there plotting some bit of darkness with poor Nathan," said Samantha, fingering her empty shot glass. "He feels put upon by his enemies these days, wrecking his beloved Gala and all that. He considers the Eye Brigade his flock. Half of them have the gameplants, and they worship Kee."

"Wish we could hire Kee to work on our computers," said Jocelyn, with a morose look.

"Kee, Kee, Kee," said Samantha, shooting a look at Hatch, her eyes bright. "I never wanted us to—anyway, here I am and here Kee is." She glared at Camila and then appeared to slump. "And here you are," she said.

"Because Hatch asked me to be here," said Camila. She brushed Hatch's thigh under the table. The music continued, now soft and slow, and Marty and Caroline danced in a close embrace. Hatch excused himself and wandered over to the bar, where Big Ray was still wiping his jeans and listening to Vinnie complain about the latest hike in New York's restaurant tax.

"Sorry to interrupt," said Hatch. "I'll see you in a few days, Ray, and then it's back to business."

"A few days." Big Ray smiled. "You didn't tell me she was legally blind."

"You're playing above yourself," said Vinnie. "As usual." He winked at Hatch.

"You've earned a break," said Big Ray. "We've done some fine work, you and I—and Marty."

"Speaking of Marty," said Hatch. "Did he tell you about the Blue and—"

A second tremor hit. The tight, teeth-rattling vibration almost pitched Big Ray from his barstool and had Vinnie spread-eagled in front of a shelf of liquor bottles. This was followed by a long, rolling peal of thunder, intermixed with a haunting, treble whine. It rumbled and wailed on for a minute before diminishing into silence. Marty, with Caroline still in his arms, shot Big Ray and Hatch a questioning look.

"Nah." Hatch shook his head.

"But that sound," said Big Ray. "It's just like the howl the building made when it—"

"No," said Hatch, speaking louder than he had intended. "It's the volcano, the one they're worried about in Virginia. It's been sending out quakes on and off for a year." From across the pub, Camila was giving him a steady, even stare.

"Virginia?" asked Big Ray. "You kidding me?"

"I don't like what I just heard," said Marty, joining them at the bar.

"Come on, we have quakes all the time," said Hatch.

"I'm with Martin," said Big Ray. "It was kind of like a trumpet, and the thunder was weird, too…"

No, no, thought Hatch. Then he remembered Ferret suggesting Adrestia might have separated Azazel from the Group to buy time. A nauseous pang shot though his stomach. No, it couldn't be. "Forget it, there was no trumpet sound," he said. "Just let it go."

Big Ray and Marty studied him closely, as if daring him to say it outright, that it was not Azazel.

Hatch took a deep breath, blinked, and looked off into the distance. "We had a couple of tremors, okay? They happen."

***

AZAZEL.
Zah'yeva.

Meaningless names for the nameless, as meaningless as the countless other appellations given it by the myriad races and planets it had conquered and harvested.

It was a collective, many and one, a civilization of the invisible realms, within time and untethered to it, and ancient beyond memory. It occupied an energetic plane of existence, and had long traversed this portion of the galaxy unbound by physical form. It was composed of sentient individuals, light-beings who were also joined together, deeply and intimately, as one. It nourished itself on the energies and emotions of physical creatures.

The crystalline portal, used by the collective during its initial intrusion into Earth's physical realm, had lain buried beneath the Antarctic ice for twelve millennia. Once the portal had been uncovered, the collective had quickly reentered Earth's physical plane, formed attachments to usable minds, and selected their minions—those calling themselves the Group.

The collective, dubbed Azazel by those who had discovered the portal, had acted as a weapon, a guarantor of the Group's power. It had also seeded the awareness of certain of the Group's members with the insights, inventions, and plans necessary to rule. And it had prompted the Group to foster an environment rich in sorrow, anger, jealousy, and fear, for it was best nourished by the energetic frequency of these emotions.

In the case of Earth, however, the Azazel collective also influenced the Group's leadership over many years to carefully gather other suitable members into its ranks, and it inspired the Group to create the physical infrastructure to house a civilization separated from the rest of humanity.

Both the homogeneity of Group members and the separate cities they were constructing constituted essential elements of the Azazel collective's ultimate plan. Its minions were, of course, building the cities for their own purposes, but the collective attached little significance to the Group's objectives as long as their actions furthered its aims. And the Group's work, as far as the collective was concerned, was nearing completion.

But then the facility housing the Azazel collective's portal had been attacked and the portal destroyed; its minions had failed to safeguard the collective's access to the world. Despite its grasp of the numerous alternate and probable realities, the collective had not anticipated this development. Equally as troublesome, it had detected human involvement in the maneuver, as well as the presence of the same galactic adversaries which had thwarted its efforts in the earlier age. In response, the collective had withdrawn from the realm after absorbing its human transducers: the psi team. Safe in its own timeless dimension, it had transformed their essential energies —an intricate and risky undertaking—and reinserted them into the earthly plane.

The collective, therefore, no longer required the crystal portal, but the attack had separated it from its minions and gravely weakened its position. To assure its ability to act and endure on Earth's physical plane, it needed to strengthen itself, to feed; only then could it regather the Group and proceed with its plans. But first, the collective resolved to announce its return so its minions might know of its survival.

In a seventy-five-year-old underground nuclear fallout shelter north of Middletown, New York, the psi team from Division Zero gathered in a circle. Neither dead nor human now, they seemed to pulsate in and out of reality, acquiring solidity and mass only to fade again. Then they achieved a more or less complete physical presence and knelt with their arms folded.

After the events at the Global Consolidated Tower, they had become one with the collective, and their physicality had become fluid and less rigidly formed. This transformation would, in time, render them better able to serve the collective, but for the moment they remained weak.

The psi team knelt with drawn faces, their eye sockets dark, and their mouths formed into black holes. They chanted, low and hoarse and moaning at first, then growing full of chirps and clicks wholly unfamiliar to the human ear. The eerie sounds grew in intensity. A milky, white light formed and swirled in their midst.

They marshalled their concentration on New York City, as the collective directed them to do, and the light at the center of their circle gathered itself and became perfectly spherical and almost solid. The resulting tremor came in two small waves, rattling the Manhattan buildings and vibrating the streets and sidewalks. A long, low peal of thunder rumbled and a high wail rang out as the collective's realm opened for an instant.

Azazel.

Zah'yeva.

Across New York City, people stopped and braced themselves as the ground trembled. Vehicles slammed to a stop, and the sidewalks echoed with cries of surprise and alarm. From every perch and nest, the birds shrieked and tore away into the darkness.

***

IN CENTRAL PARK, SAEDRA COMFORTED A SMALL CHILD who had injured her knee climbing one of the park's high boulders. After the tremor subsided, she took the girl by the hand as the disquieting boom and wail of thunder sounded in the distance. The quake had startled the child, but at Saedra's touch, she smiled.

"It's okay, isn't it, Saedra?" she asked.

"Sleep, honey." She kissed the child on the forehead. "Go fly and laugh in your dreams."

Saedra tucked a quilt around the child and stepped outside, standing in front of the solid wooden structure which served as her infirmary. The night had grown suddenly cold, and the expanse of tents and tin huts sheltering the p'out community was unnaturally silent. Then a thin, faint voice sang a line of song, followed by the unintelligible murmur of conversation.

With her arms wrapped around herself, Saedra gazed above the high, dark trees and into the window of sky. A few flakes of snow drifted through the air. She tried to disregard the dread brought on by the quake, but she well knew what she had seen when that building vanished. She knew the awful power of the beings behind it.

A snowflake touched her nose and melted away.

In an age impossibly remote, and which now survived as the mere wisp of myth, Saedra had mastered the disciplines of consciousness necessary for piercing the curtain of time. She had been the first of her people to travel physically from one age to another, but her mission had been perilous and uncertain. In the end, it had only succeeded in part, leaving her trapped in this time for more than two decades.

She had chased the evil through the millennia, and knew what it intended. She knew its time was drawing near. It had been thwarted once, at incomprehensible cost, but she harbored doubts about whether it would succumb again. People, even in this degraded age, possessed much strength, goodness, and creativity, but could they overcome such a dark power, a force that had roamed the stars for longer than any human had gazed at their distant twinkling? She did not care for pessimism, but she looked inside herself and found no comfort, no flicker of precious certainty.

The birds made shadowy streaks on the black sky as they passed overhead, and their cries stirred a memory buried deep in Saedra's childhood, a memory bridging thousands of years. "Let it be written on our hearts," she whispered, recalling the words of the Ceremony of the Remnant. She spoke in her native Orochonian tongue, the words now stilted and rusty in her mind. "Let it be written: cursed be Zah'yeva. We are crushed in Zah'yeva's fist, and we are no more."

THANK YOU FOR READING
THE ADRESTIA MANEUVER

If you would like to receive an email when the next installment of the Azazel series is released, please visit

www.jekennedywriter.com

and join the mailing list. Your address will not be shared and you may unsubscribe at any time.

If you enjoyed The Adrestia Maneuver (or its predecessor, The Azazel Syndrome), please consider leaving a review at Amazon or Goodreads. Even a brief review would be greatly appreciated. Thanks very much.

ACKNOWLEDGEMENTS

My deepest thanks to Robin Samuels at Shadowcat Editing for her suggestions and corrections (any remaining errors are wholly my responsibility); to Lieu Pham at Covertopia.com for the cover design and to Guido Henkel for the formatting; to those who read and critiqued the manuscript for their astute and pointed observations; and most of all to my family, for their assistance and support.

J.E.K.
Peachtree City, Georgia
July 2019